HIS SAINT

LUCY LENNOX

Cover Art by: AngstyG at www.AngstyG.com

Cover Photo: Wander Aguiar www.wanderaguiar.com

Editing by: Sandra at www.OneLoveEditing.com

Beta Reading by: Leslie Copeland at www.LesCourtAuthorServices.com

BLURB

Augie:

I don't need anyone's protection. I'm fine. But to appease my sister after a home invasion, I agree to take self-defense lessons. They just so happen to be with a big, muscled former navy SEAL who may or may not be everything I've always daydreamed about but never thought I could have.

And he's dead-set on looking out for me even when things in my life suddenly get complicated. Between the increasing threats against me and pressure from my wealthy family to be someone I'm not, I'm having a hard time keeping it together. As I begin to fall apart, I lose faith I'll ever meet anyone who'll want a mess like me—much less meet someone strong and capable like Saint Wilde.

The more time I spend with him, however, the more I realize he's not as put together as he seems. And I begin to wonder... while Saint's busy looking after everyone else, who's looking after him?

Saint:

After my big fat mouth gets me in trouble with a high-profile client, my boss takes away the bodyguard gig and sends me back to my hometown to give one of society's elites a few lessons at a local gym. Babysitting an antiques nerd is hardly my idea of a good time, but as soon as the attractive, petite man walks into the workout center, I nearly trip over my own feet.

He's effing adorable.

And absolutely scared to death.

He won't tell me what's spooked him, but I won't rest until I find a way to take the fear out of his gorgeous eyes. Even if defending Augie means I have to stop protecting my own heart.

ACKNOWLEDGEMENTS

My books are always better because of the input of certain special people:

Leslie Copeland for being my right hand and my beloved beta reader.

Sloane Kennedy for ~~putting up with~~ reassuring and encouraging me.

AngstyG for going above and beyond to get the keys right.

Sandra at OneLoveEditing for working overtime to help me make my release date and allowing me to leave navy all lowercase.

Chad Williams for giving me a little suggestion that made a big difference.

My family who heard "I can't right now—I'm finishing the book" for a solid three or four weeks. And knows it'll happen again next time.

THE WILDE FAMILY

Grandpa (Weston) and **Doc** (William) Wilde

Their children:

Bill, Gina, Brenda, and Jaqueline

Bill married Shelby. Their children are:

Hudson (book #4)

West (book #1)

MJ

Saint (book #5)

Otto (book #3)

King

Hallie

Winnie

Cal

Sassy

Gina married Carmen. Their children are:

Quinn

Max

Jason

Brenda married Hollis. Their children are:

Kathryn-Anne (Katie)

William-Weston (Web)

Jackson-Wyatt (Jack)

Jacqueline's child:

Felix (book #2)

CHAPTER 1

AUGIE

There was someone in the house, and this time I didn't even kid myself about it being my great-aunt Melody's ghost. This was completely different from the usual creaks and groans of the ancient rambling farmhouse, and I felt in my gut it was an intruder.

I rolled out of bed as quietly as I could before squat-walking to the master closet.

Please don't let the hinges screech.

After opening it as slowly as I dared, I made my way in and closed the door behind me before pushing through my hanging suits and button-downs to find the built-in ladder on the back wall of the tiny space.

I remembered a visit to Melody's old house the summer after I finished first grade. She'd shown me the secret passage to the tiny attic space as if it was my very own Harry Potter understairs hide-away. I'd fallen so in love with the nook, I'd secreted blankets, pillows, and picture books there as often as I could. And each summer after that, when my parents sent me "to the country for some fresh air," I'd spend hours curled up in my own private hideaway, not even caring that them sending me there was an excuse to have my beloved sister to themselves for a little while without her awkward brother trailing behind.

Only this time instead of being relaxed and happy, I was shaking with fear and terrified. Was this what it was like living all by oneself in the middle of the Texas countryside? Had my great-aunt ever had to fend off intruders? Was I going to have to actually consider purchasing a firearm to defend myself?

I shuddered at the thought. Due to a debilitating fear of firearms, I was the kind of person who'd more likely become a statistic of having one's own weapon turned against him.

Bang.

The sharp crack of the front door slamming back against the living room walls was recognizable only because I'd accidentally done the same thing the day I'd moved in three weeks before. The movers were busy carrying my giant writing slope display case, and I was so nervous about damage to the ancient beauty that I accidentally threw the door open to make sure they had plenty of room.

Oh, why hadn't I thought to grab my cell phone before coming up here?

The hatch to my hiding place was closed, and I sat as heavily on top of it as I could just in case someone was savvy enough to find it. As if my pint-sized frame would really keep an intruder from popping open the old wooden door and tossing me to the side.

I brought my knees up to my chest and hugged them, burying my face in my arms and trying not to hyperventilate. More thuds and crashes sounded from far below me on the main level of the house. What could they possibly want? Surely rural Texan burglars had no idea the worth of my antiques collection. Maybe they hoped to find the three sets of vintage sterling I owned? If so, they'd be disappointed to learn the sets were stored in a giant floor safe in the barn.

Melody hadn't trusted banks. She'd kept half her fortune under the damned horse shit. While I was usually grateful there wasn't horse shit in the barn any longer, I thought for a brief moment the old gal had been smart. Maybe I needed to get some horses after all, if only to add another layer of protection over my most valuable antiques in the vault.

There were plenty of other fence-able valuables in the house. My writing slope collection, for one. If those assholes took my favorite sixteenth-century Elizabethan slope from the center slot of the display case, I'd lose it. I could only thank my past self for having the foresight to keep my most treasured one with me instead of in the case.

I felt my jaw begin to wobble remembering my time curled up reading the ancient love letters with Melody.

Crying is for babies and women, August.

My mother's words were as clear in my head today as they'd been in my ears when I was twelve and had lost my father in a sudden, unexpected way while on vacation in Manhattan. He, my little sister Rory, and I had been walking back to our hotel after seeing a show on Broadway when we'd ducked into a convenience store to grab some drinks. It had all happened so fast. One minute Dad was humming one of the songs from the show while deciding what color sports drink to pick out of the cooler, and the next minute two armed men were waving guns around and screaming for everyone to get down.

My dad shoved Rory and me to the ground and huddled on top of us, moving the three of us into a far corner of the store and as far away from the violence as possible. It wasn't until all the noise was over and the cops came in that I realized Dad wasn't moving anymore.

Mom had allowed me exactly one week to mourn him after the accident before insisting I was now man of the house. It hadn't even been enough time for Dad's body to have been shipped home from New York. I remembered cursing our family's wealth because without it, we never would have been able to afford to leave Texas. He never would have been in the store that night.

By the time his body had arrived home, I'd done as Mom had asked. I'd stopped crying. In fact, I'd stopped feeling altogether. Numbness had been my stalwart friend in those days, carrying me through the following years at boarding school in a padded haze. What little emotion I had left was spent making sure my sister knew how loved she was since neither my mom nor my grandfather were the affectionate type. When I wasn't with Rory, I was like an automaton.

If only I could have that numbness back now. Then maybe I wouldn't feel like I was going to piss myself in terror. Hundreds of visits to a psychologist during my early adulthood finally helped me come to terms with most of the effects of my father's murder, but tonight it was as if I was back in that horrible moment listening to violence surrounding me.

Crash, thunk.

The wretched noises were followed by the telltale sound of glass breaking. I prayed it wasn't the few remaining original exterior farmhouse windows or my great-aunt's beloved Tiffany lamp in the study. Anything else could be replaced, and I'd never been a fan of the delicate crystal in the dining room corner cabinet anyway.

It took hours for the noises to stop. At least it felt like hours. In reality, I had no way of knowing. I sat curled up in a scared ball for a long time after the sound of gravel spitting indicated whoever it was had left. I still didn't have the guts to emerge from my hiding place until I heard the distant sound of the train passing by. Since the train rumbled through around half past six in the morning, I realized I was most likely safe to come down and assess the damage.

The first thing I did after scrambling for my phone was to call 911 and promptly hide under the bed until the dispatcher told me the responding sheriff's deputy was at the front door.

I threw a big hoodie sweatshirt on over my lounge pants and T-shirt before slipping on running shoes and making my way out of the bedroom to greet them.

The house was just as wrecked as I'd feared. I felt guilty for being grateful most of the damage was to my great-aunt's shabby old farmhouse furniture rather than the truly valuable pieces still in her penthouse in Dallas. Even though my great-grandmother had grown up on the Hobie farm a million years ago, it hadn't been anyone's primary residence for over eighty years. I'd only ever known it as Melody's summer home—a place to kick back and let go of real-life stress like

4

worrying about protecting the surface of a Louis XV occasional table or hiring housekeepers specially trained in how to care for antique walnut and mahogany surfaces.

I'd fully planned on bringing all the nice furnishings to the farm-house in Hobie since it was my permanent home now, but I hadn't yet secured the appropriate systems and insurance yet to move the most valuable pieces from the city.

Thank god.

Before answering the door, I spared a glance toward the far wall of the living room where my giant display case stood seemingly untouched with the exception of every writing slope it had held in its open cubbies. They all lay in broken pieces on the floor beneath the armoire—hundreds of years of history and thousands of dollars of precious antique collectibles as good as gone thanks to some North Texas assholes who didn't even know what the fuck they'd had their hands on.

I let out a shaky breath and made my way to the front door. The uniformed sheriff stood in the open doorway with a deputy off to one side.

"August Stiel?"

"That's me," I said.

"I'm Sheriff Walker and this is Deputy Diller. We'd like to make sure the premises is secure before conducting an assessment of what's missing. Would you mind stepping outside with my deputy while I get started?"

I nodded and stepped out of the house, already wondering what it would take for me to ever feel safe in my own home again.

It was only a few days before my sister came up with a suggestion.

CHAPTER 2

SAINT

BEING ON THE RECEIVING END OF MY BOSS'S ANGER WAS NOT GOOD.

"Goddamned motherfucking imbecile!" Lanny railed at me and paced behind his desk. I remained seated in the chair opposite his desk with my back straight and my hands clasped in front of me like a good little soldier.

"Tell me why you're such a fucking idiot, Saint? Why? Your job is to keep your goddamned opinions to yourself and keep the client safe. Was that too much for you to grasp? Really?" Lanny's face was red, and he couldn't look right at me. I'd already felt like a royal ass before he'd called me in there. "It would be one thing if this was the first time you let your fucking mouth get you into trouble, but we both know it's hardly the first time and it sure as hell won't be the last. You barely talk to anyone around here, yet you can't keep your fucking mouth shut on the job?"

He ran his hands through his buzzed hair, making a scritching sound. "Fuck," he muttered, winding down a bit. "Jesusfuckingchrist you're a complete liability to this company. Total asshole."

Lanny looked up at me finally, pinning me with a hard stare. I just looked back at him, knowing better than to speak before being spoken to.

He let out a breath. "Speak."

"That woman was an idiot," I said under my breath. And I meant it. The teeny-bopper pop singer I'd been in charge of had strutted and snorted her way through five clubs one night while I was protecting her, and she'd treated every server like shit. I had kept my mouth shut for more than eight hours of disgusting behavior and treatment of others before finally muttering under my breath, "*Spoiled fucking brat needs a spanking.*"

It was never meant to be overheard. But TMZ had aired the video clip the next day, and I quickly realized someone had caught it on film. Lucky me.

Lan sat back down behind his desk. "I should fire you."

"Maybe."

"You cost me a good client."

"If you say so."

He rolled his eyes. "This is where you apologize, beg for your job, and remind me of why I can't afford to lose you, jackass."

I did my best to remain calm. No matter how angry he was, I knew Lanny wasn't going to fire me. He was a good man. And he knew if I'd said what I had, it was because I'd truly been pushed to the limits. It didn't make it right, but it made it understandable.

"I'm adorable," I said with a straight face.

He pinched the bridge of his nose and tried not to smile. "I'm not sure you're my type."

"You should be so lucky."

"Saint, you're killing me. I can't send you out again right now, and you know it," he said.

I gritted my teeth as thoughts of hours of downtime flashed through my head. I couldn't handle being idle. "I need this job," I said in a low voice. "And I didn't lose my shit until I'd been working twenty hours in a row for the eighth day straight and she demanded I wake up a single mother of two small children so Gemma could have a particular flavor of ice cream. It was four in the morning."

"When has she ever not been a pain in the ass? You knew that going into this assignment, Saint. And I'm not firing you, but I *am* putting you on a paid leave. You're benched until further notice."

My stomach dropped. Benched? What did that even mean? I was a bodyguard. How could I guard a body if I was stuck at home?

Lanny flipped through folders on his desk until he found the one he was looking for. "We have a new client who needs private self-defense classes. He happens to live in your hometown, so I thought that might be something you could do while the media attention dies down."

I felt my nostrils flare. "What do you mean? Like teach some lady how to foil a purse snatcher?"

He pierced me with those eyes again. "No, like teach a little book nerd how to defend himself in a fight. The guy's sister is actually the one who hired us. She said he's been acting skittish lately but won't say why. She's worried about him. The young man himself seemed spooked as well, but when I tried to talk him into regular bodyguard services simply due to his family's wealth, he said that was ridiculous. At the very least I was able to talk him into learning some self-defense."

Something about that seemed off to me. "That's... odd," I said. "If he's suddenly skittish, there must be a reason."

"I agree, and I think you should look into it. But the man's grandfather is Jonathan Stiel, so this is a big fucking deal. Making him happy with these sessions could lead to a much more lucrative full-service contract for us. As you can imagine there are inherent facility and personnel security needs involved in running a company like the Stiel Corporation."

"Stiel like the Stiel Foundation? The Stiel building downtown? Jesus. That would be a huge contract. Good for you, Lan," I said, taking the file he handed me.

"Yes, the Stiel building houses the global headquarters of their billion-dollar family real estate development company. Jonathan's daughter, your client's mother, sits on the board of directors as well and is a highly regarded, very well-known socialite in the elite Dallas circles. Do you understand how important this is? How important it is that you don't call August Stiel a *spoiled fucking brat who needs a spanking?"*

I felt my hackles rise. August? What kind of name was that? Sounded like a stereotypical trust fund brat. "Shit, Lanny. Maybe he's the kind of guy who *enjoys* a good spanking." I glanced up from the file and caught him pinning me with a glare.

"Keep your filthy hands off the clients, Saint. Self-defense moves only. Help me make this man happy," he warned.

"Dude, I believe I have a proven track record of making men happy," I said dryly before standing up.

"Get the fuck out of here. You're due in Hobie at five. I've arranged for you to use a room at a local fitness studio, and I assume you can stay with your crazy-ass family."

AFTER HEADING NORTH TOWARD HOBIE, I realized I already knew the owner of the fitness studio where I'd be working with Lanny's client. Twist had been founded by Neckie Birch, who was by far the hippiest bohemian to ever come out of Hobie High. She'd been the super-chill girl my twin sister had crushed on the entire four years we were in school with her. MJ would have died if she'd found out I was spending time with Neckie Birch for the next few weeks. I wondered if I could convince MJ to take some vacation time to come hang with me in Hobie to get her flirt on.

I was surprised to see Twist had quadrupled in size since the last time I'd been in. Apparently the fitness business was good in the growing town of Hobie, which was a far cry from the tiny Jazzercise studio and ramshackle rec center the town had sported while I was growing up.

After introducing myself to the receptionist, I glanced through a glass-windowed classroom to see Neckie herself conducting the cooldown sequence of a stretching session. I was shocked to discover her smuggling a beach ball under her yoga tunic, but as much as I wanted to grill her about the unexpected pregnancy, I stepped out of the way so as not to interrupt her current class. My fingers immediately flew across my phone screen.

Me: *OMG Nectarine Birch is knocked up!*

MJ: *Liar.*

Me: *Swear. I'm at Twist and she's as big as a yoga ball.*

MJ: *Photos. NOW.*

I tried surreptitiously taking photos of the lovely preggo before sending them to my sister.

MJ: **sigh* she's so fucking hot. Even round like that.*

Me: *Meh. If you're into that kind of thing.*

MJ: *I didn't think I was, but damn. Why are you at Twist?*

Me: *Long story. Work. I'm in Hobie for a month.*

The phone rang. "Well hello, baby sis."

"I'm older than you are, idiot," MJ said.

"Only because I was a gentleman and let you exit first."

"Please tell me Neckie isn't in any danger, Saint."

I could hear the worry in her voice, and it squeezed my heart. MJ was a pretty stoic person in most cases, but she'd always had a soft spot for the free-spirit woman currently giving new meaning to the term child's pose.

"No. No, she's fine. Sorry to worry you. I'm not here for a bodyguard gig. Just using the studio to teach a self-defense lesson. I've been assigned to this pissant duty as punishment for running my mouth."

She let out a sigh of relief. "Serves you right. Suck it up and be glad he didn't fire you."

"Come hang out with me," I whined. "I need my baby sister to entertain me. Plus, you can flirt with the human incubator."

"What's the point? She's brewing some guy's kid. All hope is lost. Leave me alone to stew."

"There's no ring on her finger…" I teased.

"Her fingers are probably swollen. Seriously, Saint. Don't mess with me. I'm really upset about this. I… I always kind of…"

She didn't need to say the rest. I already knew she'd always held a torch for Neckie. But hearing the hopeless tone in her voice made it real.

"I'm sorry, Em. I shouldn't have said anything."

"Nah. It's good. Maybe that's the sign I need to get out there and go on some dates. I'm thirty-one for god's sake."

"Law school and the partnership track at the firm have kept you pretty busy. But I thought you were seeing that chick from Hallie's party."

"Pfft. I wasn't the only one. I found out when I met Hallie for drinks and her friend Dawn went on and on about her hot new girlfriend with the tiger tattoo and ear gauges. But it's fine. She was a little too high-strung for me. I need someone relaxing to come home to after a long day at the firm. Not someone who wants to run right back out and party all night."

I was prepared to give her a pep talk about finding the right woman when I heard the receptionist say my name. "Gotta go, sis. My client just walked in. Please consider coming up to Hobie this weekend if you can. Love you."

"Love you too. Keep an eye on her, Saint," MJ said in a serious tone.

As I hung up, I tried to psych myself up for the boring task ahead. I'd already researched the guy on the internet and read up on him before our session. He owned a little antiques shop in Hobie near the pub my brother had helped open. I wasn't sure exactly what had brought him to my tiny hometown from Dallas the year before, but it seemed a far cry from the rest of his family who seemed to own half of Dallas and flaunted their wealth in all of the social spheres in the city.

The photos I'd found showed August himself to be an attractive guy maybe in his late twenties. He wasn't the elegant, glamorous yacht-riding douche I'd pictured when I'd read Lanny's client file, and I had to admit something about the man's photo drew me in. I decided it wasn't possible for him to be that geekily adorable in real life, but I had to hand it to the guy, he employed a genius in the Photoshop department. And according to the articles online, he wasn't neces-sarily as wealthy as his mother or grandfather, but he did have a significant net worth nonetheless. August's great-aunt had passed away almost a year earlier, leaving him a penthouse in the city and a farmhouse in Hobie, but I hadn't realized what else they were involved in until I did the research on them that afternoon. The Stiel family had a charity foundation, which was essentially a multimillion-dollar conservative think tank and contributor to every far-right organization in Texas. The Stiel Foundation had enough money to impact elections, research, and policy. The sheer amount of money they managed was breathtaking. The family name was such a big deal in Texas social circles, August's father had taken the Stiel name upon marriage rather than Jonathan Stiel having to become a lowly Smith.

In addition to money and connections, online rumor had it August Stiel was also in a long-term relationship with the gorgeous news anchor at one of the largest television stations in Dallas–Fort Worth. I wondered if that was another potential feather in Lanny's cap. Providing security services to a local celebrity would pull in lots of great visibility for the company.

When I walked to the front desk to greet him, I learned just how wrong I'd been about August Stiel's photo. No Photoshop in the world could improve upon how attractive he was in real life. He was specifi-cally sent by the devil to tempt me as punishment for calling that last client a brat.

I'd landed another spoiled rich client to babysit. Only this one was...

This one was... *ungh.*

My feet froze in place, running shoes making a squeaking sound on the floor, drawing his attention. I stared at him. He wasn't large by any means, but he carried himself erect as if he felt the need to keep even his body under strict control at all times. Dark-rimmed glasses framed his hazel eyes, and his forehead had quotation mark furrows in the center between his brows. His lips were red and sensual like a woman's, but his jaw was angled and tight like a man's. He had thick, dark hair and five-o'clock shadow that made him look moody and mysterious in his dark business suit. Everything about the man looked wound up tight enough to snap.

Which just made me want to snap him as soon as I could.

"You must be Mr. Stiel," I said, reaching out a hand to shake as I forced myself into motion again.

"I am," he said. His voice was decisive but quieter than I expected. His eyes seemed to be studying me from behind his glasses, and I wondered what he was thinking. A sliver of need snaked through my gut, and I mentally slapped myself. Was I for fucking real? *Seriously, Saint, he's a goddamned client. Keep your fucking distance. Be professional.*

"My name is Saint Wilde. I'll be training you. Welcome to Twist."

"Thank you," he said.

"Why don't we start by getting you out of those clothes," I suggested. *Way to go with the professional talk, asshole.*

His eyes flared for a microsecond before his brow furrowed deeper. "Excuse me?"

Get it together, Saint. "Unless you wanted to work out in your suit? Fine by me, I guess. *Suit* yourself."

The receptionist rolled her eyes at my pun, but Mr. Stiel didn't seem to have noticed it. The man looked down at himself as if realizing for the first time he was not dressed for the task at hand. "Oh crap."

I couldn't help but stifle a laugh. "It's okay. I brought clothes you can wear."

He looked up at me, his own face flaming, and something stupid happened in my stomach.

Stupid fucking stomach.

"Shoes," he blurted. "I don't have the right kind of shoes either."

Okay, so awkward antiques geek was awkward. And cute as a fucking button.

"It's okay. We're going to be barefoot on the mat anyway. And you'll be spending more time on your back than your feet, so it's a moot point, really." Apparently I couldn't help myself. The innuendo was coming out of my mouth whether I liked it or not. The receptionist widened her eyes at my brazen behavior, and the client himself blushed an even deeper shade of pink.

God, this was going to be weird.

CHAPTER 3

AUGIE

I THOUGHT MAYBE I'D MADE A HUGE MISTAKE. I'D AGREED TO RORY'S suggestion of the self-defense class to feel empowered and strong, but I was already feeling off-kilter and dizzy. The man with... the man with all the *muscles* seemed to delight in teasing me.

That wasn't going to make me feel more powerful. Perhaps I needed to request a new trainer.

I turned to the woman at the reception counter and raised a finger to speak. Before a single word came out of my mouth, Gigantor stepped closer and put his humongous paw on my back to nudge me deeper into the building. I swallowed my tongue and tried to keep up with his long strides, which wasn't easy considering I was walking on little toothpick legs.

The feeling of that large warm hand through my coat sent shivers through me as we walked. I wondered what the hell was wrong with me. Was he so big and strong that I was having some kind of caveman fear response? I refused to think of any other explanation. I sure as shit wasn't attracted to the beast. He wasn't even close to being my type. I didn't enjoy being overpowered. I'd had enough of that in school growing up with an asshole cousin. The only thing that had

15

saved me then was having a bigger brain and quicker wit. I wondered if the same tools could best this muscleman.

I allowed him to lead me to the small men's locker room where he grabbed a similar getup to the one he was wearing: black athletic trainer pants and a matching Landen Safekeeping top. He handed over the small stack of items and looked at me expectantly. I took them and asked where the restroom was.

"Over there," he said, pointing to a doorway behind us. I nodded as if it was a totally normal dude thing to bail on changing in a locker room and made my way to a stall. I didn't care if he thought I was a weirdo; I was not changing clothes in front of that bodybuilder.

He was like eleven feet tall and ripped. No freaking way. I had enough body issues as it was without revealing my little-boy body to this manly man. I was what people would generously call "lean." But what that really meant was "skinny as shit and breakable."

I changed as quickly as I could and tried not to think about walking barefoot out of a men's room. The entire time I tiptoed across selected clean-looking tiles, I chanted to myself, "You're here to kick ass, you're here to kick ass, you're here to—"

"Follow me," Saint said as he took my pile of clothes and chucked them in a locker before leading me out to the workout center.

The fitness studio was larger than it looked from the street. The rear portion of the building held the locker rooms, an empty classroom, and a large space that seemed set up for other types of training that required mats like boxing or martial arts. Maybe there was even a gun range or something. Just the thought made my stomach lurch, but after the break-in, I couldn't help but wonder if I should consider buying a gun.

"Do you shoot?" I asked suddenly, feeling my face heat with embarrassment.

"I'm sorry, what?" Saint asked, looking back over his shoulder in confusion.

"Guns, I mean. Do you shoot guns?" *Oh my god, is it possible to sound this stupid in real life?*

Saint held the door open to the large area with soft mats lining the floor. I entered the room and felt my arm brush against his as I walked past. A tingly feeling bloomed over my skin where our bodies connected, and I felt myself blush yet again. What was it about this man that made me super-aware of his body? Of my *own* body? Was it because he was so big? Was he intimidating me?

He should be intimidating me based on his size, his looks, and how I'd always felt fearful around bigger guys like my cousin Brett and his football friends. But for some reason, the man in front of me seemed harmless. Maybe it was his messy blond hair and baby face. It was too bad, really. But it most likely explained why he was a self-defense teacher instead of a real bodyguard out in the field.

Saint looked at me with a funny quirk to the edge of one of his lips. "I do shoot guns. I was in the military for several years, and now I'm a personal security specialist. It sort of comes with the territory."

Embarrassed for asking, I quickly looked away, muttering, "Never mind."

"Okay," Saint said. "Then let's get to the point of why we're here. Self-defense. Can you tell me a little bit about what made you want to do this?"

I looked at the man and thought about how to answer. Could I really tell this human Mack truck the answer to that question? That I'd hidden like a coward while some unknown thugs took away any feeling of home and security I'd had at my family farmhouse the week before? That after years of being bullied as a child, I was finally having to come to terms with the fact that my tormentors had apparently been right? I was a coward. I was weak and scared—all the fucking time. But I also had plenty of experience pretending I was fine.

"Just thought it was time to mix up the workouts and learn some moves, that's all," I said.

I saw Saint frown. He didn't buy what I was selling, and I didn't give a damn. I wasn't about to tell someone like him what a chicken-shit I was.

"Okay then. General fitness and defense moves. Gotcha." Saint gestured for me to follow him to the center of the mat. "First let's warm up a little while I talk about the most important part of self-defense—prevention." He led me through some movements and stretches while he spoke.

"The most important part of keeping yourself safe is avoiding dangerous situations in the first place and being smart about how you move through your day." He continued to talk about being alert and things like that—all pieces of advice I'd heard before. I rolled my shoulders as he talked and started some jumping jacks when he indicated.

The muscle-jacked blond man could do any series of moves without getting remotely out of breath while he spoke. Meanwhile, despite being a regular jogger, I felt my heart rate increase and my breathing speed up.

I tried to pay attention to his words, but my eyes kept insisting on checking out his form. He was tall with very little body fat, and his muscles seemed tight like industrial rubber bands. Saint wasn't overly bulky like a professional bodybuilder, but he was definitely a protein shake–drinking, weight-lifting kind of guy. I wondered how much time he spent in the gym.

"One of your biggest advantages is catching your attacker off guard with the speed and aggression of your response. If you've tried all the other things I've mentioned, including yelling for them to back the fuck off, and they're still coming at you, it's a whole different ball game. If you actually get attacked, don't think, and don't show any mercy."

I looked at him and wondered what it would look like for a man his size to not show mercy. I couldn't even begin to imagine.

"Once someone is in your personal space, it's hit or be hit. You go for vulnerable spots, and everyone has them. Size doesn't matter. The eyes, the nose, the ears, neck and throat. The groin."

I inwardly winced, and he must have sensed my thoughts. He nodded. "You could take me down with one well-placed kick or grab and pull."

Just the thought of grabbing and pulling anything in his groin area made me shudder. *Kicking, yes. Grabbing? I don't think so.*

My face began to flame in embarrassment at all of the talk of

Saint's groin. Why were we talking about his groin? Why was I thinking about his groin? When was my brain going to stop repeating the word *groin*?

The first thing he demonstrated was an ear clap. As the large man stepped closer to me, I caught a hint of a fresh scent coming off his body. Deodorant maybe, or a lingering aftershave smell. There was something about it I liked, and I felt silly when my mind immediately wondered if I could ask him what it was so I could buy it.

You're not asking the dude why he smells so good, you idiot.

As he described the way to cup the hand and keep the fingers safe, my eyes focused on his mouth. He had a canine tooth that was a little pointy and twisted, and it gave him an endearing quality that was unusual in someone with such a hard body. I wondered if he'd grown up without money for braces.

As he brought his cupped hand to my ear, I noticed his eyes were a combination of gray and the lightest blue. He had a thin vertical scar on the edge of his upper lip, and I felt my tongue come out to test the same spot on my own lip. Saint's eyes followed my tongue, and his pupils seemed to grow darker.

"Huh?" I asked.

"What?" His mouth was right in front of my eyes, and I tried hard not to stare at it when he spoke.

I blinked. "I missed that last part. About the cupping, I mean." *What the hell? Did I just really say that?*

His lips parted in a soft smile, and I saw that silly tooth again. Jesus, what the hell was happening to me?

"The ear clap. Let me start again," he said.

I had a stern conversation with myself about the reasons why I was there that included a reminder to myself that I was most definitely not interested in how that man, or any other man for that matter, smelled or looked. Or anything to do with groins.

"The ear clap," I confirmed. "Yes."

He ran through the maneuver again, and this time when he put his hand over my ear I definitely did *not* feel goose bumps rise up on my neck and scalp at his touch. I also did not notice the warmth of his skin or the tingle of his touch.

Maybe it had been a little too long since someone had touched me sexually, so now I was interpreting any touch as sexual. I thought about reactivating my hookup app to see if there was a decent opportunity for a casual connection out here in little Hobie, but I quickly dismissed the idea. Based on how high my anxiety was these days since the break-in, I could only imagine the panic attack I'd have in a stranger's bed.

As Saint stepped closer to me, I inhaled his scent and let my eyes drift closed for the briefest moment.

At least for now, I was completely safe in his company.

But I'd be damned if I'd let him see how much that meant to me.

CHAPTER 4

SAINT

AS SOON AS MY HAND WENT OVER HIS EAR AND MY FINGERTIPS BRUSHED against his hair, I knew August Stiel was going to be a problem for me. Hell, I'd really known it the minute I'd seen him in the lobby with those little furrows of worry in his brow. There was something about him that seemed tucked away and vulnerable, and fuck if that didn't strike a chord with me.

I wanted to rub my thumb over those two frown lines on his forehead and smooth them out. For good.

As my fingers slid into the hair behind his ear, I closed my eyes and swallowed. *The job, Saint. Focus on the contract Stiel could bring to Lanny. Remember who this guy is. Rich kid like the spoiled pop star— Trouble with a capital* T.

I cleared my throat. "So, once you hit and push with the ear clap, you use your other fist for the punch. The ear clap is meant to push them off balance so you can surprise them with the punch," I explained. I demonstrated with a slow-motion punch that landed as softly as a whisper to his jaw. His skin was warm and scruffy against the backs of my knuckles, and I pulled my hand away.

"Now you try."

August looked down at his feet and gulped, sending out massive insecurity vibes. That was bad. Just as he began to cup his hand and swing his arm around, I reached out to stop him.

"Wait," I said, surprising him. "I might have rushed into this part. Let me go back to the part about carrying yourself with confidence and surety. You want to almost strut—back straight, head held high, making eye contact with those around you. The best thing to do is to give off a *don't fuck with me* vibe as you move through a potentially dangerous situation."

"I know," he said, looking up at me and narrowing his eyes. "You already explained that part. I got it."

"Then why do you look scared of me?" I asked before I could stop myself.

His eyes darkened and his lips tightened. "I'm not scared of you. Quite the opposite actually."

"What does that mean?"

"You don't scare me in the slightest."

I tilted my head and narrowed my eyes. "Really?"

He rolled his eyes, but I detected a slight tremor in his voice. "Really."

"Dude, I'm like intimidating," I said like an idiot.

He barked out a nervous laugh. "No. You're not. You're a kitten."

Was this guy for real?

"A kitten? Me? Are you joking?"

He crossed his arms and looked me up and down, making my skin flush and my boxer briefs way too brief.

"A sleepy, purring kitten," the smaller man concluded. "Not intimidating. You have a baby face, to be honest. Is that why you have to do this instead of security in the field like a real bodyguard?"

Oh. No. He. Didn't.

"I *am* a real bodyguard."

"Right," he smirked again. "Sorry. Sure you are. Didn't mean to offend you."

I must have been wrong. Maybe this guy was as much of a snob as my pop star client had been. "Oh my god, are you for real right now?"

"It's okay, Saint. I still trust you to teach me self-defense. You probably have to use these moves sometimes too."

I felt my lips open. "Mr. Stiel, *sir*," I said with a tight jaw, "I'll have you know in addition to being what you call a 'real' bodyguard, I was a navy fucking SEAL. I'm taller than most humans, and I'm trained to kill. There's not a single moment of my life when someone is stupid enough to think they can take me in a fight."

The little man fucking shrugged. "Okay. Whatever you say. What's next?"

I wanted to punch the guy. Just goddamned deck him and walk away. Well, maybe after kicking him too. But there was something in his eyes for just a brief second that exposed the truth. He was terrified. Not of me, clearly, but of something. And he was trying every coping technique in the book not to show it.

I let out a breath and smiled. "Okay, tough guy. I guess this is your way of asking me to stop going easy on you, huh?"

He set his jaw at me, but his eyes skittered away. "Bring it on."

AN HOUR LATER, we were both pouring sweat from practicing basic defense moves over and over until they were second nature for him. I'd grabbed his wrist, engulfed him from behind in a bear hug, and locked him in a choke hold. At every turn, I couldn't help but feel his sleek, lean body beneath my fingers and the smell of his clean sweat as my nose pressed against the back of his head. Had Fate planned to fuck with me that evening, she could not have sent a more perfect temptation. He was beautiful but prickly. And I wanted nothing more than to run my fucking hands all over him. Preferably naked and in bed. Or, hell, against a wall would be fine too.

"Now I know why there's such a thing as Gronk Flakes," my client muttered under his breath as he threw himself down onto the mat on his back. I'd announced our session complete after the fourth time he'd taken me down to the mat. "I used to think it was awfully egotistical to have a cereal named after you, but if his workouts are anything like this, I get it."

I couldn't help but snort. "What are you talking about?"

"Gronk Flakes. Well, and Flutie Flakes too. Then you've got the ice hockey ones like Hull-O's. But who in Texas is really going to get their hands on those?"

"Are you talking about Wheaties?"

He looked at me like I was dim.

"No. These are specially branded… you know what? Never mind. It's not like I'd ever eat them. I only eat cereal out of mini boxes."

I stared at him until his nostrils flared in defiance. "What? It's not weird. Cereal tastes different in mini boxes. It's the opposite of mini champagne bottles. With champagne, the smaller the vessel, the poorer the quality. It has to do with surface area in the storage and fermentation stages. But with cereal—" He stopped himself and looked up at me in horror. "Sorry, stupid. Never mind."

"Cereal in small boxes is less likely to crush. Less weight on the bottom pieces," I explained. "Less crumbly mess."

"Yeah, but how do you know that?"

"I only eat cereal out of mini boxes," I admitted. "My siblings think I'm crazy."

August Stiel studied me from his position on the mat. "Liar."

"Did you know that there are two types of cereal box flaps, and they're gendered?"

He sat up. "Slotted and slotless."

I nodded and grinned at him. "Female and male."

"That sucks. Why the hell do cereal boxes need to be gendered?"

"But mini boxes…"

"Don't have tabs!" His face lit up with a giant smile. "Enby flakes. Who knew?"

I wanted to keep that sunshine smile on his face. It was the most relaxed I'd seen him all evening.

"My brother once talked my mother into buying a box of Hannah Montana cereal. Since we normally ate generic bran flakes or plain oatmeal, it was a big deal."

August's eyes sparkled. "You're kidding. How did it taste?"

"A thousand times better than bran flakes but not nearly as good as the Snoop Loops a buddy in the navy picked up on shore leave somewhere in the South Pacific. Came with a free rap music CD inside and everything."

It took him a minute to realize I was pulling his leg, but when he did the giggle that came out of him was enough to make the entire Gemma punishment worth it. What I would give to hear it again and again.

"You're such a bullshitter," he said. "But I know Hannah Montana cereal actually existed because my sister had some. She also convinced our housekeeper to get Bart Simpson Peanut Butter Crunch cereal."

"Gross."

"No kidding. Then my cousin thought it would be a funny joke if he brought me Sprinkle Spangles. I guess at that time he already..." He paused and took a deep breath before looking at me with a fake smile. "You know what? Never mind. Mini cereals for the win, right?" He held out a hand to high-five but then quickly turned it into a fist to bump.

We ended up with an odd kind of accidental secret handshake before he jumped up and mumbled something about needing to get out of there.

I led him back into the locker room for a shower and showed him where everything was. There was no way I could take my shower in the large open room at the same time without getting a giant hard-on in front of him, so I told him I was going to find us some bottled water while he showered and dressed. For some reason he looked relieved that I wasn't going to be showering with him, and I wondered if he'd somehow pegged me as gay.

In my internet search of him, I'd seen many photos of him with the same beautiful woman on his arm, so I assumed he didn't play for my team. Even if he wasn't dating the television news reporter, he was clearly into women. I hoped he wasn't homophobic, but the way he seemed to relax after I announced I was going to leave him be to shower alone wasn't a good sign. Then again, he'd referred to the nongendered cereal box as nonbinary, which was a sign he at least had some passing familiarity and comfort with sexual identity terms.

As I left the locker room to grab some water, I saw my brother Otto walking out of the weight room with his husband, Seth. We clapped palms in a kind of shake before walking to the water fountain between the two locker room doors.

Otto's big toothy grin was a sight for sore eyes. "Dude, that pop star? Really?" he accused.

I rolled my eyes. "Don't. It's bad enough Lanny pulled me out of the field."

"What do you mean?"

"I'm stuck here in Hobie until the media shit with Gemma dies down," I confessed. "I'm lucky to still have my job, to be honest."

Otto looked sympathetic. "I can't say I'm surprised, but you have to know you're the only person he'd let get away with that kind of shit."

"Yeah. I know. He's been great. I don't know why he gives me so many chances," I said.

Seth looked at me with a twinkle in his eye. "Because you're cute and you have a tight ass?" he teased.

"Hey!" Otto barked with a scowl. "That's my brother you're talking about, and you're taken."

Seth grabbed Otto's butt. "I was talking about you, Wilde Man."

I laughed at his blatant attempt to rile Otto up. "Plus, Lanny's straight as an arrow. But speaking of, you two want to go out later and maybe find some trouble? I could use a little action tonight to help drown my sorrows. Doesn't Fig and Bramble do LGBT night on Wednesdays?"

"Yes. And there's actually more action there than you'd expect, especially since the resort opened up by the lake. I'll see who else wants to go. Give us a few minutes to talk to Neckie about something, and then I'll walk over to the pub with you while Seth checks in at the sheriff's office. You staying at the ranch?"

I shrugged. "I guess. Doc didn't pick up when I called him on the way to town."

"Well, you can't stay with us. Tisha is at her mom's, and we have *plans*," Otto said, making the last word sound positively filthy.

"Gross. If all else fails, I'll sleep in my truck," I muttered as I reached to fill two paper cups with water from the fountain.

The two of them wandered off, flirting and touching as if they were still the teenage lovebirds they'd once been.

Seeing them together like that was heartwarming but strange too. When Seth had moved away in high school and dropped my brother with little explanation, it had gutted Otto. He'd wound up joining the navy with me after graduation to get away from his broken heart. After watching him mourn the loss of his soul mate, I'd vowed to myself to never, ever fall in love. It wasn't worth the heartbreak if things went wrong.

As I watched the two of them walk away, I felt emptier than normal. It was a feeling I'd never noticed before until recently. Otto reconnecting with Seth had been a dream come true, but it had also caused me to rethink everything. How could I not believe in love after seeing them together?

And then when my brother Hudson had fallen for a quirky Irishman earlier this year, I'd been shocked. Hud had been the only straight one of us brothers. But watching him find someone to love the way he loved Charlie had awoken a need in me. Maybe it was my age. Or perhaps it was that my life was finally less chaotic now that I was out of the navy. There was something obviously missing now. And it had never been more apparent than when I'd spotted little August Stiel standing at the front of Twist looking lost and nervous.

After shaking off the ridiculous self-pity, I took the cups of water back to the locker room and set them down on the bench by August's workout clothes before stripping my own off and striding into the showers. Regardless of how the client felt about showering with me, I was going out for drinks tonight and needed to wash the sweat off before getting dirty again with a cute trick.

I tried to stay far away from him and not look at his body, but who was I kidding? His bare ass was right there, and it was gorgeous. High and tight, rounded and pale. I imagined lowering to my knees and sinking my teeth into those firm cheeks before sinking my—

Fuck.

Just as I began to look away, he turned and saw me. I quickly put my hand over my cock as if I was rinsing it or washing it. It wasn't fully hard yet, but it wouldn't take long if I kept looking at my client's body under the shower spray.

One more hour, Saint, and you can flirt with someone at the pub. Stop thinking about the client. Just wait one more hour.

CHAPTER 5

AUGIE

When Saint had left me alone to shower, I'd been relieved as hell. Every teasing word I'd ever heard about my body growing up clanged in my ears most days, but when I stood next to what most people considered a perfect male body, it was especially awful. If I'd been naked in the shower with him, I'd have felt even more humiliated and mortified than I normally did in a communal shower.

But I wasn't ready to go home to a dark house all alone. Another night home alone, sleeping in my hidey-hole despite the state-of-the-art security system Rory had arranged to be installed the day after the break-in was not my idea of a happy night ahead.

The new alarm system had been enough for the first few nights. Between that and the extra locks on my bedroom door, I'd felt somewhat secure.

Until I'd had a terrible nightmare in which the intruders not only broke into my house but also dragged me out of bed and tortured me for hours. I'd spent the next night in a hotel a few towns over before getting up the nerve to return to Hobie the following day. I'd finally allowed Rory to talk me into self-defense classes, but one measly session surely wasn't enough to give me the guts to sleep in the wide-open bedroom that night when the hidey-hole was so much safer.

I wondered if I'd ever be able to sleep in my own bed like a normal person again. Regardless, I knew I wanted to put off finding out for several more hours. The pub next to my shop had a popular happy hour, and if I wanted to stop by and check it out, I'd need to take a shower first. So, after Saint walked out of the locker room, I stripped out of my clothes and walked into the tiled space. The water slid over my sweaty skin, and I just stood there for a while, letting the warm spray pound against my neck and shoulder muscles. I faced the wall and closed my eyes.

All I could think about was how strange I'd felt during the session. Every time Saint had touched me, it had felt like something was happening to my skin. Like my body was a divining rod and his was a secret underground well of rich, cool water. I'd vibrated when he came near me and felt the loss of him when we parted. The whole thing was weird, not just regular physical attraction, and part of me wondered if that was how identical twins felt—like there was another body on earth that was somehow mystically dialed into theirs to the point of having an intense reaction when near each other.

I shook my head and felt the shower water slide down the sides of my face. Memories of times in my adolescence when I'd had a crush on my math teacher surfaced in my mind. What had made me think of Mr. Randolph now? Was it attraction I was feeling for Saint? Of course it fucking was.

I'd tried very hard to squelch all inappropriate feelings for other men years ago when my grandfather had caught me staring in a year-end school awards assembly and asked me about it at the restaurant later that night. My mother's reaction had been swift and harsh—enough to send my balls deep into hiding and my fantasies about other men completely out of my mind. From then on, my mother had taken every opportunity to warn me about dire consequences for tarnishing our vaunted family name with tawdry modern "lifestyle choices." I'd decided then and there to just stick to dating women like I was expected to. Women were easy. Women were lovely. Women were *safe*.

But my attempts to squelch those feelings hadn't quite worked. I didn't find women attractive in the same way men were. I'd gotten a crush on the wrong boy junior year in school and made the mistake of flirting with him one day after lunch, not realizing he was dating a big kid from the wrestling team who made it his mission for the rest of high school to remind me that I was small, weak, and ugly as hell. His campaign to make me feel worthless had been a raging success and had dovetailed quite nicely into my own cousin's bullying.

Did I still fantasize about men? Hell yes. Did I act on it? Rarely. But when I did, I stuck with the same, no-strings-attached, anonymous blowjobs and hand jobs I always had. Period.

As far as the world and my family knew, I was in a serious relationship with Katrina Duvall. This worked well for both of us since neither of us wanted the world to know our secrets. But now that I was building a life outside of Dallas, maybe it was time to consider living life out of the closet. Surely I could be out in Hobie and still keep things quiet in Dallas with my family. Katrina had always encouraged me to find someone, even though it could mean the end of our arrangement one day.

After remembering the pub's LGBT night was tonight, which meant maybe there'd even be an opportunity for me to meet someone, I opened my eyes and reached for the soap. Movement caught my eye, and I turned to see Saint's tower of inked muscle and naked beauty staring at me.

My heart stuttered to a stop in my chest, and I stood frozen at the sight of him. Surely he was wondering how a scrawny-ass such as myself could ever hope to defend himself in the case of an attack. Maybe he was right. Maybe I was too small and weak to do any justice to these lessons.

A little voice in the back of my head reminded me that Saint hadn't actually said that; it had been my own insecurity speaking.

By the time my heart kicked back into gear, he'd turned away from me to his own showerhead, and I noticed his magnificent body. He was like one of those guys on the cover of a fitness magazine. All shapely defined muscle and raw masculinity. I wondered what it was like to be that kind of man. To walk through the world with confidence and power, knowing you intimidated most of the people around you.

I'd teased him earlier about not being intimidating, but of course he was. Anyone would be an idiot to find themselves in a dark alley with Saint. But I'd also been telling the truth. For some reason, to *me*, he put out a purring kitten vibe. Did other people see it?

My eyes fell to his thick, muscular ass cheeks, and I saw them flex as he shifted his weight from one foot to the other. Fuck. *Not looking.* Not looking at another man's ass in the shower. Did I have a death wish? That guy could squash me like a goddamned bug.

I turned back around and focused on washing myself, ignoring the thickening of my cock and closing my eyes in embarrassment. Did I really want to be caught staring at him in the shower so he could take me out back and beat the shit out of me later?

Just wash and get the hell out of there, Augie. Jesus.

I washed as fast as I could, pretending I was alone. After I dried off and slipped on my trousers, I saw Saint round the corner into the locker room with a towel wrapped around his waist. Multiple tattoos covered his chest and upper arms.

"I brought you a cup of water," he said, nodding to the cups on the bench. "You need to hydrate."

"Thanks." I grabbed one like a lifeline and took a sip. The cool water helped dissipate the dry throat that had suddenly appeared at the sight of the tattoos running along Saint's back and down into the towel.

"What did you think about the session?" Saint asked as he reached into a nearby locker for his own clothes. My eyes stayed riveted on his large biceps as they contracted and stretched.

I blinked and swallowed while I gathered my composure. "Good. It was good. Especially everything you said about focusing on maintaining balance so you don't end up on the ground."

"The next time we meet, I'll show you what to do if you do end up on the ground and also how to get your attacker on the ground first," he said. His face was serious, and I tried not to think about an attacker trying to get me on the ground. Or Saint trying to get me on the ground. Both of those images seemed equally dangerous in very different ways.

I turned back to my locker to grab my undershirt and slip it over my head. I needed to get control of the situation and put us squarely back on professional terms. Neither of us was there to make friends.

"August?" he asked.

"I don't remember telling you to use my first name," I said over my shoulder as I slid on my dress shirt. It was in a crumpled ball from when Saint had tossed it into the locker earlier. My heart hammered as I did up the buttons. Out of the corner of my eye, I saw Saint startle and glance at me before looking away.

Fuck. What did I just do? I knew that look on his face because I was usually the one sporting it. It was the look of embarrassment at being called out. I owed him an apology.

"I—"

Before I could continue, Saint interrupted me with a clearing of the throat. "Why self-defense? Did something happen to make you feel threatened, *Mr. Stiel?*"

I turned back to face my locker and closed my eyes. I was screwing everything up as usual. This was a question I'd known I was going to get, and I really didn't want to have to admit what a fucking scaredy-cat I was.

I shrugged. "Everyone should be able to defend themselves," I said. I wondered if he recognized it as the nonanswer it was. My fingers finished fumbling over the final buttons of my shirt.

"True. But—"

"Good night, Mr. Wilde. See you next time," I said with a nod before grabbing my wallet, car keys, and phone and exiting the locker room.

As I made my way out to the parking lot behind the building, I remembered his words about keeping my back straight and my eyes up. The autumn evening was brisk and gloomy, and it reminded me Halloween was coming.

I clicked the fob and saw lights blink on my SUV. As I slid into the clean leather seat, I breathed out a sigh of relief.

I'd done it. I'd taken a step toward eradicating this ridiculous weakness I'd been feeling since the break-in. Hopefully the self-defense classes would help me establish some form of self-confidence. And now for the next step. I would drive my car around to park behind my shop so I wouldn't have so far to walk in the dark later.

After shifting the car into gear and pulling out of the parking space, I dialed Rory, but Katrina answered.

"Hey, sweetie," she said with a smile in her voice. "Your sister's out grabbing us dinner. How'd your first lesson go?"

I saw Saint walking out of the building next to another man about his same size. The guy with him was also good-looking. Did they only hire models at that fucking place?

My chest tightened as I saw Saint reach out to wrap his beefy arm around the other guy's shoulder. They were both laughing, and I noticed Saint's wide open smile and the crinkles in the corner of his eyes. It was such a far cry from the chastened version of him I'd ditched in the locker room. What must it feel like to be that free and happy, hanging out with another person you felt that comfortable with? I wanted to be the guy sharing the joke with him—and for some reason, I didn't want the other guy anywhere near Saint. I wondered if they were more than friends.

"Augie?" I heard through the car's Bluetooth speakers.

"Shit, sorry. Hi, Kat. It was good."

"Tell me everything." Her familiar voice was reassuring, and I slid down into my seat to enjoy the temporary company.

"The guy is cute as hell. Like... I wanted to climb him and touch him all over," I admitted. She and my sister were the only people on earth I'd have the guts to admit that to.

Kat's laughter filled the car. "Describe. Surely the guy is built if he teaches self-defense."

I sighed. "He's a million feet tall with thick blond hair. Maybe in his late twenties or early thirties. Total baby face but the most beautiful light blue eyes. And yeah, totally built. But not overly veiny or anything like a bodybuilder dude."

"Sounds like a blond version of Marco," she said, referring to her younger brother. "Hopefully, your guy has better manners though."

Marco had been the one who'd brought my sister and Kat together five years before. He'd been Rory's lab partner in a college science class, and when Rory'd discovered his sister was the gorgeous anchor on television she'd always lusted after, Marco had offered to introduce them. It had been love at first sight between my sister and Katrina. They were perfect for each other despite the ten-year age difference. Besides my homophobic family, the only problem was Kat's career. She worked for a network that would drop her like a hot potato if a whiff of her sexuality became public.

One night when Rory was supposed to accompany me to a charity fundraiser, she'd sent Kat in her place. Media speculation of the lovely news reporter and one of the wealthy Stiels together in a relationship was like catnip. Our denials somehow made it seem even more true.

After a while, we finally realized the rumors got my mother off my back even better than it got the network off Kat's. Win-win. As far as the public knew, Kat and I had been together for over two years.

"He's different from Marco..." I tried to articulate what I was thinking. "Less refined. More... raw strength or something. Marco is like a sleek panther. Elegant. Saint is like..."

"Hold up. *Saint?* His name is Saint?"

"Don't make me yell *Polo* again," I griped. "Anyway, Saint is more like an overgrown puppy who doesn't know where his own feet are."

There was silence on the other end of the line for a few moments. I hardly noticed since I was still picturing the cute kitten I'd just spent so much time with.

"You like him." Her voice was softer and seemed to hold a tinge of concern.

"Isn't that what I said? It's a problem. You're not supposed to have a crush on the guy who's teaching you to punch shit."

"Why not? What's wrong with a little crush?"

I groaned and closed my eyes, leaning my head back on the headrest. "Ugh, Katrina. You make me sound like a kid. What's wrong is springing wood in the middle of a lesson."

Her laughter made me snort too. "Sounds like a personal problem," she said after she got her chuckling under control.

"He's so hot," I whined. "So, so hot."

"So, why don't you flirt with him? See what happens?"

"No. Not him. He'd kick my ass. But it kind of made me think about going to our local gay night at the pub."

Kat's squeal almost burst my eardrums. "Oh my god, Augie! That's a great idea! I've been so worried about you. I'm thrilled to hear you say you're going to put yourself out there. It's about time."

"Now you're making me sound like a charity project," I said. "With friends like you, who needs enemies?"

"Shut up. Go get a drink and call us after. I expect you to sit down and have at least one conversation with a cute guy. Understood?"

I took in a deep breath and held it before letting go.

"Understood."

CHAPTER 6

SAINT

I WALKED OUT INTO THE CHILLY OCTOBER NIGHT WITH OTTO. MY BRAIN whirred with thoughts of August Stiel. The man was somewhat of a mystery. One moment he seemed like a stereotypical rich kid who wanted everything a certain way, but during other moments, he seemed incredibly unsure of himself and insecure.

I wondered if even he knew what he wanted or who he was. Part of me felt a little sorry for him. He clearly didn't seem comfortable in his own skin. I hated that for anyone, even if they were a little distant like he was. It was clear he'd built a massive stone fortress around himself and I wasn't one of the lucky ones he'd let in.

"Aren't we walking to the pub?" Otto asked as we approached my truck.

"Yeah, I just need to toss my stuff in here. Is anyone else joining us besides Seth?"

"West said he'll meet us there. He needs to go home and change, which I think was code for sneaking in a quickie with Nico. I texted Sassy to see if she wanted to join us, and she said she'll try. Who else is there?"

"What about Hudson?" I asked.

Otto's laugh was warm and rich in the dark evening air. "You

37

kidding? He'll be there. It's rainbow night. Ain't no way he's letting Charlie flirt with all the cute guys without supervision."

"He's so fucking whipped," I said with a smirk.

"Pretty much. It's still hard for me to wrap my head around him being with another man."

"Agreed," I admitted before unlocking the doors and throwing my bag in the truck.

"We should actually get Stevie over there to flirt with Charlie. Get Chief Paige and Hudson both fired up with jealousy," Otto said with a chuckle as we turned to walk across the square.

We were still laughing when we entered the pub. The music was turned up louder than usual, and there was way more skin showing than on a normal night at the pub. My brain flashed briefly on the memory of August Stiel in the locker room shower, and I felt my lower belly squeeze. Lean muscle stretched over a trim frame. Smooth skin slick with shower water. The rounded cheeks of his ass bunching as he turned to look at me. The memory clip was short but sweet, and it had been playing on a repetitive reel since I'd walked out of Twist.

God, I needed to get laid.

I forced my eyes around to find someone to strike my fancy while Otto took off toward where Seth stood ordering drinks at the long bar. I didn't even need a drink at this rate. I just needed to feel a hot mouth on my cock as soon as humanly possible.

I looked around and followed my nose until I saw a man who caught my eye. There was a small but crowded dance floor in the opposite corner of the pub from the dart boards. Men moved to the music and took advantage of the small area to touch each other as much as at any crowded club in Dallas. I was pleasantly shocked at the pickup scene our little local pub had managed to create in only six months of being open. The man I'd spotted saw me watching him and smiled a knowing smile. *Bingo. Target acquired.* I made my way closer until my hand landed on his hip, and I began to match his rhythm. His hands grasped my sides as he leaned closer and brushed my ear with his lips.

"Are you looking for someone to throw around tonight?" he asked in a voice that sounded nothing like I'd imagined. I felt myself stiffen and looked at him, quirking a brow. He smirked. "I hope to god you like it rough because your size is really doing it for me."

It wasn't an unusual response to my size, but it took me off guard anyway. I looked down at the man and wondered what had drawn me to him. He was much smaller than I was, which, agreed, was my type, and he had thick dark hair that looked messy in the very best way. He was wearing a blue button-down and charcoal suit pants. It wasn't until he tilted his face up that I realized it was the dark-framed glasses that had caught my attention. The same type of glasses worn by a certain geeky client of mine.

Fuck, was I really that obsessed?

I stood for a moment, trying to decide whether my reasons for picking that particular man really mattered in the grand scheme of things. No, they didn't. But the fact that my dick was as soft as a marshmallow did matter.

"Sorry, man. Just looking to dance a bit," I said. We danced for a couple of songs until I excused myself to go to the bar and say goodbye to my brothers.

Charlie looked across at me with a wide grin. "Not taking him home? That kid was cute enough. What happened?"

"I have a headache," I lied. "I'm heading to the ranch. You guys don't mind if I bail?"

Hudson and Otto looked at each other before glancing back at me. "Of course not. But are you sure you're okay?"

They were my brothers, and I knew they could see right through me.

"I'll be fine. See you tomorrow." I turned to go and saw August Stiel walk through the door looking like a terrified bunny frozen in front of a vicious wolf.

Did the poor man have any idea what he'd just walked in on?

"Hi," I said after quickly making my way over to where he stood. My stomach twisted in a knot seeing him so out of place and nervous.

He blinked at me, and if it was possible to look even more uncomfortable, he did. My heart went out to the guy.

"Let me get you a drink and introduce you to my brothers," I said quickly. The sooner I could get him some liquid courage, the sooner my heart might stop squeezing from his discomfort.

"Oh. Okay," he said quietly, looking around at all the men in the pub. "No... I should go."

There was no way I was letting him leave like that. Even if he wasn't gay, I didn't want him to feel unwelcome in my brothers' pub. I put my hand on his lower back and steered him toward the bar where I'd just said good night to everyone just a few moments before. The warmth of his body met my hand through the starched shirt, and I pressed a bit more firmly to feel more of it.

"Just stay for one drink?" I asked. "It's on me."

"You looked like you were leaving," he said.

"I... well, I was, but... then I saw you."

His eyes met mine, but before he could ask me what the hell I'd meant by that, Otto called out to us. "Back so soon?"

"Guys, this is..." I lifted a brow at him, wondering how to introduce him.

He blushed and murmured, "You can call me Augie."

The warm rush of victory heated my skin as one tiny chunk of his defensive walls crumbled at my feet. "August Stiel, this is Otto, Hudson, and behind the bar is Charlie."

The three of them stared at us before Charlie spoke. "Saint, love... we know Augie very well. He owns the antique store next door."

I felt my face heat. "Oh. Right. Well, I didn't know him before tonight, so... can he get a drink?" I turned to him. "What would you like?"

"Pint of Auld Best please," Augie said, shifting on his feet. I realized when I felt his movement under my palm that I still held a hand to his back. Pulling it away was excruciating, but I forced myself to do it anyway.

"I'll take the same," I said to Charlie. "And can we please get some of that beer cheese dip you have? That stuff is awesome."

As soon as Charlie gave me a nod and a wink, I led Augie over to a small table in the corner, away from the dancing and louder groups. I held out his chair for him and pushed it in as he took his seat.

Once I sat down too, we stared at each other, and I suddenly realized I'd usurped whatever plans he'd had for coming.

"Oh god, I didn't mean to steal you," I said quickly. "Did you… were you meeting someone here?"

Augie looked around as if still in a daze. "No. I was just going to grab a drink before heading home. I remembered it was rainbow night or something."

"Is that why you decided to leave? You remembered when you saw all the guys?" I tried not to let the thought disappoint me, but I had to admit to remembering what a conservative family he came from.

"What? No. That's why I came in the first place. But I'm not used to being…"

He paused long enough for me to consider prompting him, but then he finally finished his sentence.

"Out."

Oh. *Ohhhh.*

"I thought you were dating a woman in Dallas?"

His face registered surprise before he shoved his glasses up with one long finger and sat forward. "I am. I mean, I was. Well, I am. But not really."

I felt my mouth widen in a grin. He was fucking adorable. And now I knew he was gay.

Score.

"You're dating her but not really dating her," I said with a chuckle. "Clear as mud."

"She's a close friend. We went together to a big fundraiser a few years ago in Dallas and the media jumped to conclusions. When my family and Kat's work friends got all excited about it, we decided to let them believe whatever they wanted to believe."

"I guess it isn't easy to be out when you're from a conservative family."

Augie snorted and took a sip of his beer. "Hell no. That's an understatement. I learned early on, being gay isn't something a Stiel man does."

I leaned in like I was confessing a secret. "You should become a Wilde. Being straight isn't something a Wilde man does."

He barked out a laugh, which got the attention of my brothers and Charlie behind the bar. Otto and Hudson meandered over and pulled up chairs to our little table. The irrational part of me was annoyed at sharing Augie's company, but I'd also missed my brothers since I'd been on the road so much with Gemma.

As soon as they sat down, the conversation went to the success of LGBT nights at the pub, gossip about the elementary school principal sleeping with one of her kindergarten teachers, and the upcoming bonfire night out at Walnut Farm.

Augie laughed when Charlie popped into the conversation and acted like he didn't know what a bonfire was. His fake American accent sounded like a melodrama cowboy act and had all of us in stitches. Hearing August Stiel cut loose and relax was enough to make me feel buzzed. When he smiled that much, the very corner of one side of his mouth curled up, making him appear ten years younger.

As the next couple of hours wore on, I found myself sitting closer to Augie and resting my arm on the back of his chair. When Hudson told the story of me stealing a horse from Grandpa's barn one night when I was twelve and getting as far as the second pasture before getting bucked off, Augie turned to me with a raised eyebrow and leaned in to bump me with his shoulder. I wondered if the beer was responsible for bringing him more out of his shell.

"See? Even that horse wasn't intimidated by you, kitten," he teased.

"Ha! Smart man. My brother's a total kitten," Otto said, his face splitting into a grin. He puffed up and got close enough to loom over Augie as if to show he was bigger and more intimidating than I was. But the minute Otto approached with a pretend menacing look, Augie shrank back against me with the soft hiss of an indrawn breath.

A fear response.

Otto didn't notice and sat back down laughing. Augie tried to laugh it off, but when I put a reassuring hand on his shoulder, I felt a slight tremble in his body.

I leaned in to whisper in his ear. "Hey, you okay?"

He nodded quickly and smiled at me, but it didn't reach his eyes. "Yeah. I just think it's time for me to head home. I have to be at the shop early to meet a delivery."

"I'll walk you to your car," I offered.

"No, that's fine—"

I met his eyes and shook my head. "Please let me. I'm heading out anyway."

He nodded and leaned forward to say good night to the rest of the guys at the table. I followed suit and then led Augie out of the pub and into the cool night air. As the breeze ruffled through his shirt, I caught the barest whiff of the gym shampoo scent from his hair.

I wanted to touch him, to lean in for a sniff and place a kiss behind his ear. My self-control and desire to keep my job warred with the sudden need to be closer to him, to watch over him. I considered offering to follow him home just to make sure he got there okay, but then I had to remind myself the man was an adult. And for all I knew, the well-educated antiques expert had no interest whatsoever in a gym rat who'd barely made it through high school.

Augie made a squeaking sound before stopping in his tracks. I was so lost in my head, I nearly knocked him to the ground, stopping just in time to grab him around the waist to keep him from launching forward upon impact. Up ahead was a dark SUV with its passenger door hanging open and papers spilling out onto the ground.

"Is that your car?" I asked, scanning the area around it to see if I could find anyone nearby who may have seen what happened. My arm tightened around his front automatically.

"Yes," he said breathlessly. "Oh god."

I released my hold around his waist and reached for his hand. He was shaking again. What the fuck had happened to this guy to make him so scared? And why hadn't his car alarm gone off if someone had entered it illegally?

We approached the vehicle together and peered inside.

"Did you leave it unlocked?" I asked, getting closer and peering inside.

"I mean… it's possible I forgot to lock it," Augie said quietly. "But that wouldn't be like me. I'm kind of… careful about stuff like that."

"There are no signs of forced entry," I noted. "Should we call the sheriff's office?"

"No, god no. I just want to go home," he said. The poor man sounded defeated.

"I'm sorry this happened. Do you want me to follow you home?"

The edge of his lip quirked up. "No, thanks. I'll be fine. I have my new ear clap skills, remember?"

I turned him toward me and put my hands on his upper arms to force him to meet my eyes. "You call me if you need anything at all. Okay?"

He looked so lost in that moment, worried and unsure. I wanted to scoop him up and take him somewhere safe, reassure him that whatever had him feeling off-kilter was just in his mind. But I didn't know that. Hell, I didn't know much of anything about the guy. I did know that these feelings were new for me. I'd felt very protective in the past of my family members, the other members of my SEAL team, and even the civilians we'd been tasked with keeping safe during different missions. But it had never felt quite like this.

Looking out for those other people had felt like my job, my responsibility, whereas looking out for Augie felt like some kind of ridiculous inner need that came from my gut.

I forced myself to go against every instinct and let him go. Once he'd pulled out of the lot, I made my way to the truck and headed toward the ranch.

As I made my way out of town, I cursed my fickle nature. I'd gone to the pub tonight looking for a quick fix. Yet, the last thing I needed was to get a reputation in Hobie or even in my own damned family of being more interested in a hookup than in spending time with my brothers. What the fuck was wrong with me that I'd even considered a quick fuck with a stranger at Hudson and Charlie's pub? Hadn't I already had enough meaningless fucks with strangers to last a lifetime? Hell, I'd spent the first year after leaving the navy finding as many men to fuck as humanly possible. It was like making up for all the lost time when I was balls-deep in mud and live fire during my time as a SEAL instead of balls-deep in a tight body like other men my age.

Maybe instead of trying to find sexual satisfaction in Hobie, I needed to get to the bottom of what had spooked August Stiel in this tiny quiet town. Instead of heading straight to the ranch, I turned toward the address listed for August Stiel in the contact info Lanny had given me. It wasn't too far from my grandfathers' place, so I simply passed by slowly enough to make sure he'd gotten home safely and turned on some lights inside before making my way to the ranch.

As soon as I settled into my bed in the bunkhouse, I planned to take out my laptop and start digging. I hadn't had enough time earlier to really get to the good stuff, and something about Augie's skittishness made me antsy enough to want to learn more.

When I arrived at the ranch, my truck tires crunched over the long gravel drive before coming to a stop in front of the low, wide house with the wraparound porch. Doc and Grandpa sat together on an outdoor love seat with a big flannel blanket wrapped around them and Doc's head resting on Grandpa's wide shoulder. It was a sight so familiar and comforting, I felt it deep into my bones.

I was home.

CHAPTER 7

AUGIE

I REALIZED I'D ZONED OUT IN THE MIDDLE OF CHARLIE'S STORY ABOUT whatever Netflix series he and Hudson were hooked on these days. "I'm sorry."

Charlie reached a hand across the battered wooden surface of the antique farinier I used to check out customers at the shop. "It's okay. But you've been drifting off more than usual lately. Is everything okay?"

The man had become the closest thing to a friend I had here in Hobie in the six months since I'd moved back.

"Someone broke into the farmhouse," I admitted, pulling off my glasses to swipe them clean with a cloth from one of the drawers in the farinier. I didn't mention the car thing from the night before. "It happened last week. I guess it still has me a bit rattled. I'm not sleeping very well at night."

Charlie's expressive face dropped into surprise. "Does Seth know?"

I laughed. Hobie was small enough that half the town was related to the sheriff, including Charlie's partner, Hudson. "Yes, he knows. I called 911 and they came out immediately. There wasn't much they could do. The burglar took the usual. Laptop, wallet, etc. The only other things missing were a jar of old keys and some antique writing boxes from my slope collection."

Charlie looked at me like I was speaking Greek. I tried to clarify. "The boxes were each worth several hundred dollars and easy to grab."

He blinked at me. "And a country boy looking for easy money would know that how?"

It was the question most on my own mind. I shrugged. "I don't want to think about it. The only place around here to fence something like that is with me. So now, I'm terrified I'm going to turn around one day to check out a customer and come face-to-face with my own burglars here in the shop."

"Shit, Augie," Charlie said, reaching down to pluck my cat, Milo, up from where he was running figure eights through Charlie's legs. "Maybe you need some extra security around here. You know... Saint is a security special—"

"Saint can't know about the break-in," I blurted.

"Why not?"

I tried toning down the freak-out. "I just don't want everyone knowing my business, that's all."

"But while he's in town, you might as well take advantage of his knowledge about security measures."

"He doesn't normally live in Hobie?"

"He lives and works in Dallas. You didn't know that?" Milo's loud purr and face-bumping distracted Charlie while my head spun. Why was Saint the one in Hobie giving me self-defense lessons if he didn't normally live and work here?

The shop door opened with the tinkle of a bell. I scurried over to help the mail carrier with a stack of boxes. "Mrs. Parnell, let me grab some of those," I said to the older woman. "If they're the books I've been expecting, they're probably super heavy."

"Good morning, Augie," she said with her usual energy. "I heard about the break-in at Melody's old place. Any leads yet on the perps?"

In addition to being one of many town gossips, I suspected Mrs. Parnell was also an avid television watcher. If she knew about the burglary, I could forget any expectation of privacy.

"You'd have to ask the sheriff, I'm afraid," I said, grabbing the entire stack of boxes from her and turning to take them to the back room. I didn't see Charlie's dog, Mama, dart out to greet our visitor, and I tripped over her, tipping toward the wooden floor face-first. With my arms full of boxes, there was no hope of surviving the fall without major damage.

I heard Charlie's high-pitched screech as well as Mrs. Parnell's shout of warning before two strong bands of muscle grabbed me and pulled me upright. One of the boxes tumbled out of my grip, but while I bobbled the other two, I caught the familiar scent of Saint Wilde's unique aftershave. Before I could accidentally pitch the remaining boxes onto the floor to join the third, Saint reached around and took them out of my arms, stepping over to the cashier stand to set them down on a steady surface.

"Good morning, Charlie," he said as if he hadn't just saved me from breaking my face on the rough wooden boards of the antique shop floor. "I was hoping to find you here." That last part was mumbled into my ear rather than said to Charlie. The deep, low voice set all the hair on my body into high alert.

Out of the corner of my eye, I caught Mrs. Parnell batting her ancient eyelashes at Saint. I wanted to growl.

"Well, if it isn't one of the Wilde boys," she tittered. "I didn't know you were in town, sweetheart. What brings you home? I thought you were touring with that famous... what's her name? Carla? Rosita? Lolita? The pop star you were guarding. You know the one. Barely wears any clothes." She whispered that last part, most likely so Jesus didn't hear her. It was a common affliction among Texan busybodies.

I sensed Saint's body stiffen.

"Gemma, ma'am. I've been removed from her service."

"Oh, what a shame." Clearly, she didn't think it was a shame at all.

"Not a shame. I'm working with another valuable asset now. One whose company I much prefer." His eyes slid toward me, and I could have sworn I saw him take in a sudden breath before he winked.

Winked.

At *me*.

I gulped. Surely I was mistaken. I cleared my throat and moved to the table where the boxes were sitting so I could begin opening them. After tugging on the edge of one of the stubborn things with no success, I walked around the table to find a pair of scissors. Saint continued chatting with Mrs. Parnell while reaching for the box and ripping it open effortlessly. He swiveled it toward me and continued his conversation.

I stared at him.

Milo jumped up to see what was in the package. Within seconds, Saint's big hands were all over my cat, stroking and caressing his tortoiseshell coat. Milo preened under his attentions while I stared in a jealous stupor.

"Hey, sweetie," Saint murmured. "Who are you?"

Before I could say anything, Charlie spoke up in his lovely Irish lilt. "That's Milo. A rare male calico. Mama's been having an affair with him for many months now. It's quite awkward considering your grandfathers' dog Grump is her baby daddy." Charlie turned to me with a frown. "Is that the right phrase? Baby daddy?"

I nodded, but before I could open my mouth, Mrs. Parnell cut in. "Oh *you*. Those puppies were so beautiful. I see at least three of them on my route every day." She leaned over to scratch Charlie's border collie on the head. "Well, I must be off. Augie, stay safe and get yourself one of those alarm systems on the old place, okay? Good to see you back, Saint. Don't be a stranger, you hear?"

"Yes, ma'am," he responded, smiling and waving until she was gone. His forehead crinkled as he turned back to study me. "You okay?"

I looked behind me to see who he was talking to. The only thing there was the Edwardian stand mirror that always showed movement in the store and assisted me regularly in scaring the crap out of myself.

"Who, me?" I asked.

Saint's expression softened. "Yes, you. When I came in you were three inches from a broken nose. You all right?"

"Oh, uh... yeah. I'm fine."

He studied me for a moment as if making sure I was telling the truth. His scrutiny made me squirm, so I busied myself unpacking one of the boxes of books onto the counter.

"Charlie," Saint said. "I need to speak to Mr. Stiel about something private. Do you mind...?"

Charlie looked between Saint and me. "Mr. Stiel? Who the hell is—"

I looked up and caught Charlie's eye.

"Oh, hmm. Well, okay. I guess." He watched us over his shoulder as he sauntered out of the shop. "Come on, Mama. Augie, call me."

I nodded, even though I'd never called the man before in my life. I'd spent the first six months living in the room over the shop until I got up the nerve to move into the farmhouse, but even then, I was usually too nervous to pop around to the pub for a drink by myself. The sum total of my visits with Charlie were when one or the other of us was fetching or returning Mama to the pub from my shop or the handful of times I'd ventured out for a beer at his pub.

When Charlie was gone, I suddenly realized the obvious. I was alone with Saint Wilde. My heart thumped and my stomach flopped around like a dying fish. I looked around frantically for the bottle of cold water I usually kept in the shop. Was it under the counter of the farinier? No. On the bookcase with the provenance files? No. Was it—

"Looking for this?"

I whipped my head around to see Saint holding out my water bottle. "How did you know what I was looking for?" I reached out and took the bottle, being careful not to let my fingers touch his. The daydreams I'd had about touching Saint Wilde had kept me up half the night jacking off. I was afraid if I touched him for real, my dick might get the wrong idea.

And then the big navy SEAL would know the resident loser had a giant crush on him.

"You sounded like you were choking."

Water shot out of my nose, making his assertion come true. "Crap," I sputtered. "Shit."

I grabbed a few tissues out of a box in a nearby drawer and wiped my face. "Sorry. No. Well, I mean, yes. Now I am."

I wasn't even sure what I was saying. Being around Saint was suddenly impossible if I wanted to keep any semblance of dignity.

"What do you need?" I asked in my haughtiest voice.

His eyes were like lasers, and his nostrils flared. "Why didn't you tell me about the break-in?"

"Oh. Ahh… it was just a random break-in," I began, picking at the edge of the lip of the water bottle with a fingernail.

"Bullshit."

I blinked up at him. "What do you mean, bullshit?"

"Tell me about the antiques that were missing."

My heart was suddenly in my throat. I didn't want him or anyone to imply it was something other than a regular home invasion. The very idea I could be a deliberate target for violence was something I couldn't handle. "No," I whispered.

Saint's stern face softened into one of concern. He reached out slowly and clasped my shoulder with a large warm hand. I wanted to lean into him and feel more of his strength.

"Augie, please tell me. I saw the police report online. Why do you think they took those specific items?"

It was the first time he'd called me that. The nickname was somehow extra intimate spoken in his voice. I felt myself begin to shake. "They looked old. Maybe they thought that was the same as valuable. It was just… you know, random stuff. It's fine. I'm fine."

Saint's eyes again. Fuck. I looked away, fiddling with the cap of my water bottle and looking for something that needed doing in the shop. I heard him take in a breath like he was preparing to ask me more questions, make the connection between the home invasion and the vehicle entry the night before, but what came out wasn't what I expected.

"Okay. Well, I just wanted to make sure you knew you could call on me if you need anything. I mean… If you want me to check your house or help install extra security… I'm happy to help in any way. I don't want you to feel—"

Thankfully, he was interrupted by an older couple pushing into the store in the middle of an argument about the difference between a soup tureen and a punch bowl. I greeted the pair with a pasted-on smile and quickly ignored Saint in order to help explain the features of both the tureen and the punch bowl. By the time I explained several rare pieces of cutlery and helped them purchase a sterling silver gravy boat that was neither tureen nor bowl, Saint was gone.

It wasn't until later that evening when I went to close the shop that I found his note.

Augie, call me if you need anything at all. Sheriff Walker is my brother-in-law. It's natural to be nervous after the experiences you've had, and it wouldn't hurt to make sure they're not anything specific to who you are. Let me know how I can help. I realized last night I never gave you my number. - Saint

PS - Remind me to tell you about my grandfathers' vintage cake breaker and ice cream knife set. But if you dare say the phrase "marrow scoop" in my presence again, I'll insist on an extra twenty push-ups at our next session.

I chuckled at the mention of the marrow scoop and noticed he'd included his phone number at the bottom in small, clear print.

Specific to who I was? Was I a target because I was a Stiel?

I resisted seeing myself as the child my family seemed to think I was, but I couldn't deny feeling off-kilter and freaked-out by the implication. I was determined to find a way to get my confidence back and feel strong after the burglary. I'd agreed to take the self-defense lessons, but secretly wished I had my very own bodyguard. Someone to keep me safe so I wouldn't feel like I always had to watch my own back. If only I had the kind of job that could justify hiring one.

But that obviously wasn't happening, and besides, I didn't need anyone else to protect me. As my grandfather would say, I simply had a weakness that needed to be annihilated.

That was all.

CHAPTER 8

SAINT

WHEN I LEFT THE SHOP, I HEADED TO THE FIREHOUSE TO SEE IF I COULD catch up with Otto. Out of all my siblings, Otto was the one I was closest to besides MJ. We'd joined the navy together and even lived together in Dallas for a time after getting out. Now Otto was married to Hobie's sheriff, and I needed to see if I could pull some strings to get inside information about Augie's break-in or find out if there was suddenly an uptick in home invasions in Hobie.

Once inside the main bay door, I spotted Chief Paige talking to a young recruit. The woman was looking up at the chief as if he was some kind of superhero, which I guess around these parts he was. When the chief spotted me, he grinned. "Hey, Saint. Looking for your brother?"

"Yep. Was hoping to steal him away from you for a coffee break if that's okay."

Chief Paige nodded. "Sure thing. It's been slow around here today. Just bring me back a coffee if you head to Sugar Britches."

"What kind do you take?" I asked as I spotted Otto coming out of a door in the back.

Chief Paige's entire face softened into a lovesick smile. "Just tell Stevie it's for me. He knows what I like."

Since Stevie Devore and Evan Paige had been dating hot and heavy for almost six months, I couldn't skip the opportunity he'd just handed me on a silver platter.

"Oh, I'll just bet he knows what you like, Chief. But I wondered about the *coffee*."

Otto snorted as he approached us, and the woman standing with the chief looked back and forth between us all with a confused expression. Chief Paige looked down at her. "Stevie's my boyfriend," he said. I couldn't help but notice him stand up straighter and puff out his chest a bit. "He's the manager of Sugar Britches bakery on the square."

The woman's eyes just about bugged out of her head at the news her beloved fire chief had a male lover.

"O-oh. Well… oh!" she stammered and looked to Otto for help. "I didn't… that's… great?"

The chief's nostrils flared in irritation, but his smile remained plastered on. "Better than great. I'm the luckiest man in Hobie. I'm sure if you stick around, you'll see lots of Stevie at the firehouse."

"Yes, sir. That's… I mean, I look forward to meeting him," she said quickly before looking down at her feet.

I kind of felt sorry for the young woman, but it was better she get over her surprise quickly since Chief Paige wasn't the only person on her team who wasn't straight. I winked at my brother. "Let's go grab a coffee."

After making our way out of the station and heading toward the town square, Otto turned to me. "What's up?"

"Can you see if Seth can join us?" I asked.

Otto's brows furrowed, but he pulled out his phone and dialed Seth's number. "Hey, babe, you have time to meet me and Saint at Sugar Britches right now?"

He gave the sheriff a chance to answer before grunting and ending the call. "He'll meet us there in a few. Now spill. What do you want to see Seth for?"

I sighed. "You remember Augie from last night. It turns out his house was broken into, and the perp or perps took some portable antiques that a regular burglar wouldn't have known were particularly valuable. The man comes from serious money. I want to ask Seth what he found out after the break-in."

As we continued to walk the couple blocks to the square, Otto asked more about how I'd come to be giving the guy self-defense classes. I explained everything to him, including Augie's reluctance to consider personal security which really pissed me off.

Otto stopped walking and stared at me. "Seriously?"

"What?" I asked. "Clearly there's something serious going on." For some reason I sounded defensive even to my own ears.

"Saint, the man's house was broken into. It's hardly the making of a dangerous conspiracy."

"He needs someone to watch his back," I insisted.

"He needs a can of mace and an alarm system," Otto rebutted. "Why are you turning this into... oh shit." His grin widened as much as his eyes did. "You like the kid."

"What? No."

"You do. You like him. Can't blame you. He's goddamned adorable."

My teeth ground together. "You already have a partner."

I didn't know it was possible for Otto's eyes to get any wider. "I called the guy cute. I didn't say I wanted to fuck him."

Just the word out of my brother's mouth made me want to punch him. "Don't talk about him like that." My heart was pounding harder than normal in my chest. "Plus, as far as the world knows, he's straight. Has a girlfriend and everything." I might have done some more internet research about that late last night for the sake of... whatever. The photos and gossip columns were quite convincing. Katrina Duvall was a news anchor for one of the big stations in Dallas. She was stunning and elegant, the exact type of woman I was sure his family would love to see on his arm.

"He didn't look at you the way a straight man does, brother." Otto laughed. "You really fucking like this guy. Admit it."

"No I don't. He's a client."

"He may be a client, but he's pushing all your protection buttons for damned sure."

"Can we change the subject, please?" I asked.

"Your entire purpose for bringing me to the bakery was to talk about this."

Fuck.

As we turned the corner to head to the small storefront, Seth Walker approached in all his uniformed glory. I wolf whistled at him just to pay Otto back for being a prick.

Otto ignored me and jogged the last couple steps to take Seth into a big bear hug. "Fuck. You're a sight for sore eyes."

Seth kissed him while chuckling. "I saw you this morning at the breakfast table."

Otto pressed his face into Seth's neck and inhaled. Something about the gesture made my stomach hurt, and I quickly looked away.

The last person I'd even come close to having an intimate relationship with had fucked right off and slept with my cousin Web when he'd come to visit me in San Diego the first year I was in the navy. I hated the feelings of anger, betrayal, and resentment I'd felt toward both of them. No relationship had been worth fucking with my family.

After that, I'd decided I didn't have the time nor the inclination for relationships with feelings. I was a navy man. A SEAL for fuck's sake. It was A-okay for me to fuck, but love? Pfft. No need for that nonsense. I had a world to see and people to save.

After that, quick fucks before the next mission were my specialty. And when I'd come out of the navy almost two years ago, I'd embraced my reputation as a playboy even more. It wasn't until I began seeing my brothers fall in love that I wondered how long I could continue to fool myself into thinking casual sex would meet all my needs.

I heard Seth smack a kiss on Otto's lips, and I tried to shake off my moment of envy.

"I only have about fifteen minutes, and don't let me forget to order something for Luanne or she'll kick my ass," Seth said before pulling out of Otto's embrace and opening the door to the bakery for us.

We chatted with Stevie for a few minutes while ordering drinks and pastries. Once everything was ready, we found a spot in a quiet corner to talk. I explained that I was concerned for Augie's safety after what had happened.

"When we walked out of the pub last night, his car door was open. Someone had been through all his shit."

"You think he was specifically targeted?" Seth asked.

I shrugged. "He's a member of one of the wealthiest families in this part of Texas. It's not a stretch to think so. Did you know that the Stiel Foundation just pledged half a million dollars to the Second Amendment Foundation and 1.2 million dollars to Texas Right to Life? That's some serious money for two organizations involved in volatile media campaigns right now, not to mention the money they regularly contribute to other conservative groups. Lots of people are, excuse the phrase, gunning for the Stiels right now in this state. No matter what side of these issues you fall on, you have to admit, it's big money and big emotions tied together. That's dangerous."

Seth glanced quickly at Otto before looking back at me. "Has Landen Safekeeping been hired to look into this?"

"No."

"Then what's your interest here?"

I stared at him. "My interest is in keeping the man safe. Clearly, he's terrified, but he doesn't want anyone to know how much."

Now Otto and Seth both glanced at each other with one of those silent spousal messages. I grunted and looked down at my cookie, annoyed as hell at their stubborn personalities.

Seth's hand landed on my shoulder. "Have you asked him about it? Because the last I knew, he thought it was a standard residential burglary. We don't have evidence of it being anything else."

"How many other houses out that way have been burglarized lately?" I asked.

Seth paused for a beat. "None."

"See? Jesus. This isn't normal for Hobie. Can't you at least consider that there's something else going on here?"

"Saint, I get your frustration, but the standard items were missing from Augie's house as would be missing in any break-in. Small electronics, keys, wallet, a couple of portable antiques. Whoever did this had no specific knowledge of the safe hidden on the property or the high value of a small painting on the wall. They were smash-and-grab types looking for an easy fix probably. I mean, thank god his great-aunt wasn't still living there. Can you imagine if they'd found her alone and tried to ask her where the valuables were?"

It hadn't occurred to me the burglars might have confronted Augie. My stomach twisted painfully. "Did they approach Augie?" I asked. "Did they come into his bedroom?" I felt light-headed at the very idea of little August Stiel being awoken by thugs in his own room.

"No, they didn't approach him, but they did ransack his bedroom. He heard them break in and was able to hide in his closet I think."

I felt like I was going to be sick. Everything in me was screaming to go to him and make sure he was okay even though I'd only seen him an hour before. No wonder he was scared to death. He'd had to hide for his own damned safety while criminals were in his house going through his stuff. And how had they ransacked his bedroom without finding him in the closet?

"I have to go," I said, standing up and reaching for my wallet. I handed Otto some cash. "Don't forget to grab Evan something." They both stared at me like I was crazy, but I didn't wait around long enough to even apologize for acting weird.

I went straight back to Augie's Antiques.

CHAPTER 9

AUGIE

I WAS ON THE FLOOR TRYING TO COLLECT THE LAST OF THE ANTIQUE keys I'd spilled when I heard the bells tinkle over the door.

"Be right with you," I called.

"Need some help?"

I turned in surprise to see Saint. "What are you doing back so soon?" I asked.

He knelt on the floor and began picking up keys. "What happened?"

"Oh, I uh… I was unpacking an urn and didn't realize it was full of all these keys. I guess the broker included them in the package as a gift for me, but when I pulled out the urn upside down, they all tumbled onto the floor."

He glanced at me in confusion. "Why would he include a bunch of keys? What do they go to?"

"Nothing, really. I collect them. It's a personal thing. The man I bought this lot of urns from knows how much I love them." I hesitated for a second before continuing. "I… I love the mystery of old keys."

"What do you mean?"

I felt my face heat. "Ever since my great-aunt gave me a special antique key on a childhood visit to Hobie, I've always enjoyed daydreaming about what antique keys go to. As if maybe there's some ancient collection of interesting items in an old chest somewhere that no one knows is there because they don't have the right key." I swallowed, trying not to notice how close Saint's large body was to mine on the wooden floor of the shop. "It's silly, I guess. Simply the product of a wild imagination."

"I think that's really interesting," he said softly. "Like buried treasure without the map to lead you there."

I looked up at Saint, stopped short by his clear gray-blue eyes. "Exactly."

We were interrupted by the sound of my cell phone ringing. I pulled it out of my pocket to see my mom's photo lighting up the screen. "Excuse me," I murmured before answering. It was a long-ingrained habit not to keep my mother waiting.

"Mother," I answered before standing up and stretching my back.

"Augie, I need you to come to the city tonight. Meet me at Dakota's at seven."

Her high-brow sense of entitlement that I would jump when she said jump annoyed me immediately. "I can't. I have to work. The shop is open until six, and then it would take me a couple of hours to get to the city. Sorry."

I closed my eyes in frustration hearing the apology come out of my own damned mouth. Why was I sorry for doing my job?

"Find someone else to close the shop. It's important. Aurora will be there as well. I'm sure your sister misses you since you moved to the countryside."

My mother liked to refer to Hobie as "the countryside" as if it were a summer estate in an old English romance novel. Which was better than what my cousin Brett had always called it. But my mother slipping Rory's name in there to guilt me was a hot button of mine. And she knew pressing it worked every time.

I did have a part-time employee who could close for me, but he had a second job working evenings in a restaurant. When he closed, it left him precious little time to make it to the Pinecone for his shift. "I can't. What's so important that you need me there tonight?" I assumed it was most likely an investor or friend who particularly liked antiques. That was my mother's favorite time to trot out her knowledgeable son.

"I heard about the break-in. You need to tell me what happened. Why didn't you call me right away?"

Saint finished grabbing the last of the keys and stood up next to me to put them in the box with the others. His big muscled body was close enough to dwarf me, but instead of being intimidated by his size, I found myself wanting to lean into his sturdy frame.

I cleared my throat and tried to concentrate on my mother's words. "What?"

I tried ignoring the little smile that quirked up the edge of Saint's lush mouth. The man was sexy as hell. I let out a breath.

"August," she said in her clipped tone. "This is serious. You should have had a proper alarm system in place. Why did someone break into your house?"

I threw up my hand. "How the hell should I know? Why does anyone ever break into a house, Mom? To steal stuff, I guess."

Silence.

Saint shifted closer to me. I wanted to turn and bury my face into the front of his shirt. I was so fucking tired from not getting any decent sleep, and now my mother was making me feel like the burglary had somehow been my fault.

When the silence from the other end of the line became unbearable, I did what I always did with my family. I caved.

"Sorry for my outburst," I mumbled, turning away from Saint. "And I had a security system installed right after it happened. I didn't expect to need it in the countryside. Hobie has an insanely low crime rate."

"Have you seen Brett at all?"

The sudden change of subject threw me. My cousin and I didn't get along. Brett had been a complete terror to me growing up, and I avoided him as much as possible now that it was in my power to do so. "Um, no? Why would I have seen him? I've been here in Hobie since I met you for lunch at Grandfather's office a couple of weeks ago. The burglary happened after that."

"You should have told me," she continued. "Had I known Melody's house had been broken into, I would have insisted—"

"I'm sorry, Mom. I need to help some customers who just came in. Sorry about missing dinner tonight." I hung up before she had a chance to say another word. I turned to ask Saint why he'd come by.

He studied me with wrinkles of concern on his forehead. "Augie..."

"Why are you here?" I pushed my glasses up and looked around at the shop full of things Saint could have zero interest in. Surely he wasn't there as a customer.

"I wanted to ask you some more questions."

As much as I would have loved to have cried all my woes to the big protector, I resisted the urge to rely on a perfect stranger, and I knew that even talking about it would reveal just how upset the topic made me. The idea of transforming into the trembling, cowering weakling in front of Saint that I already saw myself as in general was untenable.

"No, thank you. I need to get back to work."

Saint took a slow pan of the shop which was empty of any customers. "I can see how slammed you are," he said flatly.

"Saint... I can't... I just don't want to talk about it anymore. It's over. I'm fine."

"Could the break-in have anything to do with your family's... money or... involvement in political issues?"

I could tell he was trying to be professional, but the implication rankled. "No."

"How do you know for sure?"

"Because I don't have anything to do with the company or the foundation. That's all my grandfather."

We stared at each other for a beat. I could see the man's frustration at not being able to solve the mystery behind my intruders. Leave it to a professional self-defense instructor to get annoyed at not being able to account for all factors and secure all angles.

"Let me take you to Dallas," Saint blurted. By the almost comical widening of his eyes immediately after, I could tell he'd surprised himself as much as me with his offer.

"What? Why?" Was he asking me out? No. Surely not.

Saint cleared his throat. "Well, your mother wants you to come to dinner, and I'd love a chance to meet her."

Oh. Oh, right. It wasn't me he wanted to spend time with in the city. It was either my beautiful, elegant mother or my famous, rich, and influential family. My heart tumbled to the floor like an idiot. I had so much experience being used for my connections, there was no telling why I was surprised by this.

"No. I'm not going. I have to close the shop."

"I'll get my sister Sassy to come hold down the fort. She's worked a ton of retail and lives just a few blocks away over the doctor's office. I'm sure she wouldn't mind."

"Why in the world would I need you to drive me to Dallas? And how exactly would I explain your presence to my mother?"

My head was reeling with the conflicting emotions of disappointment that he didn't want me for me and the temptation of getting him alone in the car for several hours just so I could have an excuse to be near him. Plus, I had to admit to myself the idea of having him beside me at John's house filled me with a strange kind of relief.

"You could tell her I'm your personal security. Maybe it would make her feel better knowing someone was looking after you since the break-in and everything."

"Don't be ridiculous. I don't need a bodyguard."

I may have *wanted* one... but I didn't *need* one.

Saint stepped closer, overwhelming me with the same fresh scent I'd imprinted on during our first self-defense lesson. It made me dizzy with the effort not to actively sniff him like a dog.

"I'd like to take you to Dallas, Augie," he said in a low voice. The rumble went straight to my dick like a traitor. "Please."

I bit my teeth against the whimper that wanted to escape. "We'd be stuck there for hours. My mother never shuts up."

"If it's too late to come home, we can stay at my apartment in the city and drive back in the morning," he suggested.

My knees began shaking. Did he have a one bedroom? Would we be forced to share a bed? *Don't be ridiculous, Augie. The man would put you on the sofa before sharing a bed with you.*

"Augie?"

"Huh?" I sounded breathless even to my own ears.

"Can I call Sassy to come help?"

"Um…"

Saint's hand came up as if to touch me. I stared at it, tracking every millimeter of movement with my eyes and accelerating heartbeat. When his fingers reached out to pluck a piece of lint off my shirt, I almost cried out my disappointment.

"No," I said with a cough, shaking myself out of the daze I'd fallen into. What the hell was wrong with me? I didn't appeal to men like this. And I didn't have open crushes and flirtations. I had Katrina. And a hookup app if needed. "No, I'm fine. I'm not going to Dallas tonight. But thank you anyway for offering."

I turned around to move the box of keys… somewhere. Anywhere, really. I simply needed to get away from the magnetic pull that was Saint Wilde.

"I'll see you for our lesson tomorrow night," I said over my shoulder. "Thanks for stopping by."

I pretended not to see Saint's expression of concern and disappointment. I pretended not to care that the man had wanted to use me to get to my wealthy family the same way people had been doing to me for years.

And as usual, I pretended I was fine. Until two hours later when I got a text from my mother.

Mother: *Dinner tonight is nonnegotiable. I expect you to be here. And bring Melody's old writing box with you.*

I closed the shop early and made my way to Dallas, not realizing until I was halfway there that I'd forgotten the writing slope. It was a good thing I did though. During dinner at the restaurant, my car was broken into again in the parking garage attached to my grandfather's office building.

When I came outside after the interminable dinner where Mom's friend Merlina Giordano grilled me about the provenance of several small pieces of personal grooming items she'd bought at an auction, I discovered the smashed passenger-side window and the explosion of items that had been pulled from the overnight bag on the front seat. Nothing seemed to be missing except the box of old keys I'd brought from the shop to keep at home with the rest of my collection. Since I hadn't paid for them, it wasn't really a monetary loss, but it pissed me off nonetheless. What the fuck did someone want with a bunch of old metal keys? Was I just being harassed? If so, by whom?

As soon as the cops were done taking my statement so I could claim the damage on my insurance, I got my scaredy-cat ass in the car before speeding home to Hobie with the October wind freezing me into an ice cube through the broken window.

And I holed up in my attic nest without sleeping a wink all night.

CHAPTER 10

SAINT

WHAT THE FUCK HAD I BEEN THINKING?

Offering to take Augie to Dallas was the stupidest thing that had ever come out of my mouth. I was officially trying too hard to butt into business that was not my own while Augie was doing his best to make it clear my efforts were unwelcome.

So I'd nodded and left the shop with my tail between my legs. Unwilling to head back to the ranch with too much day left to think about my client, I took a detour to Twist to check in with Neckie. She'd called me earlier to ask if I could help cover some of her classes now that her pregnancy was taking its toll on her energy. I'd told her that wasn't a problem, so I had a good excuse to stop by and find out if there was any way I could help her that afternoon and evening.

"Hey, Saint," she said when I walked through the front doors of the studio. "I thought you weren't coming till tomorrow morning's stretching class?"

"I was free, so I thought I'd stop and see if you needed any help this evening."

She studied me for a minute before surprising me. "How's your sister?"

Her eyes were hard to read, but I noticed fine lines near her mouth.

"Which one?" I knew which one, but I wanted to be sure.

"MJ. I haven't seen her since Hudson and Charlie's pub opened. And I didn't even get a chance to talk to her before she bugged out of there."

I remembered MJ getting an emergency call from a client and having to head all the way back to Dallas late that night.

"She's okay. Working too hard, as usual."

"Oh." Neckie looked down at her belly where her hands roamed affectionately over her pale pink sweater. "Is she... is she seeing anyone?"

My brain whirred in vain, trying to determine how to play this.

"Um... no? I mean... she's..." I ran out of stupid words and just stared at her.

"Will you... ah, tell her I miss seeing her? I'd like to..." Her voice faded. "You know what? Never mind." She took a deep breath and plastered on a fake smile, rubbing the giant belly in front of her. "I'd love for you to help in the weight room if you don't mind. Several people have had dangerously bad form lately, and it's getting harder for me to correct them myself."

"Yeah, no worries," I said quickly, taking the out she'd offered me. I wasn't great at awkward conversations.

When I got back to the ranch much later that night, I told Doc and Grandpa that I suspected Neckie and MJ were star-crossed lovers. Doc's eyes got hearts in them while Grandpa's narrowed in concern.

"Don't mess with your sister's love life, Saint," Grandpa warned. "Nothing good will come from that."

"I disagree," Doc said, reaching over from his spot on the sofa to squeeze Grandpa's knee. "We should at least get them in a room together and see what happens."

"Liam," Grandpa groaned. "No one wants their grandfathers to set them up on a date."

"Pfft, how would you know? And I'm not suggesting we set them up. I'm only suggesting we facilitate a conversation. Saint, get her on the phone."

"Which one?" I asked.

"MJ. I'm going to tell her to come home."

"Wait. How do we know Neckie's available? She's pregnant. Doesn't that kind of imply she's with someone?" I asked.

My grandfathers exchanged a look before turning to me.

"Saint," Doc said. "It's not her baby. She's a gestational carrier for someone else."

The information surprised me, but ultimately it seemed to be good news for MJ. "Okay. Why are you acting like it's some big secret?"

Grandpa met my eye. "The secret is whose baby it is. We can't tell you that. But Neckie is single as far as we know."

That's all I needed to hear. I picked up the phone and told my sister to get her ass to Hobie.

I SPENT the next day before Augie's lesson helping Neckie as much as possible at Twist. Assisting with a yoga class was a harsh reminder of how little patience I had for meditation and calm stretching, so by the time Augie turned up that evening, I was wired for some true physical work. Anything to get out of neighborhood gossip and soccer moms doing downward dog. I wondered idly how to get more men to sign up for the yoga class.

When Augie entered the building, I was standing at the reception counter chatting with Leona, who was one of the personal trainers at Twist. She'd been telling me about her sister's wedding that weekend and how she'd caught the bridal bouquet.

"Leona," I said. "You'll make a gorgeous bride."

I heard a surprised sound and looked up to see the startled hazel eyes of my client. They were framed by inky smudges indicating poor sleep.

"Mr. Stiel," I said with a nod. "Welcome back."

Augie looked from me to Leona and back again. "Sorry to interrupt," he said in his quiet voice. The sound of it set off little vibrations of interest in my gut, and I straightened up from where I'd been leaning on the counter.

"You're not. Leona and I were just talking about tying the knot. Have you two met?" I asked.

Augie shifted a gym bag to his other hand before reaching out to shake Leona's hand. I wondered if he found her attractive as another potential fake girlfriend. She was petite and elfin-cute with a tumble of dark curly hair. The two of them would make an attractive couple, but just picturing it irked the hell out of me the same way seeing him with Katrina Duvall had in all the photos online.

He's gay, jackass. But you're going to have to get it through your thick skull he doesn't want someone with a thick skull.

They shook hands and Leona seemed to pop a few candy hearts out of her eyes when she noticed him smile at her.

Shit.

"Well," I said a little too loudly, "let's get changed."

Augie looked over at me, revealing the quotation mark divots in his forehead above the dark frames of his sexy glasses. Was he confused or worried? Either way, I hated seeing them and had the now-familiar sensation of itching to press them away with my fingers.

Instead, I shoved my hands in the pockets of my pants and tried to maintain some professionalism.

We walked to the locker room, and I held the door open for him but didn't follow him in this time. "I'll wait for you here," I said. As much as I'd have loved to watch him change, I didn't think it was acceptable for me to sit and drool as a client revealed his hot little bod to me in the Twist locker room. I still hadn't forgotten what his naked ass looked like or the smooth stretch of back muscle leading down to it. Not to mention his shapely calves and the soft slender curve of his hamstrings. Did he run? He looked like he ran. I wondered if—

"Dude, what are you standing in the hallway for?" I turned to see one of my coworkers from Landen in Dallas.

"Rex, what are you doing here?"

"Lanny sent me up here to upgrade the security system. I think it's part of how he's paying Twist for use of the space. The receptionist said I could take advantage of the facilities while I was here."

"Oh," I said, still thinking about Augie.

"Dude, you look like you're daydreaming about Chris Hemsworth," he said with a laugh.

"Caught me," I said. "Totally daydreaming about a hot piece of—"

Just then the locker room door opened and Augie walked out. He was wearing well-fitted gray trainer pants and a black tank top that revealed small but muscled rounded shoulders and shapely biceps.

"Ready?" he asked, before noticing Rex. "Oh, hi. Sorry."

Rex's smile turned predatory as he glanced over at me. "Well, hello," he said in his sultry Rexian way.

Fuck.

"We've got to get started," I said quickly, grabbing Augie's wrist and pulling him toward the training room. Augie almost tripped before catching his balance and falling against me. He craned his head back around to make eye contact with Rex.

"Sorry. Ah, it was nice to meet you," he said.

"Likewise, *Chris*. Hope to see you around much more in the future."

Goddamned jackass. I was going to challenge him to a shooting contest later just so I could beat him at something.

Augie followed me through the doorway to the room with the training mats, and we found ourselves blessedly alone like the last time. I realized I was still holding his wrist and dropped it like a hot potato.

I let out a breath and ran my hands through my hair. "Sorry," I mumbled.

"What for? He seemed nice. Although maybe not so good with names."

"Who, Rex? Nice? Nah. Not really," I said.

Augie coughed out a laugh. "Really? It looked like you two were friends."

"We are. Well, more like brothers, really. We served in the navy together. Several of us did. We came to work for Lanny's security company at the same time. As a team."

"That's cool. It must be fun to work together with your friends," he offered with a raised eyebrow.

I felt myself relax. "It is. Unless one or more of them are on a dangerous assignment, and then it's just as stressful as it was in the service."

"I can't imagine. They're all bodyguards? Is that hard for you?" Augie asked.

"What do you mean?"

He looked down and brushed a wrinkle out of his shirt. "Sorry. I didn't mean to make you feel weird about it."

"Weird about what?" I asked, feeling confused about what he was getting at.

"The fact that your friends all work in the field and you're stuck doing fitness classes."

I stood there and just stared at him while I tried reworking his words in my head to make sense.

"What... what do you mean fitness classes?"

His cheeks bloomed a deep red, and he kept his face down. Fuck, he was cute as hell.

"Sorry, *self-defense.*"

"I'm a personal security specialist," I corrected.

"Landen lets you have that title?"

"Augie, what are you saying?"

He looked up at me, the divots on his forehead again. "I didn't mean to make you feel bad. I just wondered if it was hard for you to be stuck teaching civilians like me while your teammates are out on security details or whatever. Especially since you seem to have the same background."

"I'm only 'stuck teaching civilians,' as you put it, for a few weeks as punishment for something stupid I did. I'm normally out there with my guys in the field."

Augie looked up at me, eyes widening. "Really? They let you go on missions?"

"Why wouldn't they?" I asked.

"Oh my god. Never mind. I shouldn't have said anything. I feel like an idiot. Forget it."

The red splotches on Augie's cheeks moved down to his throat.

"Are you saying I wouldn't make a good security specialist out in the field for some reason? Why?"

"Because you're not very threatening. I thought maybe you weren't intimidating enough for that kind of work," he said, lifting a brow up.

I couldn't help but bark out a laugh. "The kitten thing again? You really don't think I'm intimidating enough to be someone's body-guard? Seriously?"

"Sorry. Like I said, I didn't mean any offense."

"Augie, I'm six foot five and can bench-press any one of my team-mates. I was a navy SEAL for god's sake, and I carry a weapon most of the time. If I'm not intimidating enough to protect a celebrity from a few rabid fans, you have pretty damned high expectations," I said. "Or you've seen way too many movies."

"Can we just get started?" he asked, turning his back to me to do some stretching.

"Sure. But just so we're clear, no one has ever in my life made me feel so much like a child as you did right now. I'm not quite sure how I feel about it. Part of me wants to laugh, but the other part wants to apologize for some reason," I admitted with a chuckle.

"No need to apologize to me. It's not like I need your protection. Hopefully if and when the time comes, I can protect myself."

I suddenly realized he was putting up a front. He was trying to act tough when in reality, he was scared.

"Augie, do you think someone is going to confront you? Do you know what this is about?"

The man turned back to look at me and I could see the truth in his stormy eyes. "Do you mind if we skip this part and go right to learning the moves?"

Oookay then. Less talk, more action. Action, I can do.

I stepped closer to him to begin the move I wanted to teach first. His eyes locked on mine as I moved into his personal space, and I realized it was probably a good thing he didn't find me intimidating. That day's session involved me throwing him around a bit, and I didn't want it to freak him out.

After reaching one of my hands to his shoulder, I noticed his lips part. His eyes flared to life, and their color deepened. The skin of his shoulder was warm, and I felt my fingers tighten on it. A sudden flash image of throwing him down on his back on the mats raced through my mind and a sharp pang went from my belly to my groin in response.

"I'm going to throw you down on your back and lie on top of you," I said in a voice too rough for a professional setting. "And you're going to learn what to do to get out from under me or at least flip me over and get into the dominant position."

I saw his Adam's apple bob, and I wondered what he was thinking. Was he intimidated now? Surely it wasn't attraction... was it?

"Okay," Augie said in a noticeably squeaky voice. Shit. Maybe it was attraction. That would suck. It was bad enough for me to fantasize about my client but would be ten times worse if the client was actually interested in return. The last thing I needed was to get in trouble with Lanny again. "How? How can I defend myself against you?"

"I'm going to show you some moves, but remember one of the biggest rules: do whatever it takes to get away. Whatever it takes to catch them off guard. In general, you don't want to ever end up on the ground, right?" I asked.

"Obviously."

"What would you normally do to defend against me trying to put you down?"

I placed my hand on his shoulder while I spoke, facing him, and I moved my right foot around behind his right leg. After I began pressing his shoulder, he pushed back and fought to remain standing. Since I was larger and stronger, it was easy to overpower him and force him back over my leg and off balance. I reached out with my free arm to cradle him around the back as he fell.

"Dammit," he breathed, still trying to scramble against me and right himself. Once I had him on the ground, I lay over him, gently but firmly pinning his wrists to the mat beside his head and his legs to the mat with my legs and feet.

"'S'okay," I said softly. "Stop fighting it." After he forced himself to stop struggling against me, I continued. I couldn't deny enjoying the feeling of lying on top of him and looking down at him beneath me. Just the thought of getting him beneath me in bed made my cock fill.

When I spoke, my voice sounded foreign and rocky to my ears.

"The best thing to do when you feel like you're going to go down is to go down, but do it under your own power so you control the outcome. Remember what I said about using the element of surprise. Instead of fighting, pull the attacker toward you, and then roll when you drop. He will go over your head and lose his grip on you while you get some much-needed distance and pop back up."

I locked eyes with him and belatedly noticed my libido getting into a fistfight with my desire to stay gainfully employed. A part of me truly wondered which one would win if I stayed almost hip-to-hip with August Stiel on the mat.

He was still breathing heavy as he peered up at me with dark pupils. His chest brushed against mine on the inhale, and a sweet puff of air caressed my neck on the exhale. My eyes fell to his lips before I forced myself to look away and let him go.

I cleared my throat. "Just remember, flip your attacker and roll through the fall. Let's try it again," I said, standing up and reaching out a hand to pull him up. I must have pulled a little too forcefully because he came slamming into my chest with a grunt.

"Jesus, Saint," Augie said against my shirt before pushing off me. "Did you double dose on the steroids today?"

"For your information, this is 100 percent natural, Mr. Stiel. Determination and hard work," I corrected with a small grin.

He let out a reluctant laugh. "Duly noted."

This time when I tried to topple Augie, he immediately yanked my arm forward and dropped his weight down, creating a little speed bump of sorts that rammed into my shins. I went tumbling over him onto the mat. By the time I jumped back up, he was in a defensive stance backing well away from me.

"Much better," I said. "How did that feel?"

"Pretty awesome," he said with a giant grin. I felt my mouth turn up in a similar smile. It was the first time he looked proud of himself, and my heart leapt. I knew that feeling well. Accomplishing something you set out to do was invigorating.

"Try again. This time I'm not going to go easy on you," I said, assessing him as I stalked closer.

CHAPTER 11

AUGIE

I FELT ADRENALINE COURSE THROUGH ME AS SAINT APPROACHED ME. This time he didn't go easy on me. He grabbed my arm and spun me around until my back was against his front and his arms were around me in a reverse bear hug.

He was so much bigger than I was that his giant body engulfed mine and wrapped around it like a shell. My arms were pinned, and I frantically tried to remember what to do. I tried throwing my ass back into his groin, but he bent out of the way in anticipation. I tried throwing my head back, but his arms were like tight bands around me, limiting my range of motion.

I could hear his heavy breathing in my ear, and it was making me hot. Sweat poured out of me as my body's nerves fired sensations rapidly into my memory banks. The feel of his strong thighs pressing in behind my hamstrings, the sight of his thick forearm across my chest, the smell of his unique, fresh scent wafting off his hard body, only this time it was mixed with masculine overtones from our workout session. The combination was banging all kinds of pots and pans in my head, begging for my attention.

I struggled in his tight hold again, and his face came closer to rest against the side of mine with a scratch of beard against beard.

My eyes squeezed closed, and I tried everything I could think of to convince my body to try and get out of his hold. But how the hell could I be expected to fight him when all my body wanted to do was stay right where it was—feeling the intoxicating man against me?

"Stop and think," Saint murmured into my ear. "Do whatever it takes."

"I don't want to hurt you," I muttered as I reached up to grip the forearm he had tight around my upper chest.

I felt more than heard the grumble of a laugh. "Think I can't defend myself against a little antiques dealer?"

As I continued to struggle without making any progress, my eyes strayed to the muscled forearm I held. I moved before I could stop myself, leaning my head down until my mouth landed on his warm skin. I teased the skin first with the tip of my tongue and felt his entire body stiffen before I opened my mouth and bit down.

"Fuck!" he grunted, jumping back while still trying to hold on to me with the other arm he had around my waist. I followed his momentum toward his center mass and threw my body weight against his massive chest. We landed together on the mat in a heap of arms and legs with me lying on top of him but moving as fast as I could to scramble off.

Once I was moving away from him in a defensive crouch, I finally noticed his shocked expression.

And the red bite mark standing out angrily on his forearm.

My eyes snapped back up to his, and I felt my stomach drop as the reality set in. I'd hurt him. I'd hurt a man who could pound me into the ground with one fist.

"Saint," I said. "Oh my god." I raced back toward him and carefully reached out my hand for his arm. "Shit, shit. Saint, I'm so sorry. Fuck."

"It's okay," he said gently. "That was a really good move. It worked, didn't it?"

"No. I mean, yes it worked, but no, it wasn't a good move to use when we were just practicing." I lifted his forearm up to inspect it closely and run my fingers over it. The little hairs around it on his arm stood on end, and I felt another wave of embarrassment at doing something so childish. Had I really *bit* him?

"I'm sorry," I said again—only this time it was a whisper.

"Augie," he said, using his own fingers to tilt my chin up so he could see me. "I'm fine. You didn't even break the skin. Do you remember me telling you to do whatever it takes?"

"Yes, but—"

"And don't you think it would have been worse if you'd gotten me in the groin?" he said, a small quirk appearing on the side of his lip.

My face suffused with heat at the mention of Saint's groin, and I looked away.

Warm fingers gently guided my face back to his. "Augie, don't you think I'd be proud to know you could do that in a real-life situation? And seeing you do it here proves that to me."

I had to find a way to ratchet down the intensity of the moment, or I was going to walk into this big man's embrace seeking comfort and reassurance like a baby.

"I just know how bad it must make you feel to get bested by a little antiques dealer," I said with a straight face.

He blinked at me before realizing I was teasing. "Well, I didn't say my *feelings* weren't hurt."

I cracked a smile and stepped back, away from the long, warm fingers on my face. "What's next?" I asked.

ALMOST TWO HOURS later we were dripping with sweat and limping out of the training room toward the locker room.

"I can't believe you bit my leg, jackass," I complained, leaning down to rub the sore spot on my calf through my pants.

"Dude, you started it," Saint said. "Payback is hell."

"Yeah, but I'm the client," I whined. "And I can barely walk as it is without being reminded of this dog bite every time I move my muscle."

"Are you calling me a dog?" He turned to grin at me as he held open the door to the locker room.

"If the collar fits," I teased. Saint seemed more open and playful than he had the first night we'd met. I enjoyed seeing the lighter side of him and wondered if he'd just been in a serious mood the other night or if that was his norm. We'd spent the last part of our session teasing each other like old friends, and it felt comfortable and fun.

"We went twice as long as I'd planned tonight. I kind of lost track of time. You should alternate ice packs and hot baths for sore muscles. I'll grab you a chocolate milk for some protein. You'll need to hydrate and get some good sleep."

"Seriously? I didn't just run the Boston marathon."

The man disappeared for a moment before coming back in with two small cartons of chocolate milk. "Here. Drink it."

I did as he said, sitting down on a bench while I downed the cold sweetness. Saint sat down next to me and did the same. I could feel the heat radiating off his thigh next to mine on the narrow bench. We didn't speak as we drank.

As my body cooled further, my sweaty skin began to chill in the tiled locker room and I shivered.

"Did everyone leave, do you think?" I asked. I guessed it was late, and the building seemed empty.

"Probably. The owner is off today because of some medical appointments. Leona gave me a set of keys to lock up if I was here later than everyone else."

"Are you and Rex dating?" I asked before I could stop myself. My teeth clamped together after the words were out of my mouth, but it was too late to get them back.

"Who?" Saint asked.

"Never mind. None of my business. Forget I asked."

He grinned. "No. Rex and I aren't dating."

"Just friends?" I asked, clearly unable to stop myself from being nosy.

"Just friends."

"Oh." I rested my forearms on my thighs and rolled the plastic bottle back and forth between my palms.

I felt Saint's eyes on me. "Do you like to dance?"

My eyes flicked up to meet his. "Oh. Ah... yeah, I guess. Well, no. Not really."

Saint laughed, exposing the twisted tooth in his smile that made me want to drop my pants and beg. "Well, which one is it? Yeah, I guess, or no, not really?"

I swallowed. "I like to, yes. But I suck at it. So I try never to do it in front of other people."

"That's too bad. Life's too short to worry about what other people think about you," Saint said in a kind voice. "You should go out to a club one night where you don't know anyone and just let go. Swing your arms, shake your ass, and throw your head back."

I imagined Saint doing that and felt my lips turn up. "You're probably a little bit crazy, aren't you?"

He laughed again. "Yeah, I guess. My mom used to call me a loon."

"I can see that. Where are you from?"

"Born and raised right here in Hobie."

"Oh. I guess I knew that if Hudson is your brother" was all I could think to say. "Are your parents still in Hobie?"

"Nope. They're halfway around the world living abroad. What about you?" Saint's smile was still there, but it no longer reached his eyes. I wanted to take back the stupid question that removed the sparkle from his eyes.

"Dallas."

"Highland Park boy?"

"Something like that," I replied. I wondered if kids who grew up with my family's kind of money were automatically assholes in Saint's book. If so, I could hardly blame him. I knew from experience those guys could be the worst of the bullies.

"Well then," Saint said, standing up and grabbing our containers to toss in a nearby recycling bin before tossing me a wink. "I'd better let you get cleaned up so you can get home and count your gold bricks."

I wanted to reach out and stop him. Stop this conversation and beg him to let us go back to a place of easy friendship and semi-equality—when we were just two guys on the mat wrestling around. I didn't want to be client and trainer or rich kid and not-so-rich kid—or whatever the hell his shuttered eyes were implying. But we *were* those things. And I couldn't exactly beg this guy to be my friend.

"Okay, yeah. Guess you're right," I murmured, standing up and walking toward the shower room. I felt a familiar numb feeling seep into my body. And feeling numb made me realize that for the past two hours I'd felt fantastically alive. Every part of my being had been awake, alert, and engaged. A day that had started with stressful memories of the shattered car window the night before had ended with a fantastic workout and enjoyable conversation with a nice person.

But, as usual, I'd found a way to fuck it up. I sucked at making friends. It was enough to make me wonder if I should just stop trying.

My muscles complained as I leaned over to shuck my pants and briefs, hanging my discarded clothes on a hook outside the shower area and making sure I had a towel waiting. Since I'd obviously said something to cause Saint to withdraw from me, I assumed he would avoid joining me in the shower.

I turned the spray as hot as I could stand it and stepped under it, facing the wall and bracing my hands against the tile so I could let the spray land on my shoulders and upper back. The hot water lulled me into a stupor, and I must have zoned out.

When Saint's voice registered from somewhere behind me, it scared the shit out of me. I screamed, jumping and spinning around at the same time I scrambled as far back away from the noise as I could.

His eyes were wide and his mouth open in surprise. "Augie?"

81

CHAPTER 12

SAINT

What the hell? I hadn't meant to scare him. I'd called out his name a few times, but he hadn't heard me. The look of fear in his eyes took me by surprise, though, since he knew I was the only other person in the building. Surely, he wasn't afraid of me.

Was he?

I wanted to go to him, to reach my hand out to steady him and reassure him I would never hurt him. To be completely honest, I wanted to gather him into my arms and keep him safe. But I was naked in a communal shower. Not the time or place to be touching another man. Especially a client. Especially a client I'd already spent some time fantasizing about naked.

"It's just me," I said calmly instead. "Sorry I startled you."

"Fuck," Augie muttered under his breath. "*Fuck*. It's fine. Sorry."

I forced myself to turn away and start my own shower spray—act like everything was cool since the alternative would have me interrogating the poor guy to ask what the hell had caused him to spook like that. Clearly there was something going on with him to make him jumpy. It seemed more like he'd been a victim of a beating than a break-in.

My eyes closed as I felt the hot water thrum against my skin. I stood under the water for a while trying to relax. Eventually, I snuck a peek to make sure Augie was okay.

Of course my eyes immediately landed on his bare ass. The same bare ass I may or may not have jacked off to that very morning. I closed my eyes again and stifled a groan. The man was beautiful. His body was lean and sleek like a cat, and his changeable personality only intensified my interest in him.

But if I was being honest, my interest at that point was being driven primarily by his ass. Just the idea of sliding my body into that tight heat had my cock perking up. I clenched my jaw in frustration. Couldn't Neckie have sprung for individual shower stalls for fuck's sake? Then I wouldn't have had to try to rifle through my mental Rolodex of boner-killing images to save my boss from losing a client.

I reached a soapy hand down to stroke my cock under the guise of washing it. *Ohhhh, fuckkk.* Couldn't the man just finish his shower and leave me in peace to finish myself off? It seriously wouldn't take more than like five seconds at this rate.

I reached my other hand to pull on my sac and gritted my teeth as the feelings in my groin only intensified. Even though I was facing away from Augie, there was still no way I'd be able to hide my growing erection from him if I couldn't get myself together.

Augie made a noise, and I turned to look over my shoulder. His head was tilted back, and his eyes were squeezed closed. He, too, was facing away, and both his hands were hidden in front of his body. Just the thought that he could be doing the same thing I was made my dick even harder.

Suddenly my brain flashed to Lanny and his warnings to me the other day in his office. I remembered how disappointed he'd been in me for being irresponsible with a client. And there I was contemplating stroking one off while I was ten feet away from another important client.

Jesusfuckingchrist, I was an asshole and an idiot.

After my dick deflated, I was left feeling like the lowest of scum. I quickly finished washing, wrapped a towel around my waist, and hurried out of the shower room without sparing another glance at Augie. As I made my way to my locker, I rolled my eyes at myself before sinking to the bench and dropping my head into my hands.

"Saint?" Augie's soft voice came from directly in front of me. I raised my face to see him standing almost between my spread legs. The divots of worry were etched into his forehead as usual, and without his glasses, he looked deliciously sleepy.

"Hm?" My hands itched to pull the towel from his waist, to trace the path of water droplets down his chest, to reach around to cup his little ass and bring him close enough to bury my face in his front. I felt my breath come in quicker draws.

"Are you... do you like guys? I wasn't really sure after last night..."

The question took me by surprise. I could see a deep blush mottling Augie's neck and cheeks, but he had the strength to maintain eye contact with me while he waited for my response.

Instead of speaking it, I leaned toward him and rested my forehead against his flat belly, bringing my hands up to rest lightly on his hips.

"More than you can even imagine," I whispered.

His fingers forked through my hair as his feet shuffled closer. The bulge of a hard cock was right below my face, pressing the towel toward me. It was so very tempting. And surprising, since I thought he wouldn't be interested in the dumb-jock type. But maybe he was willing to slum it for a night.

I lifted my head up to meet his eyes. "I can't stop watching you," I admitted. "I'm sorry."

Both of his hands slid over my cheeks to cup the sides of my face. His fingers were slender and cool against my skin. "Why are you sorry? I can't stop watching you either."

"But you kind of have a girlfriend," I said, because I'd second-guessed his declaration after seeing all the photos of the two of them together online. "And you're my client."

He came even closer and straddled me, placing one knee and then the other on the bench to either side of me. "I kind of have a *fake* girl-friend," he said in a thick voice, settling his tight bum on my thighs.

The towel opened enough for me to see the sleek, curved muscles of his inner thighs. My eyes begged to see farther up underneath the teasing towel.

"And you're fired."

Augie's smiling lips brushed against mine before coming back for more. And more. And more.

I let him play around with our lips for a little while before bringing a hand up to cradle the back of his head and kissing him even deeper. Little moans of pleasure made their way out of his throat as my tongue explored his mouth. His hands held on to my shoulders for dear life, and his hips undulated, pushing his hard cock against my stomach.

I was hard as hell and desperate to get him naked beneath me. My hands moved down his smooth back and into the back of the loose towel. His ass cheeks filled my hands perfectly.

"Augie, you have no idea how much you turn me on. I've been wanting to touch you like this since I first saw you," I murmured against his mouth.

"Please," he breathed, moving his lips in a trail along my jaw and down my neck. "Touch me."

I pulled the towel away from his hips until I had a naked August Stiel hard and begging on my lap. It was better than every daydream I'd had in the few days since we'd met. I peeked down at his erection, stiff and ruddy pink against the pale skin of his abdomen. The thatch of hair surrounding it was neatly trimmed, which didn't surprise me in someone so outwardly orderly. I reached down to run my fingers through it before taking his cock in hand and slowly stroking it.

"Like this?" I whispered into his ear. His entire body shuddered.

"Mm-hm. Just like that."

I kissed the side of his head as he took a break from kissing across my shoulder to try and catch his breath.

"I want to see you come, Augie. Want to watch you relax and let go. You're so beautiful like this, flushed and panting... letting me touch you the way I want to touch you. You're making me so hard, baby. So fucking hard."

I continued to grumble encouraging words to him as I stroked him faster, taking the precum leaking from his tip and smearing it across his velvety skin.

"Saint," he moaned. "Gonna come."

His head rested against my chest, and his legs propelled his hips forward and back, fucking himself into my hand as his orgasm drew closer. Suddenly, I had the urge to swallow his release, to take him into my mouth and make him feel as good as possible.

I lifted him off me and sat him on my spot on the bench, causing him to yelp at the hard surface under his tender ass. Instead of apologizing with words, I knelt down and took him into my mouth, bobbing and sucking for all I was worth while wrapping one arm around his hips and holding him tight. With the other hand, I opened my own towel and jacked myself off.

It only took seconds before he was arching up and shooting into my throat with a muffled grunt followed by a loud, sucked in breath. The minute I felt him come, I sensed the detonation of my own release and thrust hard into my own hand. After I finished, I continued soft licks and sucks on Augie until his body shook with the aftershocks of oversensitivity. When I finally glanced up at him, he looked stunned.

"You sucked me off," he croaked.

I licked my lips and grinned. "Mm-hmm. Sure did."

His eyes jumped down to where my cock was softening against my thighs. "You came?" His voice was still high-pitched in disbelief. Something about that was endearing as hell.

"I did indeed. You're sexy as fuck."

Augie scrambled off the bench and out of my embrace, grabbing the towel and backing up like I was some kind of threat.

"I'm sorry," he said. His eyes were wide and frightened, not at all what I would expect after such an intimate moment.

"Augie?"

"No, I mean... I just like jumped you... basically. And... well, I never do that. I never do this." He gestured with one hand wildly between us while holding the towel in front of his crotch with the other. "I don't know what came over me. I didn't mean to put you in an awkward position, and... shit, is this like some kind of 'hashtag me too' thing where I've put you in a terrible position? It's just that—"

I interrupted his babbling before he could hyperventilate. "Augie, I clearly wanted it. Why are you panicking? Do you regret what we did? Did I do something to—"

"No! Not at all. I was afraid that I was the one... because clearly you wouldn't normally do... this... with..." He seemed to run out of steam. "Someone like me."

His eyes were downcast, as if he couldn't bear to look at me anymore. For a split second, I wondered if he was referring to how much higher up the intelligence and socioeconomic scales he was than I was. But his body language was clearly broadcasting massive insecurity.

Which made my stomach hurt and my heart lodge in my throat.

I moved to the bench and sat down, facing him. I didn't want to scare him off, and I was desperate to touch him again, if only to reassure him. But I didn't want to scare him like I had in the shower.

"Come here please," I said softly, holding out my arms.

His eyes widened and he looked up before taking a tentative step toward me. "You aren't upset?"

"Are you kidding? Where is this coming from? You're beautiful and sexy, successful and smart. Why in the world, besides pissing off my boss, would I regret what we did together?"

He came even closer until he stood between my legs again. I put my arms around him and rested my chin on his stomach while looking up at his pretty hazel eyes. Augie's hands threaded into my hair almost without him realizing it.

"Will you get in trouble with Lanny?" he asked. "I won't tell anyone. You don't have to say anything. I'm good at keeping secrets."

The sour feeling in my stomach worsened. I hated knowing he was so used to keeping his liaisons a secret. And I despised the implication he didn't think he was good enough for a regular guy like me. But I also couldn't afford for Lanny to hear that only a few days after benching me for inappropriate behavior toward a client, I'd dived right in to do it again.

"He certainly wouldn't be happy about it," I explained. "But I can't say I'm sorry we did this. Are you?"

"Pfft. Are you crazy? Have you seen you?" His cheeks flamed. "I don't do this kind of thing very often."

I pulled him forward to straddle me again so I could hold him a little longer. "So you said. Why is that?"

Augie's jaw tightened. "My family. If they found out..." He shook his head from side to side. "You know what? No. I'm sick and fucking tired of keeping part of myself locked away. I swore I wasn't going to do this shit anymore. I'm twenty-eight fucking years old. Why do I turn into a wayward child when I think of coming out again to my family?"

"I can't say I understand what it's like to be in the closet with family. Hell, I have the queerest family around. But I do know that coming out is complicated and emotional regardless of your family situation. So you have to go easy on yourself. You don't owe anyone anything, especially me."

I rubbed my hands along his slender back, enjoying the smooth warm skin under my fingers. Augie's arms were wrapped around my neck, and I took the opportunity to lean in and kiss the worry marks on his forehead.

"I hate seeing you worry," I murmured against his skin. He moved his head down to tuck into my neck, and we just stayed there like that, wrapped up in each other for comfort more than anything else.

It was something I wasn't sure I'd ever had with another person. Cuddling and embracing like that wasn't something you did with one-nighters and quick hookups.

After a few minutes, I could sense Augie getting hard again. He wasn't the only one.

"Come home with me?" Augie whispered. It was so soft, I barely made it out.

I knew I shouldn't. It was an irresponsible choice considering the damage I could be doing to my job.

He shifted so he could meet my eyes. "Please, Saint. I don't want to be alone tonight."

If there was a person alive who could resist that plea, it certainly wasn't me.

"Let's go," I said, gently nudging him off my lap. "I'll follow you there."

CHAPTER 13

AUGIE

I HAD NO IDEA WHAT HAD COME OVER ME. WHERE THE HELL HAD I COME up with the balls to come on to Saint Wilde? One minute I'd been salivating over him in the showers, and the next minute, I'd been climbing all over him half-naked and shooting my load down his freaking throat.

Even though we'd held on to each other and calmed down, I still felt my heart thundering wildly in his company. And now that I knew he was coming home with me? I thought maybe I was going to lose my mind.

I'd never had anal sex. Not because I hadn't wanted to, but more because I hadn't trusted a random stranger enough to try it. But Saint wasn't a random stranger. And I wanted him to fuck me pretty damned badly.

We walked to our cars side by side, and just as we were about to separate, Saint grabbed me by the wrist and pulled me behind a large truck I assumed was his at the same time he stepped in front of me to shield me from view.

My heart stuttered from the sudden movement, and I opened my mouth to ask him what the fuck was happening. I couldn't see past the wide expanse of his back, and he had one arm holding me in place behind him while he pulled a gun from who-the-hell-knew-where.

Nerves lit up my entire body, and my eyes locked on the weapon with sudden tunnel vision. "Saint—"

"Shh," he snapped.

I felt the cold metal of the truck against my back and the warm fibers of Saint's shirt under my palms where they'd landed on his waist. He shifted his weight, inadvertently pressing me back farther into the cold metal of the truck's door until my entire front was plastered against him. He felt amazing, and I could smell the shampoo wafting off his still-damp hair.

It seemed to take ages before he must have decided the coast was clear. As he turned around to face me, he slipped the gun in the back of his waistband and reached out to run his large hands up and down my upper arms.

"Are you okay?" he asked in a low voice. "You look really pale." Concern wrinkled his brows, and I was speechless for a moment. When was the last time someone had been worried about me?

"I… ah… yeah. I'm fine," I stammered. "What happened?"

"There was a man in a car. It looked like he was watching you."

My throat tightened and my heart sped up. "What?" I stepped out of his grasp to look around the parking lot frantically, as if the car was still there and I could get some answers. "Who? What kind of car? What did he look like?" My words came fast and breathy as my brain spun through possibilities and I kept looking around the lot.

Who the hell would be following me? Could it be the person or people who'd broken into my house? The person who'd broken into my car? Surely not.

"Shit," I muttered when I didn't see a single hint of what Saint was talking about. I turned to look at him and caught him staring at me. "Are you sure?"

"Augie, what the hell is going on? What aren't you telling me?"

"What? Nothing," I said, clamping my mouth shut. "I'm sure it was nothing. Probably just someone lost."

"It wasn't nothing. And it wasn't someone lost. A man in a silver four-door sedan was definitely looking at you," Saint said. His voice wasn't harsh or anything. In fact, it was sweet and concerned. As if he was genuinely worried about my safety. While that was nice and all, I didn't need some big tough guy looking out for me. I wasn't a wuss. I could take care of myself. That was why I was taking the lessons, after all. And as my grandfather always taught me, Stiels were strong as steel. And I'd be damned if I was going to be the first in generations to prove that assertion wrong.

I shrugged. "I'm sure it's nothing. And if it is something—just think, maybe I'll get a chance to practice my new moves." I tried to smile up at him, but the creases in his forehead only deepened.

"Are you being followed, Augie?" he asked.

"Of course not," I replied, hoping like hell I was right.

He continued as if I hadn't said anything. "Is that why you signed up for this training? Something more than the break-in? Has someone been threatening you?"

The concern on his face caused my chest to tighten. I wanted to tell him I was scared. I wanted to step forward and lean my face into his chest. To ask him to take over watching my back so I could stop being nervous and scared for one goddamned minute.

Or lonely, for that matter.

But I wouldn't. I couldn't. Because Stiels were strong as fucking steel. If I'd heard it once, I'd heard it a thousand times. It was especially drilled into me by my grandfather after my dad's murder. He'd made sure I'd understood it was my job to be the strong one for Rory's sake. I was the one who was supposed to be strong, supposed to be brave. I was the one responsible for protecting my mother and sister once my father was gone. It was my job. And I could do it like I always had. I just needed to remember to toughen up.

I'd been an idiot to beg Saint to stay with me like I was some kind of baby.

"It's fine, Saint. I promise," I said. "But maybe it's not a good idea for you to come over. This whole thing kind of ruined the mood."

I walked toward my rental car without looking back at him.

"That isn't your car," he called across the space between our vehicles. "What happened to your SUV?"

Saint didn't know about the broken car window from my jaunt to Dallas.

"In the shop," I called back. "It's fine."

I ignored whatever other question he called out and got into my car to begin the drive home. It wasn't until I was a mile away on the drive home that I realized Saint was following me in his truck. Just the idea of that control freak feeling like he needed to babysit me set my teeth on edge.

As I continued down the road, I was tempted to pull over and scream at him that I was fine. But there was a bigger part of me that wanted the tall muscled Adonis in my bed more than anything on earth. I knew I shouldn't want him, but I did.

So fucking much.

It had been a long time since I'd had to talk myself down from being attracted to another man, but that was the situation I'd found myself in with Saint. I didn't want to want him. I didn't want to have to deal with this shit when everything else was blowing up in my life. Even though I was out of practice, I knew what I needed to do. Call Lanny and ask for a different trainer. Stop exposing myself to Saint. Stop tempting myself with the man I couldn't stop fantasizing about. Forget what it felt like to touch his bare skin and take his tongue into my mouth.

The idea of training with someone else made my heart thunder with a feeling of absolute wrongness. Maybe I didn't need to change trainers. And why couldn't I let myself be attracted to another man? Where was the harm in following my true desires, especially now that Rory was happily in a relationship? It hadn't escaped me that I made a terrible role model for my pansexual sister. But I'd always been torn about encouraging her to be out with our family since I knew it would bring nothing but scorn and stress.

The streets I passed grew darker as I left Hobie for the more rural area where the farmhouse was. Finally I reached the end of the small road and turned into my driveway. I glanced in my rearview mirror in time to see Saint's truck pull in behind me. Motherfucking asshole thinking I needed protecting like some kind of victim.

But it was sweet, right? I had to admit to myself it made me feel cared for, looked after. And if I ever stripped away the bravado bull-shit, I might just admit to myself, and only myself, that it was my wildest dream to have someone else take charge for once. The idea of someone else protecting me was a deep, dark fantasy that had always been there despite my wishes to rid it from my subconscious.

Instead of pulling around back to the garage, I slammed the car into park in the driveway and got out, storming over to his vehicle. His face remained neutral as he stepped out and closed the door behind him.

"What the fuck are you doing?" I shouted at him. My anger took me by surprise, and I suddenly realized I was terrified of him seeing the state of my house and learning the truth. That I hadn't been brave enough to clean up all the mess yet. That I'd pushed all the furniture around late the night before to be able to cover the doors and windows inside. "You think I can't protect myself? You think you can just follow me—show up here like you're some kind of... what? *Body-guard*? *Concerned lover*? Or were you just looking for the booty call I promised?"

"Augie—"

"No. Go home, Saint. I don't need your help. I don't need anyone's help." I turned to walk toward my front door when I heard him say my name again.

"Augie!" he called.

I spun around and glared at him, trying desperately to ignore how badly I was shaking. "What?"

"I was worried about you. That guy set off my alarm bells. He could have followed you home and gotten to you once you were alone. I just wanted to make sure you were safe. I care about you." Saint's eyes had stopped appearing neutral and now looked worried again. "Why aren't you more concerned about this?"

"Maybe it's just what comes with having lots of money and a big name, Saint. Or maybe someone is secretly lusting after me and decided to stalk me. Did you ever think of that?" The suggestion was so stupid, we both should have laughed. But we didn't.

He looked worried for another moment before his face transformed into one of determination.

"Bullshit," he said in a low growl. "You're terrified. Something's going on that has you on edge, but you're too damned stubborn to ask for help."

I wanted to tell him to go to hell, but I couldn't bring myself to say the words. Instead, some base part of me decided to forget all that bodyguard/danger nonsense and just kiss him right on the damned lips.

CHAPTER 14

SAINT

IT WAS LIKE AUGIE WAS HOVERING BETWEEN TWO CHOICES. THE ONE where he would tell me to fuck off and leave, and the one where he'd admit what was happening and let me help him.

What I didn't expect was a third, completely different, choice. The one in which he leaned forward and came up on his toes as if he was going to kiss me. My gaze traveled down to his soft red lips, and my stomach began swirling with anticipation. I felt my own lips part as my head lowered, and just before I reached to put a hand on his jaw, I heard the unmistakable sound of another car pulling into the gravel drive.

I immediately turned and stepped in front of Augie, cursing myself for leaving my weapon in the car. Warm hands came to rest on my lower back, and I felt goose bumps rising on my skin. Augie shifted behind me until he could see the car in the drive.

"Easy, killer. It's my grandfather," he murmured. The words went straight into my ear, almost making me shiver as the warm breath slid against the skin under my collar.

I craned my neck to see past the headlights, and sure enough, an older man began to emerge from the back seat of the sleek black vehicle. He was elegant and poised in a business suit that probably cost more than I made in a month. His hair was a perfectly trimmed salt-and-pepper style that made him look as distinguished as his reputation. Despite being surprised at how young he looked, I assumed I was looking at Jonathan Stiel.

For some reason I still felt the need to keep Augie behind me, but he slipped out anyway and stepped forward. As the man approached, he eyed me standing next to his grandson and looked me up and down as if inspecting me.

"August," he said in a clipped tone. "I've been trying to reach you for hours."

"Is everything okay?" Augie asked, frowning.

"I need to talk to you about something," he said, glancing my way.

"Grandfather, this is Saint Wilde. Saint, this is Jonathan Stiel," Augie said politely.

I reached out a hand to shake. "Nice to meet you, Mr. Stiel."

He seemed to pause a beat before taking my hand. His eyes were still studying me, most likely wondering who in the hell I was to his grandson. He probably didn't see Augie often with men like me. I assumed Augie's normal friends were a bit more refined than I was.

He shook my hand briefly before turning to Augie. "Why don't we go inside?"

He passed us and let himself in the front door, leaving us alone on the front porch. Augie looked up at me, and I immediately noticed a change in his entire demeanor from minutes before when we were alone. He seemed tired all of a sudden. And stressed. I wanted to reassure him that whatever was going on with him couldn't be that bad. That it would all be okay. But what the hell did I know? I was just his self-defense instructor for god's sake.

"I guess I'd better go," I said.

"Sorry about this," he said. "I wasn't expecting him."

I smiled at him. "You weren't really expecting me either, so it's okay."

Despite the dim light from the porch fixtures, I could have sworn he blushed. "But still. I should have said thank you."

"For what?"

"For giving a shit. For caring enough to make sure I got home safely. I'm sorry I was an ass about it."

"You have my number in case something comes up. Please call me if you need me," I told him.

I was afraid he was going to get angry at me again for butting in where I didn't belong, but his face softened into a smile. "Yeah, okay."

"Good night." I almost stepped forward to kiss his cheek but managed to stop myself just in time. No sense in creating trouble for him with his grandfather who stood scowling at us from the front door of the farmhouse.

I turned to walk to my truck, feeling a strange sense of apprehension at leaving Augie alone with his grandfather. Which was all kinds of bizarre. Why in the world was I feeling protective of the man around his own family? It didn't make any sense.

Just before reaching the door of my truck, I felt a vibration in my pocket and pulled my phone back out. It was a text.

August Stiel: *Thank you again. Drive safely.*

I felt the edges of my lips turn up. I lifted my head to search him out on the front porch, but I saw just the back of him as he disappeared through the front door. I looked back down at my phone and typed in a response.

Me: *Stay out of trouble. Keep your self-defense moves for our sessions only. No real-life practice allowed.*

August Stiel: *Understood. Hey - favor?*

Me: *What is it?*

August Stiel: *Text me in 20 minutes with an urgent message I can use as an excuse to boot my grandfather out?*

Me: *Should I have stayed to protect you from the old guy?*

August Stiel: *Ha fucking ha.*

I drove the rest of the way back to the ranch with a stupid grin on my face. Once I was parked and out of the truck, I leaned back against the door and typed up another text.

Me: *URGENT. I am out of milk for my cereal. SOS.*

August Stiel: *Save Our Sereal? BTW, he's never leaving. I'm in hell. I just want to go to sleep. Someone kicked my ass at the gym tonight.*

Me: *Pfft. That was nothing. Wait till next time when we start sparring.*

Once I stopped staring goofily at my phone, I realized MJ's car was parked near the barn alongside Sassy's Volkswagen Beetle and West's pickup truck. I made my way to the main house to say hello and see who all was there. I'd been staying in the bunkhouse so my comings and goings didn't disturb Doc and Grandpa, but I spent most of my time in the main house when I wasn't sleeping or in town.

When I let myself into the front door, I followed the din to the giant farmhouse kitchen with attached family room. My siblings were sprawled out all over the giant sofas and chairs, and Doc was making something in a blender. Both West and Nico were present, which probably meant their daughter was asleep in the nursery by Doc and Grandpa's room. Hudson and Charlie were snuggled together in the corner of a sofa, and Hudson's fingers were stroking down the long length of Charlie's red hair. The action seemed to be putting his man to sleep despite the noise of everyone talking and the whirr of the blender.

MJ was setting something out on a tray in the kitchen but turned when she heard me say hello.

"Fuck," she said before rushing over to hug me. I tightened my arms around her and breathed in the familiar, faded scent of Chanel No. 5 that always reminded me of our mother.

"Hey, you," I murmured into her hair. "You okay?"

"I am now that my other half is here. Where you been?"

"Long story. You staying in the bunkhouse?"

"Yeah. You promise to tell me everything when we get over there later?"

I pulled back and kissed her cheek before nodding. Her light blue eyes peered at me as if checking me for any noticeable changes since she last saw me. It had only been a week or two at the most, so I couldn't imagine there was anything to notice.

"Moose Jaw, get the lead out," Hudson called. "My man is starving over here."

MJ turned to him. "He's in a coma, Hudson. I think you mean *you're* the one who's starving. And you can hold your damned horses."

"I'll get it," Nico offered, hoisting himself off the arm of the chair he'd been perched on. "I want some of those cream puff things I saw in the freezer the other day."

Grandpa looked up from where he'd been knitting some purple monstrosity that vaguely resembled a basketball. "How'd your lesson go?"

MJ interrupted before I had a chance to answer. "Were you at Twist? Was Neckie there? How is she? Is she okay?"

I noticed Nico glance over his shoulder toward West with a raised eyebrow. West shook his head without saying anything, and Nico continued to the kitchen area.

"She wasn't there tonight, but I saw her earlier today and she was good. She left shortly after lunch for an appointment and didn't come back though," I said.

This time it was Grandpa who glanced over at West, but instead of lifting a brow, Grandpa narrowed his eyes at my older brother.

West let out a sigh and stood up, disturbing at least three dogs on his trek across the rug to join Nico by the large kitchen island. He slid his arm around Nico's waist before whispering something into his ear. After Nico nodded, West spoke up loudly enough for everyone to hear.

"We have an announcement to make."

I realized what was happening before MJ did.

"Nico and I are having a baby," West continued. "We didn't want to say anything until the baby came because we didn't want our poor gestational carrier to be inundated with Wilde family good intentions for nine months, but..."

Nico broke in. "Neckie is carrying our baby."

There was silence for a beat before the room erupted in pandemonium.

Everyone stood to surround them with excited words of congratulations and a million questions while my twin stood there in pale shock.

West noticed before I could get to MJ.

"Em..." he said. "I'm sorry, I didn't know."

"No," she said, shaking her head and trying her best to paste on a big smile. It was fake as all hell. "No, that's amazing. I'm so happy for you! Seriously. So fucking thrilled Pippa is getting a sibling." She swallowed and spoke again. "You know how important siblings are to us, West. I'm so happy for all of you. I'm just... I'm just going to..."

West glanced at me, and I shot him a reassuring look before taking MJ into my arms and leading her outside into the cool night air.

"It's okay to be pissed," I said softly. "I didn't know. I swear I didn't. You know I would have told you."

She snorted. "You couldn't keep a secret from me if you tried. Remember in eighth grade when you tried to tell me Shayla Tubbs gave you that hickey?"

"It wasn't my place to out her brother, and you know it."

She rolled her eyes at me before tucking her head against my shoulder. "I want her to be carrying *my* baby, Saint," she whispered against my shirt. "Isn't that the most selfish thing you can imagine?"

I moved her over to sit next to me on the front porch swing and tucked her back against my side once we were settled.

"It's totally understandable. And I think she actually feels the same way. That's why we got you here. She needs someone in her corner right now. Even if it's just as a friend. I think she's scared, Em."

"I want West and Nico to have a baby, I do. But... why Neckie?"

I thought for a moment before speaking. "Maybe it was a way for her to do something for you indirectly. She's always adored our family. Maybe this is her way of loving us... loving *you*. You won't know unless you ask her."

We sat in silence for a while, listening to the night rustlings of creatures and the few audible reminders of the horses in the nearby barn.

"Is it too late to go over there?" she asked after a little while.

"To Neckie's?" I checked my phone and saw it was half past ten. "Want me to text her first and ask?"

"Would you mind?"

I shook my head and punched in the text since Neckie and I had already texted back and forth over details of my schedule at Twist. Within seconds she responded she was still up and would love a visit from MJ.

"Go get 'em, tiger," I said, pulling her close in a squeeze. I felt the slight tremble of her nerves but knew she was one of the bravest of us. She'd tackled law school despite a pretty debilitating case of dyslexia and had created a name for herself in Dallas legal circles. She was kick-ass.

As we stood up from the swing, West and Nico joined us on the porch.

"Sorry, Em," West said again. "If I'd known you still had feelings for her, I would have talked to you first."

"It's okay. I promise."

"It's my sperm," Nico blurted. "I mean..." He looked up at his husband in desperation. Poor Nico hated seeing anyone upset.

MJ laughed and put her hand on his shoulder. "It's fine. The woman of my dreams is still having my brother's baby. No big deal."

West looked crushed. "Em..."

I felt a familiar tightening in my chest. Whenever anyone in my family disagreed, I always wanted to put a stop to it any way I could. Often it was making a fool out of myself to change the focus. But it always made me feel out of control and rudderless when there was strife.

MJ let out a breath. "I'll get over it, West. It just really took me by surprise. Finding out she was pregnant was one thing, but finding out you guys are the ones who get a little piece of her isn't easy."

"It's not her egg," West said. "Katie donated it for us, so there was Salerno and Wilde genetics together. Sassy's too young to make such a big decision. Winnie was going to do it, but then we realized she'd never be able to keep it from Hallie. And if Hallie knew..."

"Everyone would know," we all said together.

The tension was broken when we all chuckled at the truth.

"That was nice of Katie," I said. Our cousin had always been generous and kind. It didn't surprise me at all she'd been willing to help West and Nico out like that.

"Why didn't you ask me?" MJ asked. "I would have donated an egg for you guys."

West's face softened. "We started the process at the same time you announced landing the Bascourt case. There was no doubt that was an incredible opportunity that would require tons of extra hours and energy, Em."

She nodded, but I could feel the gears turning in her head. "I won," she muttered under her breath. "Fat lot of good that did. Those motherfuckers still haven't offered me the position I deserve at the firm."

West stepped forward and pulled her into a big hug. "We love you no matter what. Who cares if you're just vacuuming and emptying trash over there? You're still aces in our book—*aiyeee!*"

She'd reached up and pinched his nipple the same way she used to do when we were kids. Nico's jaw dropped in surprise, and he yanked West out of our sister's menacing reach.

"Don't fuck with his nips, you horrible woman! I rely on those sonsabitches for entertainment," Nico exclaimed, murmuring soothing sounds to West as he reached up to rub the injured spot.

"Whatever," she snapped. "Next time don't impregnate my woman, assholes. I'm out of here."

She stormed back into the house, presumably to grab her keys before heading to Neckie's place.

Nico looked back at me over West's shoulder. "Think she'll still set out some snacks for us before she goes?"

CHAPTER 15

AUGIE

My grandfather was in an odd mood that night and only stayed for about an hour before leaving to head back to the city. I worried about his strange behavior now that he was getting older. He seemed more worried in general and a bit further removed from my mother. The two of them always seemed thick as thieves, but lately they didn't seem to spend much time together. For as traditional and intimidating as the man was, I'd always caught glimpses of another side to him. When his sister was still alive, she had the ability to tease him about being such a curmudgeon, and she even had the ability to jolly him into laughter. When the two of them would set each other off with corny jokes, my mother would roll her eyes and mutter the same phrase every time: *Melody has a magic way with him.*

And she did. She was the key to his heart. Even though she'd been older than Grandfather, Melody had been the darling of the family. It was almost like he treated her the way I sometimes treated Rory—as the baby who deserved every bit of pampering and happiness. What Melody wanted, Grandfather provided. It wasn't until my adulthood that I realized my mother would have never approved of my summers in Hobie. It had to have been Melody requesting my presence and

Grandfather's complete inability to deny her anything that resulted in the most wonderful memories of my teen years.

When I remembered his tenderness for her, it explained a bit of his disorientation in what had been her home for years. And then I recalled it had also been his own mother's childhood home. My great-grandmother had grown up in the Hobie farmhouse before meeting and marrying Jeremiah Stiel when he came to Hobie to purchase a plot of land on behalf of the Baptist General Convention for the location of the brand-new Hobie First Baptist church just off the town square.

After Grandfather left, I reminded myself that this farmhouse had been a part of his heritage the same way it had been to his sister. While he wouldn't have been nearly as sentimental about his mother's birthplace as Melody had been, he still would have found the property meaningful.

Property was in his blood.

Stiels had been buying and selling property for themselves and others for over a century. Could that have explained his melancholy mood?

It had left me feeling so unsettled that I'd called Rory to tell her about it. We'd talked for an hour about Grandfather's recent strange behavior, Mother's shortening temper, and, inevitably, the self-defense lessons I'd let her talk me into. I told her a little bit about my instructor and even the part about me getting one over on him with the bite. After she praised my ingenuity, I had to admit to him getting me back.

By the time we got off the phone, I'd tried to gather up enough courage to sleep in my bed again, but I just couldn't. My attic nest was so much more comfortable now that I had rigged up some twinkle lights and hung some of my favorite keys among them from the whitewashed boards that comprised the ceiling of the little nook. It made it seem less like a storage cubby and more like a special secret hideaway. In addition to the thick duvet I usually kept on the guest bed, I'd brought up two of Melody's vintage quilts that were sturdy enough for use and the two squishy bed pillows from the guest room.

It almost felt like a little wolf's den or something. I could understand the concept den animals had of securing such a space.

I knew if anyone ever found this place, however, I would die of embarrassment. I would keel right over in abject horror and never be able to show my face around that person again.

The following morning, I got up early to treat myself to a fancy coffee and pastry at the bakery before opening the shop. Halfway to town, my sister called to tell me she and Kat had gotten up early to drive out to Hobie for a visit. We decided to meet up at Sugar Britches to have breakfast before heading over to the shop. I was thrilled to have the distraction of their visit to help me spend less time obsessing about a certain baby-faced Wilde.

When I entered the bakery, the line was almost out the door. Luckily, I noticed Rory and Katrina at a table in the corner and was able to squeeze past the line to join them.

"We got you a pumpkin-spiced—" Rory began with a straight face.

"Bullshit, give me the mocha," I interrupted, holding out my hand for the huge ceramic mug. She knew I hated the very idea of pumpkin-spiced anything and craved chocolate as much as coffee.

"Told you he wouldn't believe you," Kat murmured before kissing Rory on the ear. "But you were adorable with your pretend serious face. You get an A for effort, cutie pie."

Rory rolled her eyes and reached out to give me a side hug before handing me the drink.

"They're bringing out the pastries in a minute. As soon as the guy at the counter saw the last name on my credit card, he kind of squealed and did a little dance. I don't know what that means, but he told us that made us VIPs. How do people know who we are out here in the sticks?"

I glanced over my shoulder and spotted the hyperactive manager with the hot-pink faux-hawk and pale pink lip gloss talking a customer's ear off while simultaneously frothing milk and running a credit card through the machine. "Oh, that's Stevie. He runs the place. I guess he's a friend?"

There was no telling why I hesitated to call people in Hobie a true friend. Charlie and I had been friendly for at least eight months, and half the time hanging out with Charlie meant hanging out with Hudson. And then there was Jen who owned the children's boutique next to my shop and always went in with me on a Chinese food takeout order every Friday for lunch.

"Is that a question?" Rory asked.

"Well, we kind of bonded over our mutual hatred of Precious Moments figurines. You'd have to know Stevie to understand why that's a thing. And then we both discovered we secretly sponsor animals in need from that ridiculous commercial..."

"Shut up," Kat said.

"No," Rory gasped. "Augie, you don't! Tell me you don't send them money."

Katrina shot a guilty look at my sister, and Rory gasped again. "You too? Jesus, what a bunch of bleeding hearts."

"Did someone summon me?" Stevie called as he flitted to the table with a quaint white basket lined with a cotton napkin. He set the basket in the center of the table and then handed me a stack of small plates. "Tra-la! Selection of all the primo shit, my dear. Insider tip: the donut holes have a Bailey's Irish Cream drizzle on them. If you want a little relaxation on this beautiful fall morning, they're your best bet."

Before we could even say thank you, he dashed off with a wave and a "Toodles" called over his shoulder. The three of us watched his pert butt wiggle back behind the counter in a painted-on pair of skinny jeans.

"See something you like?" a deep voice rumbled from behind me. I closed my eyes and inhaled, half hoping I'd imagined the sexy voice and half hoping it was real. Saint's fresh scent enveloped me, and I opened my eyes again, spinning around to see the gorgeous specimen before me.

I may have whimpered a little bit.

My bratty sister coughed the word "beefcake" before turning on her most giant smile as if it had never happened. "You must be the biter."

"Oh my fucking god," I cried. "You did not just say that."

The rich sound of Saint's laugh rumbled through me, and his hand landed on my shoulder for a brief squeeze. He leaned in to speak closer to my ear. "It's not a lie."

My entire body shuddered, and my cock may have dripped a tiny bit. I tried to take a sip of my mocha but choked on it when Saint straightened back up and told my sister, "Don't kid yourself. This one's no kitten either. More like a feral cat."

Rory's eyes lit up like a fucking Vegas slot machine hitting the triple diamond. She'd struck brother gossip pay dirt and damned well knew it.

"So, uh. This is Saint. Saint, this is my sister, Rory, and—"

"I recognize the lovely Katrina Duvall. It's a pleasure to meet you both," Saint said, reaching an arm past me to shake. The bakery was crowded enough to push his body into mine when he reached, and I nudged my nose over to surreptitiously sniff his shirt.

Okay, his pit.

It smelled amazing.

I gulped. "Fancy meeting you here."

Oh god.

Rory lifted a brow at me like, *Really, you stupid motherfucker. That all you got?*

Kat narrowed her eyes and tilted her head at me like, *Did you just sniff the man's armpit?*

"I, uh..." Was it high-pitched in here, or was that just me? "I should get to work? At the shop?"

Rory shot Kat a look. "This is really happening. Kat, get out your phone and start getting this on video."

I shook my head as fast as I could. "Don't be ridonkulous. It's just a..."

Oh god. I didn't just say ridonkulous.

Rory nodded her head enthusiastically. *Oh yes you did. You sooo did.*

Fuck.

I glanced at Kat in desperation, but she was busy fumbling her phone out of her bag.

"I'm sorry," I choked. "I have a shopment coming. Shop ment. Ship mont. Ship… mint."

I shook my head and scraped my chair back, accidentally knocking it right into Saint's gut. His grunt of pain shocked some sense into me.

"Oh god! Saint, no. Oh no. Saint. I'm so sorry. I'm Saint sorry. Saint… so…" I looked at him in mortified horror, expecting to see either annoyance at me impaling him with the back of my chair or laughter at what a fool I was making of myself. What I saw wasn't either one of those.

He was worried about me. The concern in his face was genuine and hit me right in the solar plexus, taking my breath away with a sudden *whoosh*. Saint gave Rory and Kat a quick, polite goodbye before wrapping his big arm around me, tucking me into his side, and dragging me through the crowd and out the door.

Once we'd crossed the street onto the quieter space of the grassy square park, Saint quickly found us a bench to sit on.

"Take a breath, sweet… ah… of some sweet air. Some fresh air. Some sweet, fresh air," he said. His arm was still around me, and I found myself leaning into his solid warmth.

"It's contagious," I said with a soft chuckle after a moment.

"What is?"

"The stupid mouth. You caught it from me. Sorry about that."

"You don't have a stupid mouth," he said. "I happen to know from experience you have a sweet mouth. A soft mouth, a sensual—"

A sound in my throat interrupted him. Our faces were only inches apart, and I thought I heard myself whisper the word *please* under my breath against my better judgment.

"Augie," he breathed.

"Augie!" someone else called from across the square. We both snapped our heads around and jumped apart like guilty teens dancing too closely at a school social.

It was a regular customer of mine who was most likely itching to pick up the Rococo chaise lounge I'd arranged for him to have reupholstered.

"Is it ready?" Mr. Webster asked as he shuffled closer down the paved walkway. "I couldn't wait any longer to see how it turned out. I was just heading to the shop to check on it when I saw you there."

Saint stood from the bench and reached out a hand. "Mr. Webster, it's good to see you again. How is Gunnar?"

I gawped at the big muscly man asking the frail retired school teacher about his beloved Yorkie.

"Oh, Saint. I didn't realize that was you. Yes, Gunnar is fine. In fact, I've just left him at the groomers and ran into your grandfathers there. They were dropping off one of the little dogs. I'm not sure which one. Can never tell them apart. Salty, I think. Anyway, Augie? The chaise?"

I glanced at Saint with an apology. "Yes, sir. It's ready. Let's go see how it looks."

When I got to the far end of the square, I turned back for one last glance at Saint. He'd sat back down on the bench with one leg crossed over the other and had a bakery treat in his hands and a big smile on his face.

That was when I saw my sister and Kat, all grins, sitting down next to him on the bench.

He must have felt my eyes on him because he looked up suddenly and met my gaze. Then that sexy man smiled at me as if the entire sun had just broken over the horizon.

And damned if I hadn't been in the dark for a very long time.

CHAPTER 16

SAINT

OF COURSE I SPENT THE REST OF SATURDAY FORCIBLY RESTRAINING myself from dropping in to Augie's Antiques with some pathetic, manufactured excuse to check on the man. Instead, I met up with MJ and forced her to spill all the details from her night with Neckie.

My sister was riding high, and I could tell from the minute I saw her that the two of them had managed to come together in some way.

"Tell me everything," I said the minute she snuck into the bunkhouse after noon still wearing the same clothes she'd had on the night before. "Look at your walk of shame. Holy shit."

"There is nothing you can say to dampen my mood. I kissed her, Saint. Kissed her mouth like I've dreamed about doing for at least fifteen years."

"How did we not know she was into women?"

"She dated whatshisname in high school. Remember?"

I thought back to those years and pictured a flakey skinny dude with a buzz cut who was always dressed in camo. "Wait. Dinko? Dirk Dinko? Wasn't that his name?"

MJ snorted. "Yeah, him. Super quiet dude. But she had a soft spot for him. She told me it started out with her defending him from some bullies at a school soccer game. I guess they were ribbing him for not being able to get a girl, so Neckie sidled up to him and kissed him right on the lips, asking if he was ready to take her home. He followed her in shocked silence until finally finding his tongue in the parking lot. As soon as he found it, he vomited. She felt so sorry for him, she took him to the diner for a milkshake. They talked all afternoon and made a connection. She said it wasn't some great love, but he was good to her. I remember that, Saint. He was good to her."

"Whatever happened to him, I wonder?"

I moved a stack of sofa pillows over so she could sink into the cushions next to me. She kicked her shoes off and pulled her feet under her.

"He married the girl he dated in college. They were in the same teacher's program at UNT in Denton. Neckie said they're really happy now. They both teach high school in Austin."

"You seem pretty chill about it," I said.

She shrugged. "I was so jealous of him at the time, but I also knew that if they were together, he had to be a pretty good guy. I mean... I knew him and he was nice enough. But he was super shy. I never got to know him all that well. And when she and I did stuff together, she didn't include him, thank god. I would have been a hormonal basket case even more than I already was."

"Enough about Dinko. Tell me about Neckie."

MJ got a dreamy look on her face. "She said she's had a crush on me since eighth grade. She remembered the time Dad and I helped her mom with a flat tire. She even remembers my hair was braided on the side that day."

I'd never really seen my sister this goofy.

"Do you remember that day too?"

She nodded. "Her hair was wild. Blonde curls everywhere from driving with the windows down. I remember she had her summer freckles, and she looked so different outside of school. Like the sun shone right on her." MJ turned to face me. "She's it for me, Saint. And after last night, I truly think I might be it for her too."

My heart squeezed tightly in my chest. I couldn't think of many people who deserved to find someone special more than my sister. She'd always been the stoic one, the no-nonsense sibling who pretended all she cared about was a successful career. But I'd always known better. She craved someone to love, and she deserved someone to love her back with everything they had. I couldn't think of a better match for my orderly, straight-laced sister than the wild-spirited Nectarine Birch who basically lived in a treehouse and probably named all the squirrels in her yard.

"Did you do it?" I asked with a snicker.

MJ shot me the middle finger. "No, we didn't do it. She's a thousand months pregnant. We just made out and then curled up together in her big comfy bed and talked for hours. She's amazing. Did you know she's always wanted to be a stay-at-home mom? She wants a house full of kids she can homeschool and take on adventures. Isn't that so interesting?"

I listened to MJ go on and on about her new belle. My sister's happiness painted the most beautiful brightness on her face—something I hadn't seen there in way too long. Simply talking about Neckie lit her up inside, and I wondered how long it would take her to realize Neckie's home was in Hobie while MJ's was in the city.

The same way Augie's home was in Hobie now while mine was in the city.

Not that the two were at all similar. Augie and I were merely... what? Student and teacher? Client and bodyguard? Friends? Friends with benefits?

None of those seemed to fit.

As I had the night before, I went to sleep Saturday night with thoughts of the enigmatic antiques geek on my mind, and when I got to Twist the next morning to fake my way through a kickboxing class, I ran into my coworker Rex again. He was leaning on the reception counter sipping coffee and raised an eyebrow at me when I walked in and stopped in surprise.

"Morning," he said.

"Hey. What are you still doing here?"

"Got a flat a few minutes out of town last night. The garage is fixing it up. Thought I'd come by and fit in another workout before driving back to the city."

"Shit, man. You could have stayed with me at my family's ranch. Why didn't you call?"

He shrugged and grinned. "I found someone to stay with."

I laughed. Typical Rex. "I hope I'm not related to whoever that was. If you hooked up with a gay guy in Hobie, chances are, he's a Wilde."

"Not true. You obviously haven't opened Grindr since you've been here."

I shuddered, thinking of opening the app and seeing Hobie residents' dick pics. No, thanks. Too close to home for my taste.

That's not what you were thinking the other night at the pub.

I shook off the stupid thought and remembered something about Rex's specialty in computer stuff. "Hey, I was wondering if you could do me a favor when you get back to the office."

"Probably. What's up?"

I tapped my fingertips on my thigh as I contemplated whether or not I really wanted to open this can of worms. Rex must have sensed my hesitation but remained quiet while I made my decision.

"You know my self-defense client?" I asked.

"Chris Hemsworth?" he teased. "Yeah, what about him?"

"I think there's something going on he's not telling me about. Like a threat or something. I think he's pursuing these self-defense lessons because he's scared."

My friend studied me before responding. "And? What business is it of yours if he doesn't want to tell you?"

"I think it's possible he's being followed."

Rex just looked at me some more until I broke.

"Goddammit. Don't look at me with those eyes. You think I don't know? You think I don't know it's none of my business? I do. But I'm worried about him, man. And I don't want anything to happen to the guy. Can't you just look into it for me? Please?"

His face widened into a grin. "Ahh, there's the magic word. I'll give it a shot."

I clapped him on the shoulder. "Thanks. I owe you one."

~

LATER THAT EVENING as I was getting ready to return to the ranch, Rex called.

"I found police reports for a home invasion in Hobie about ten days ago and the auto B&E in Dallas the other night. The—"

"Wait," I interrupted. "Back up. Car break-in? When? Where in Dallas? Are you sure it was him? He has family in Dallas. It could have been one of them."

I heard the click of the keyboard before he spoke again. "No. It was a black Range Rover SUV registered to August Bailey Stiel with a Hobie address. According to the police report, the incident happened in a parking garage attached to the Stiel building downtown at 11:00 p.m. the night before last. I think I saw this car at the garage in Hobie as a matter of fact. Shattered passenger-side window."

I remembered his mother requesting his presence that night and Augie telling me he wasn't going to go. Most likely, he'd changed his mind out of guilt. But why hadn't he told me about the vehicle B&E? It certainly explained why he had a rental car.

"Does the report say what was taken?" I asked.

"That's the weird thing. There was a messenger bag inside with an iPad and e-reader. But they were still there. The only thing missing, according to the vic, was a box of antique keys."

"Keys," I muttered, remembering the box we'd put the spilled keys in. "Why the hell would someone in a downtown parking garage break in to steal a box of random old keys and leave the electronics inside? It doesn't make any sense."

"Your guess is as good as mine. Maybe the keys go to something important."

"They don't though. He simply collects old mismatched keys for fun."

Rex continued. "There were old keys missing from the home invasion too in addition to other more expected items. Seems like your client has had a pretty fucking bad month."

"Jesus," I muttered, letting out a breath. "The old keys don't go to anything though. And who gets their house and car broken into in the same month? It's not like he lives in the slums. I've been to his—" I stopped talking the minute I realized what I was saying.

I heard the sharp intake of Rex's breath and could have kicked myself.

"Start talking," he said with a tone of amusement.

"Nothing. I thought he was being followed by a weirdo last night, so I made sure he got home safely. That's all."

"Thereby confirming that he was, in fact, being followed by a weirdo."

"Shut the fuck up. I'm hanging up." I pulled the phone away from my ear.

"Be careful Saint-Michel-Devs-Saints," he said loudly in his best French accent, invoking my given name to get my attention.

"Sure thing, *Reginald Xavier*," I replied as I tapped the red button to end the call.

On my way to the truck, I was surprised by a text from Augie.

Augie: *Hypothetically speaking, how does one get blood out of carpet?*

Me: *Ah... Augie, are you okay?*

Augie: *I'm asking for a friend.*

Me: *Is your friend covering up a homicide?*

Augie: *It's probably better if you don't ask too many questions.*

Me: *Why are you asking me about blood?*

Augie: *You seem like the type to know these things.*

Me: *Is the blood wet or dry?*

Augie: *Wet.*

Me: *Augie... what's going on?*

Augie: *Never mind. I'll google it.*

After what Rex had just told me, I wasn't sure whether to laugh or worry, so I tried calling Augie. There was no answer. After fifteen minutes of no response, I decided to stop by his house and check on him just to be sure he was okay. It was probably nothing, in which case I'd be embarrassed about going to all the trouble of stopping by. But on the off chance something was going on he needed help with, there was no harm in stopping by on my way home from the gym.

After ringing the doorbell, I stepped back on the porch and waited. The longer it took for someone to come to the door, the more I felt like an idiot for coming over there unannounced. Would he think I was crazy?

Augie opened the door hesitantly until he saw it was me. His eyes grew wide, and his face paled. "Saint? What are you doing here?" he asked.

"You texted me about fresh blood and then didn't answer my calls. I was worried about you."

"Jesus, I was kidding. I'm fine," he said, but I caught sight of the edge of a gauze bandage peeking out from behind the door where his left hand was.

"You're not fine," I said, stepping forward and reaching for the bandaged hand he held behind the door. One look at the state of his foyer and I found myself pushing my way into the house to inspect the bandaged hand. There was furniture shoved every which way, and blood seeped through the bandage. My heart began to hammer as I wondered what was going on.

"What the hell happened here?"

He seemed startled, whether by my appearance or question, or both, was unclear.

"I... I just cut myself on some glass. That's all," he stammered. "I was trying to clean up."

I continued to hold his arm gently as I took in my surroundings. His house was completely out of order. Large pieces of furniture were crowded and stacked in the foyer, and the rooms to either side looked empty by comparison. Surely this wasn't still from the home invasion over a week ago. Was it?

After turning back to him, I saw a flash of defiance in his eyes. "It's none of your business," he said before I even had a chance to speak.

"Like hell it's not," I barked. "What the fuck happened, Augie?"

"I moved some furniture around. That's all."

My jaw dropped. "That's *all*? This place looks like it's been gone over by a crazy person."

Suddenly, I had a thought that made my blood run cold. "Did you get broken into again? Jesusfuckingchrist, were you here when it happened?" I reached both hands up to grip his face and make sure he was looking at me so I could see the truth of his response.

"No. No, of course not. *No*," he said. And I believed him. Before I could stop to think about what I was doing, I pulled him against my chest and wrapped my arms around him. I felt my heart hammer and my stomach twist at the thought of someone putting Augie in danger.

"Fuck," I muttered under my breath. "Thank god. Baby, are you okay?"

I felt Augie's body shudder against me, and I pulled back to inspect him again. Just before asking if he was hurt anywhere else, I noticed tears threaten to spill out of his eyes. I wanted to reach a thumb out to swipe at them, but I held myself back for fear of embarrassing him.

"I'm sorry. Did I scare you?" I asked as gently as I could. He shook his head. "Then what is it?"

"You're the first person who's asked me that." His words came out in a small rough voice that broke my heart.

"Surely that's not true. What about your grandfather? He was here last night; he had to have seen all of this mess. Didn't you tell him what happened?" I asked.

"He knows."

That's all he said, but it was enough. Anger spiked at the knowledge that his grandfather hadn't comforted him. I remembered the bandage and stepped back so I had room between us to inspect his hand. The bandage was mangled as if he'd tried to apply it himself and couldn't quite reach.

"What happened?" I asked again.

"I told you, just some glass. I was trying to clean up, and I wasn't paying close enough attention."

"Where are your supplies? I'll help you get it cleaned up. Looks like it wasn't an easy job with just one hand," I said with a frown.

Augie looked up at me, seeming to weigh the pros and cons of letting me stay to help him.

"Yeah, okay. Through here. In the kitchen," he said before turning to lead me through the debris.

The house was a lovely old two-story farmhouse with wide plank wood flooring and a warm butter-yellow color on most of the walls. I thought about all the work it would take to replace all the broken items and make it a home again.

"I'm so sorry, Augie. This is awful," I said softly as we entered the kitchen. "What did they take?"

"You mean besides my peace of mind?" His attempt at humor fell flat, and I finally knew why August Stiel had hired Landen Safekeeping.

When those assailants had broken into his home, they'd taken more than his possessions.

They'd ripped away his sense of safety and destroyed his self-confidence.

CHAPTER 17

AUGIE

Something about having Saint in my house was both nerve-racking and soothing. He made me feel safe despite the chaos everywhere, but I was still on edge around him for some reason. Like all the hairs on my body were on high alert and my heart was prepared at any minute to be launched skyward.

I'd spent the entire weekend alternatively obsessing over him and trying not to think of him. Was it any surprise which I spent more time doing?

So having him in my home had my entire body vibrating with awareness.

"Do you want a beer or something?" I asked.

His blue-gray eyes looked up at me from where he'd taken a seat at the kitchen island, and I stopped what I was doing to stare at them. Something about the soft lights in my kitchen made those eyes speak to me in a way nothing else did. He was curious and concerned, and his entire being was focused solely on me.

The realization was intoxicating, and I found myself taking a step toward him before catching myself and shaking my head.

"Beer, yeah?" I asked again before turning to the fridge and pulling out two bottles. I didn't wait for his response but opened them anyway and set one on the counter in front of him before taking a sip of the other.

I walked to the drawer with the first aid supplies and pulled them out before walking back to the island and taking the stool next to him. He gently took the supplies out of my hand and moved his beer away to make room for the kit.

While he looked for what he wanted in the box, I focused on taking some calming breaths and reminding myself that this man was here to make sure I was all right. Because he was a nice guy. Not because he was my boyfriend.

And that was okay. I could accept his help and move on without putting some stupid meaning onto the encounter. But I couldn't deny my reaction to his sudden hug by the front door. It had taken me by surprise at first, but then his body's heat had seeped into me and I'd felt completely and utterly at home in his embrace. I shuddered again at the memory and tried to remind myself he was just being thoughtful. The embrace didn't mean anything.

At least that was what the adult in me tried to tell the twelve-year-old in me who was beginning to have a massive crush on the handsome guy with the bandages.

"Fuck," I muttered under my breath before taking another sip of my beer.

Saint's brows lifted and he looked at me. "That bad?"

Yeah, dude. Apparently, I want you that bad.

"Just hurts a little," I said. And that was true also.

"Okay, let me get this other bandage off first. Hold still."

As he worked the bandage off gently, I studied his face up close. The golden stubble on his jaw after a full day, the thick light lashes setting off his blue-gray eyes, a freckle on the sharpest point of one of his cheekbones. He was so beautiful, and I wondered if people told him that all the time.

He shook his head and grunted.

"What?" I asked.

"This mess happened over a week ago. I can't believe I was here last night and didn't know you were coming home to this. Why didn't you say something? I could have come in and helped you clean up or something," he muttered as he tore open some cleansing wipes.

"It's just the furniture out of place. And besides, it's not your problem."

He looked up at me, pinning me with a glare. "Does it have to be my problem for me to give a shit?"

"No, but why would you? You don't even know me," I pointed out.

Saint rolled his eyes and went back to treating the cut on my arm. "You're an idiot," he murmured as he cleaned my open wound with an alcohol solution.

I winced from the pain. "Why am I an idiot?" I snapped at him, letting the sting get the better of my self-control.

"I like you, Augie. I care about what happens to you. Is that so hard to believe?"

"You don't even know me," I repeated.

The corner of his lips turned up at that. "And whose fault is that?"

He went back to tending the wound and finished up with some fresh bandages before looking back up at me. "Where is the glass so I can clean it up? I don't want you getting cut again."

"Don't worry about it. I can handle it," I told him. Saint lifted an eyebrow at me, and I began to squirm under his attentions. "Fine. It's in my bedroom." I stood up and began walking out of the kitchen, Saint trailing behind me.

I wondered what he thought of my house. Despite the mess, I was proud of it. It had been in my family for a long time, and now it was mine. Over the years of spending summers here with my great-aunt Melody, the place had become a part of me—the closest thing I had to my very own haven—and having it invaded and destroyed had wrecked something inside of me.

When we walked through the doorway to the master bedroom, I felt my heart speed up as it had every time I'd seen it since the night of the break-in. The bed was undisturbed since I hadn't tried sleeping in it since that night, but clothes were strewn all over the place, and the large mirror over my dresser was shattered.

"Jesus Christ, Augie," Saint said from behind me.

"Yeah."

"What were they looking for?" he asked.

"I don't know."

He turned around and studied me. "Are you sure? This wasn't done by some kids looking for drug money. This was a serious search-and-destroy mission. They were looking for something."

I felt nerves in my gut and wished I hadn't had those few sips of beer moments before.

"I honestly don't know what they could have been looking for, Saint. I'm an antique appraiser for god's sake. Not the keeper of the nuclear codes."

"Did they take your computer?" he asked.

"Yes, but there wasn't anything really important on there. I keep everything stored in the cloud."

Saint looked around and stepped over piles of clothes on the floor. "Where is the glass? It looks like the mirror glass is all still in the frame."

I stepped up behind him and pointed to a broken picture frame on my bedside table. He sat on the edge of my bed and pulled the photograph carefully out from the broken frame.

It was my favorite photo of my father and me when I was little. We were swimming in the ocean, and Dad had me propped on a hip. I was tanned and freckled from the summer sun, and our faces were wide with happy smiles. There was an enormous wave right behind us getting ready to crash over our heads, but for that brief moment, we were untouchable. I can't remember who took the photo. Probably a nanny of some kind or maybe my mom. I remembered that trip to the beach. Dad helped me make sandcastles, and I swam and played in the sand all day—not a care in the world.

"Is this you and your dad?" he asked quietly. "He died when you were growing up, right?"

My throat felt thick, so I just nodded.

"I'm so sorry, Augie. I read about your dad on the internet. It sounded like he was a good man."

"He was," I said, my voice sounding rough to my own ears. "My mom moved us into my grandfather's house as if he could replace my dad in some way. They were nothing alike. Grandfather is more like my mom, so... yeah. Needless to say, I haven't gotten over losing my dad."

I turned away, intending to look for a cardboard box or something to collect the broken glass in when Saint stood up, grabbed my wrist, and pulled me back. I stumbled and fell against his chest before his arms came around me. The physical contact when I was already feeling so raw was enough to push me over the edge. I let out a muffled sob against his shirt and felt his arms tighten.

"It's okay, sweetheart," he murmured against my hair. "It's okay."

I shook my head against his chest. It sure as shit wasn't okay. Nothing was okay and it would never *be* okay again.

"I miss him so fucking much, Saint," I admitted. "He was larger than life, you know? Just a good man. He always thought the best of me. Encouraged me. Believed in me." I was babbling, but they were thoughts that had been on my mind so much in the past year since my great-aunt's death. "He was different from the rest of my family. It's so unfair."

"I know."

The reality of the situation hit, and embarrassment slammed into me. I tried to pull away, but Saint's arms didn't budge. I looked up at him, intending to tell him to let go. But the look in his eyes stopped me. Concern was there, for sure. Worry too. But something else was clear in those aquamarine eyes.

Lust.

My heart was jackhammering in my chest, and I saw a pulse point on his neck jumping.

"Saint?" I whispered.

CHAPTER 18

SAINT

I WANTED TO KISS HIM DESPERATELY. AUGIE'S LIPS WERE RIGHT THERE IN front of me, soft and full. I'd never seen a man's lips so naturally tempting. Just one quick taste. I knew it was a bad idea because of the work connection. But god, those lips.

Before I had a chance to decide either way, Augie brushed his lips across mine and I was gone. His mouth was soft and tentative, so I leaned forward and grabbed the back of his neck to keep him from changing his mind. My mouth took charge, eliciting a moan from Augie as my tongue sought entry into his mouth.

He tasted so damned sweet, and I felt his hands fist the front of my shirt. As he stepped in to my body, I wrapped my free arm around his waist to pull him in closer. Our mouths explored each other, tongues tangling as our breathing quickly turned into panting.

Finally I pulled away and leaned my forehead against his to catch my breath. I brought both hands up to cup the sides of his face and tilted it so I could look into his eyes.

His eyes were dark with need. The intensity was so much, I took a step back to catch my breath.

I closed my eyes and breathed in. Before I even had a chance to open my eyes, Augie's body pushed against mine, forcing me back against the bedroom door until our entire bodies were pressed together. Slender-fingered hands came up to hold my face still, forcing me to look at him.

When he spoke, his voice was deliberate and held a definitive tone I hadn't heard before. "More."

My stomach dropped and my eyes flicked to his lips, still red and moist from the previous kiss. Augie's hands pulled my face down until our mouths met.

The kiss started off sweet and tentative, the way I thought of the man himself, but it wasn't long before I couldn't keep it soft anymore. I wanted him. When my mouth was on his, all rational thought flew out of my head and I lost control. Gone were responsible reminders of my job security. Gone were warnings about moving too fast with someone who probably didn't have all that much experience with guys. The only thing in my mind was getting more—getting inside of his delicious mouth and devouring him.

I reached around and cupped his ass, pulling him even tighter to me until I could feel the hard ridge of his erection shift against mine through our clothes. A groan escaped me, and I heard him whimper in response. His hands moved from my face to the sides of my neck, and within moments, I felt him begin to climb my body, pulling himself up until his legs were around my waist. I stepped away from the door and began moving toward the bed.

I didn't want to move too fast, so instead of lying him down, I turned and sat, landing with him in my lap and pulling our faces away from each other long enough to look at him.

"What do you want?" I asked in a gruff voice.

He just looked at me, caught in a haze of lust for a few beats before speaking.

"You."

I rubbed my hands up and down his thighs where they straddled my own. Lean muscles curved under my hands, and I was itching to feel them without the barrier of his clothes.

"Augie, I don't want to rush you…"

His jaw tightened and his eyes shuttered. "That's fine. We don't have to." As he spoke, he began shifting off me, but I moved my arms around his back in time to stop him.

"That's not what I meant," I said gently. "I just want to understand what you're thinking—what you're feeling. Talk to me. I don't want to do something you'll regret later."

He seemed to relax against me again until I felt like I could move my hands back to rubbing his thighs without him escaping.

Augie's own hands came up to my chest, and he seemed to lose himself in tracing a finger over my collarbone as he gathered his thoughts. After a few moments, he looked back up at me.

"I've been with other men, Saint. Just no one I cared about. And I've never... had anal sex. Just blowjobs and hand jobs. I've never been with someone long enough for more than that."

"Why not?" I asked, although I had a pretty good idea.

He sighed and looked up at the ceiling. "If I actually dated someone, then I'd have to eventually introduce them to my family, you know? And I always assumed it would be impossible to get someone to understand the way I was raised. My mom has a brother. Did you know that? His name is Eric, and his son, Brett, is basically my nemesis. He and his friends made it their mission to treat me like the runt growing up, and when they found out I had a crush on a boy? God, it was hell. Anyway, my crazy family, childhood bullying, the expectations of my family's reputation, just... typical bullshit. My grandfather's voice is so loud in my head, Saint... God, it sounds so ridiculous saying out loud right now. It's so embarrassing."

He was rambling, but I thought it was better for it all to come out than stay crammed in.

"It's pretty common, Augie. I get it."

"It's pathetic. I'm an adult and I'm still making decisions about my love life based on my goddamned family? Jesus Christ."

I leaned forward and brushed a kiss across his lips. "It's okay."

"No, it's not. But thank you for saying so anyway," he said, leaning in for more kisses. They turned light and playful until I glimpsed a smile tilting up the edges of his lips. Just the sight of it made me smile too, and I finally leaned back to grin at him.

"You're smiling," I said in surprise.

"You're really fucking fun to kiss. Don't stop."

I'd never seen this side of him. The smiling, happy Augie whose nose deliberately poked me in the ticklish spot below my ear and whose fingers began seeking my armpits for the same reason. When I couldn't stop laughing, I pulled away again.

"Who the hell are you?" I asked through the laughter. "The quiet shop owner was body snatched and replaced by a goofball."

His face bloomed red, and he looked down. "I'm sorry. I'm just so... giddy." He put his hands over his face, but I could tell he was still smiling through his embarrassment.

I wrapped my arms around him in a big bear hug. "Don't be sorry; I like giddy Augie," I said softly into his ear. "He's sexy as hell."

He moved his hands away, and his lips started kissing again—this time on my neck, trailing a path to my ear to suck on my lobe. My heart stuttered in my chest, and my dick pressed painfully against my pants. I wanted release. I wanted to get naked. I wanted to shove my cock into Augie's tight little body.

But want and need were two different things. And what I *needed* was to get my head on straight. The image of Lanny's disappointment in me, the entire team's disappointment in me, if I lost this client and his influential family for the company, came roaring back to the forefront of my mind. I pushed it down, desire for the man in my arms taking over from any rational thought. We kissed and teased for a long time until we were rolling around on the bed dry-humping each other like teenagers.

"What's that?" Augie asked when the phone in my pocket vibrated.

I dropped a quick kiss on his nose and rolled off him to pull it out. I hadn't intended to look at it, but when I pulled it from my pocket, it vibrated again and the image of my boss flashed across the screen.

"Fuck," I muttered. "It's Lanny. I have to take this."

I sat up and stepped off the bed, making my way out to the hallway for privacy while accepting the call.

"Saint Wilde," I answered in a clipped tone.

"Why is Rex looking into two police reports involving August

Stiel? And why, pray tell, did you not think to inform me of this development?"

Shit. Fuck. Damn.

"Rex told you?" I realized how petulant that sounded and quickly moved to take it back. "I mean, yes, sir. It turns out his house was broken into as well as his car."

"Well, apparently Rex tapped into the surveillance of the parking deck where the vehicle was and saw something quite interesting. Mr. Brett Stiel, your client's first cousin, was also present in the parking deck during that time."

"That would make sense. I believe Augie was in town for a family dinner," I said.

"Let me clarify," Lanny said in a concerned voice. "His cousin's vehicle wasn't noticed; the man himself was seen approaching your client's vehicle with another unidentified man forty-five minutes before the break-in. It appears he was pointing August's car out to the other man."

I glanced at the bedroom door I'd closed behind myself when I stepped into the hall. Surely Augie's own cousin didn't have anything to do with the vehicle break-in?

"Could you tell who actually broke the window when it happened?"

"No. The man was wearing dark, nondescript clothing and a ball cap, but to me—and Rex agrees—it very well could be the second man. The shoes look the same, but it's too fuzzy to tell conclusively."

"That doesn't make any sense. Why would Augie's own cousin arrange for his car to be broken into?"

"That's the million-dollar question. And by million, I mean billion. Understand? We're going to get to the bottom of this because these two events can't be random. Not when that home invasion happened in Hickville where the crime rate is at Barney Fife levels."

"I don't know what that means," I said. Which was a lie. But all of us enjoyed making Lanny feel old. It was left over from serving together when he was our team leader.

"Shut the fuck up. Yes you do," he grunted. "Are you at a computer? I want to send you this surveillance video and see what you think."

"Um, no. I'm not at home."

"Well, get somewhere you can pull it up and call me back ASAP. Actually, no. Come here to the office if you don't mind. I'll pull together a crew to start work on this tomorrow."

"Yes, sir."

After disconnecting the call, I opened the door to the bedroom again and saw Augie lying back in his bed with his head on the pillow. His glasses were folded neatly on the bedside table, and his eyes were closed. I had to force myself not to go to him. The minute I touched him, I'd break all the unspoken promises I'd made to my boss.

This was ridiculous. I was skating on such thin ice as it was, and this job with Lanny was all I had. It was the only reason I'd left the navy in the first place. I'd wanted to go home when Otto had decided he was done, but I wouldn't have felt like I could if Lanny hadn't been there offering me a job. Being one of his trusted men at Landen had given me something to focus on, something to take the place of my identity as a SEAL. I was a personal security specialist. And my job was to keep Augie safe, not to get him naked and do naughty things to his body.

I sighed and cursed the act of maturing. It was so fucking overrated.

"Augie, I'm sorry," I said, holding back all the things I really wanted to say. That he was beautiful and kind, sweet and sexy. "I have to go."

CHAPTER 19

AUGIE

I SAT THERE IN STUNNED SILENCE JUST STARING AT SAINT AS HE PACED in front of the doorway. "Wh-what?" I finally managed to sputter. "What the hell?" Had he just been fucking around with me for some reason? Was I the butt of some big joke? Humiliation bloomed harsh and fast throughout my entire body, strangling me with its familiar hold.

Saint's face was flushed, and I wasn't sure if it was from the kissing or something else.

"Augie, I can't," he said, running fingers through his hair and moving restlessly around the room. "That was my boss, okay? And you're my client. You're *Lanny's* client. I can't do this. I'll lose my job. We shouldn't have—"

"Don't you fucking say it," I warned, a mixture of relief and embarrassment beginning to fill my face despite knowing I'd done absolutely nothing to be embarrassed about.

"I'm sorry," Saint said. And the look on his face was awful. He looked miserable—such a far cry from how he'd looked just moments before when we were laughing together. I wanted to climb back on his lap—kiss him again and tell him it was all okay. I was so relieved that it wasn't some big joke—that he really seemed into me the way I was into him. But maybe he was right. "My boss wants me in Dallas by morning. I can't stay here with you and face him, Augie. I can't."

"Okay," I said instead. "Go."

Saint stood staring at me, forehead crinkled in confusion and indecision. I could tell he was torn between wanting to stay and needing to go.

"It's okay," I repeated softly. "I understand. You have to know I wouldn't want to do anything to put your job in jeopardy, Saint."

"Augie..."

I made my way toward him slowly, careful not to step on any of the debris on the floor, until I was standing in front of him.

"One more kiss good night?" I asked with a smile.

He swallowed and stepped into me, wrapping his strong arms around me. Instead of kissing me though, he tucked his face into my neck and hugged me tightly. My entire body relaxed into his arms immediately, and I felt my throat tighten with an unfamiliar emotion. A possessive feeling I'd never had before as long as I'd lived.

You belong with me.

THE NEXT DAY at work I found myself daydreaming about that last kiss with Saint. Well, all of the kisses with Saint, really. But that last one had been the most heart-wrenching mix of sweet and desperate, and it somehow left me feeling an aching emptiness inside way worse than anything I'd felt before. Saint had pulled back from the hug and kissed me with everything he'd fucking had. And the kiss had burned away any final suspicion I'd had about him playing me.

There was no way on earth someone could have faked what that kiss had been between us.

Earlier that morning, I'd thought back to the dinner I'd had with my family a few nights before. Brett had only stayed long enough for one drink before disappearing for some kind of meeting at work, but that hadn't stopped Mom and her brother from being just as annoying as my cousin.

Uncle Eric had asked me for Melody's antique writing slope, which she had left me in her will almost a year before. I'd had to explain accidentally forgetting it at home.

That writing slope had been in my family since it was handcrafted in 1790 for a distant ancestor named Margaret Baker, who at the time had lived in a small village in Buckinghamshire called Penn and had a passionate, forbidden love affair with a local craftsman. I'd spent hours reading Margaret's small collection of love letters inside the ancient wooden box, along with the diary she'd kept after her lover's untimely death only two years later. It had been the central romance story of my young years until I'd discovered the Jude Devereaux paperbacks stashed in a shoebox under Melody's bed one summer at the Hobie farmhouse.

In fact, the tiny intricate key Margaret had used to lock her writing slope had become the first key of my collection. Melody had given it to me years before, and I now wore it on a chain around my neck under my clothes. The only times I took it off were for things like my self-defense lessons when I feared it would get snagged on something. There wasn't much monetary value to the items inside the box, but the words were raw and pure, private and intimate. I held the key near my heart more as a symbol of respect than anything else, as if I was guarding someone's innermost desires, and in Margaret's case, innermost pain as well.

When my grandfather had delivered the slope into my possession after Melody's funeral, it had come with a lecture about under-standing its value and keeping it safe. As if I didn't know that. I had multiple degrees and certifications in art history, antiquities, and appraisal. And all of it had been born out of a genuine connection with my own family history and artifacts. To finally have Margaret's slope in my possession was a bittersweet feeling.

So when Grandfather had asked to see it the other night at my house, I hadn't been surprised. I'd assumed he was checking up on how well I was keeping it safe. I'd never known him to be particularly sentimental, but maybe he had feelings I was unaware of. After retrieving it from my bedroom closet, I'd brought it out to him for inspection. To my surprise, he'd pulled a duplicate key out of his pocket to open it.

"Just want to make sure everything is still here," he'd mumbled, almost to himself. I'd rolled my eyes, trying not to flash back to all the times in my childhood he'd been a controlling, micromanaging bastard, and I'd headed into the kitchen to put water on for tea while he'd rifled through the letters or took whatever ridiculous inventory he'd felt he needed to take in order to determine whether or not I was an irresponsible good-for-nothing.

When I'd returned to the living room, the box was locked back up, and Grandfather looked noticeably more relaxed.

At the time, I'd truly thought of it as an annoying checkup on me the same way he'd once made me bring home every single assignment from boarding school one semester to prove I was working to "Stiel potential."

But now I wondered what the hell he'd wanted with a bunch of old love letters. When he'd left that night, he'd strongly suggested I keep the slope in the floor vault in the barn.

"You can never be too careful, August," he'd said with narrowed eyes. "After the break-in, I would think you wouldn't want to take any chances."

It took me until now to wonder why he hadn't suggested the same care and safekeeping for the set of ten Japanese Meiji chargers I had on display in the glass-front George III corner cabinet in the dining room. The charger collection alone was worth over twenty thousand dollars, and Grandfather knew it because he had purchased the set as a gift for Melody on her eightieth birthday. Or why he hadn't insisted I present and properly store Melody's 1940s Cartier Art Deco enamel and jade bracelet that had to be worth over forty-five thousand dollars. The amount of high-value items in my house right now was shocking, really. The last of Melody's belongings from the Dallas penthouse had been delivered to the farmhouse as soon as the new security system had been activated. I'd quickly stored many of the small valuables like jewelry in the barn safe, but there were plenty of expensive collectibles still on display around the house.

Was he envious that I owned this piece of family history? That concept didn't hold with the Jonathan Stiel I knew. He'd sold his wife's wedding dress when someone had requested it to use in a movie. For enough cash, my grandfather would do almost anything. So why be more concerned about the love letters than the expensive antique jewelry and collectibles?

I pondered over it for several hours until I received a call from my cousin Brett.

"It's my mom's birthday today," he said without preamble.

"I know. I already called her this morning," I said. "We're having dinner next Friday night at Grandfather's house, right?"

"She wants to have dinner *tonight* at The French Room. She's craving fois gras. I suggest grabbing a burger on the way since their portions are the size of a grain of rice. At least, that's my plan."

"Grandfather said there were no plans to celebrate on the day because Aunt Prima was going to a charity fashion show or something. I can't just leave work again on short notice." It was a lie. My part-timer was due to arrive any minute, but Brett didn't need to know that. I was annoyed at the repeated command performance so soon after the last one.

"You know what a cow she'll have if you're not there. Persona non grata and all that. Suit yourself, Augustine."

And with that, he hung up on me.

"Fuck," I spat. I fucking hated my family, but even worse, I hated how ingrained it was in me to not rock the boat. I knew without stopping to even argue with myself that I'd be there. For all the hassle my uncle had given me over the years, Aunt Prima had never missed my birthday.

When I arrived in Dallas a few hours later, I decided to valet park my rental car at a nearby hotel so I wouldn't have to go into a parking garage alone. As soon as I approached the restaurant, I felt like I was being watched. It wasn't the first time I'd gotten that eerie feeling, but because of everything that had been happening to me, it was the first time I'd actually thought there could be something to it. Sure enough,

I looked around and spotted someone looking at me from twenty yards away.

The man wasn't much to look at, actually. Normally he wouldn't have stood out at all, but he was clearly watching me. When he saw me notice him, he looked away quickly. Did that mean he was watching me for nefarious reasons? Surely not. Maybe I had wet paint on my ass or something. Maybe he thought I looked like someone he knew. Hell, maybe I *was* someone he knew. But the encounter left me feeling shaky and unsure nonetheless. Instead of heading into The French Room, I ducked into the nearest place I could find which was a cell phone store.

Once inside the store, I debated about whether to call Saint but quickly dismissed the idea. I was being paranoid and ridiculous. And besides, the whole reason I'd signed up for the lessons was to be able to defend myself without needing someone else to do it for me.

After nodding a kind of apology to the cell phone worker, who looked at me with a questioning glance, I exited the shop and was relieved to see no trace of the man. I made my way toward the French Room and tried to put it out of my mind.

Just inside the restaurant, I saw Brett waiting. I approached him and was surprised to hear him say Eric and Prima had canceled.

"Mom decided to go to the charity thing after all, so we're back on for Friday night. Hey, you want to grab a burger around the corner since you're here anyway? My treat," Brett said.

I side-eyed him. He'd never in my life wanted to have a meal with just me. But I had to admit, I was starving. "Ah, sure?"

Once we were seated at Chop House Burger, I finally allowed myself to take a breath. I'd sped to the city and then hustled from the valet stand to the restaurant like someone was after me. But now that I was sitting in the burger place, I realized how ridiculous my paranoia had been.

"Where's everyone else?" I asked. "Weren't my mom and Grandfather coming too?"

Brett shrugged. "No idea. Hey, how are things going in the shop? It's been open a couple months now, right?"

I stared at him. Why was I surprised he didn't know better? "It'll be a year in January," I corrected. Even though January was still a couple of months away, I wanted to make the point that it had been much longer than a "couple months."

"Oh right. You started it with Melody's inheritance."

I nodded and took another bite of my burger, unwilling to babble some apology or excuse as to why she'd left me so much and him only her hunting rifle collection. I wondered if he knew that had been a joke from beyond the grave. He was a terrible shot, and even into her eighties, Great-Aunt Melody had taken great pride in outshooting him at the range. I hadn't gotten to see any of those victories in person since I had a paralyzing fear of guns, but I'd heard the stories and they were entertaining as hell.

But Brett, like the rest of us, had shares in the Stiel Corporation, which meant he had plenty of money to live comfortably. He had a job in the accounting department at Stiel as well, which meant Grandfather had an excuse to funnel even more money to him without inheritance tax one day.

I hadn't actually planned on opening my own shop, but Melody's death had coincided with me landing a promotion at an auction house that meant reporting to an old family friend of my mother's who'd had a crush on her for years. After the first two weeks of working for the guy, I learned he was telling her every little detail of my life and work. It took an already nosy family into extreme intrusion territory. Now I had a much more peaceful life in Hobie, away from the Stiel name and family. I loved it there. The small town was much more my speed, and the people were incredibly friendly.

"Have you sold that, um, what's that thing called again? That writing box deal she used to have?"

The food turned to a clump of lead in my gut, and my skin began to tingle. I looked up at him. Brett was munching on fries and doing his best to look nonchalant.

He failed.

"Oh, yeah," I lied, making shit up on the spot. "I sold it the other day. A nice older couple bought it with a silver gravy boat."

I took a sip of my sweet tea and eyed him as I swallowed.

His eyes widened. "Really? I thought you loved that thing."

I shrugged. "Yeah, I did when I was a kid, you know? But I got five hundred bucks for it, so I figured what the hell. I'll find another one like it at auction one day if I decide I miss it that much."

There was no way he'd have any idea how significant the box was to my great-aunt. If he was asking about it, something seriously weird was going on.

"Huh. You sure? I can't see you parting with it. You and Melody were close."

"We were. But now that I have the house and everything, I don't feel as sentimental about the little stuff," I said, hoping like hell my voice was steady. I wasn't the best liar in the world.

"Weren't there papers inside? Where did you put those? I kind of wish I'd asked to look at that stuff before she died. My dad said there were letters or something?"

What could my idiot cousin really want with a bunch of antique love letters? I couldn't for the life of me think of anything. But an idea popped into my head.

"There's an old wooden steamer trunk in the apartment above the shop. I tossed them in there with some of Melody's nicer vintage clothes until I have time to go through them."

"Cool. I'm sure the old broad had some amazing dresses from like the twenties and stuff."

I stared at him. "Melody was born in 1931, Brett. I don't think she had flapper dresses."

"Oh. Huh. Well, that's too bad. I'm sure all you guys love that kind of thing," he said while checking out the ass on a passing female server. "I wouldn't know."

"Well," I said, putting down my napkin and standing up, "if by 'you guys' you mean antique appraisers, you'd be right. We do love that kind of thing, especially if we can confirm provenance, valuate the item, and find out interesting history attached to a particular garment. Thanks for the burger."

I left him sitting there with his jaw hanging down in surprise. Of all the Stiels, I was definitely the least likely to make waves. But not only was I sick of his stupidity, I was also nervous as hell that everyone in my family seemed to want to get their hands on the writing slope I had stashed away in my nest back home.

Before I got back to the valet stand to collect my car, someone grabbed my elbow hard enough to bruise. I whipped around and saw my cousin with a nasty look on his face. It was only there for a brief second, and then he was all smiles and fake friendliness again.

"You should have offered that box to one of us before selling it, Augie."

"Why? You never cared about family history before." I hoped my voice didn't sound as shaky as it felt.

"Things like that are more valuable than you think. I'd like you to bring me the contents at least."

I yanked my arm out of his hold. "Stop touching me," I said loudly enough for passersby to hear. I followed it with two giant strides away from him the way Saint had taught me. "And you're not getting the contents. Melody left it to me to do with as I please. There's nothing in a pack of old love letters you could have any interest in. Goodbye."

I turned and stepped quickly to the valet stand, hoping he'd let me go without grabbing me again. My elbow still smarted from his tight grip. He'd always been a bully, but this was just plain weird. Even for him.

Brett called out to my retreating back. "See you Friday."

"Said the lion to the lamb," I muttered under my breath. Voices in my head began clamoring for attention and action, but the strongest one must have taken charge of my body because the next thing I knew, I was on the road, halfway to the Dallas office of Landen Safe-keeping.

And Saint.

CHAPTER 20

SAINT

When Lanny called me into his office to ask how things were going with Augie, I felt the slinky coil of guilt in my gut. I'd been nervous all day about this since Lanny had needed to put off our meeting till mid-afternoon.

"Fine. Good, I mean. *Good*," I said.

Lanny raised his eyebrows at me in question. "What the fuck was that?"

"What was what?" I asked, despite knowing what he meant.

"You did a thing. With your face and your mouth. I can't decide if you were lying to me or lying to yourself. Wanna try again?" His eyebrows were still raised, but he seemed to be more surprised than upset.

"I just... I wonder if maybe you should assign someone else to work with him," I said even though the mere thought of another person working with Augie, *touching* Augie, made me want to beat the shit out of something.

"Explain," Lanny demanded. "What happened?"

"Nothing," I lied. "Nothing. I just... he's..." I felt my jaw tighten, and I looked away. "He's really cute."

There. If I was looking to lose the respect of my mentor, that oughta do it nicely.

God, I was a total jackass.

"Oh hell," Lanny muttered.

"Yeah. Sorry."

And then he laughed. Like I'd said the funniest thing in the fucking world. I couldn't help staring at him like maybe he'd had a psychotic break.

"Lan...?" I asked.

"Dude, seriously? That's all? You can't work with him because he's a hot piece of ass?"

"Don't call him that. And no, it's not just that..." But really, it was mostly that.

"Then what else is it?"

I stared at him, desperately trying to think of what other problems there were besides the hot piece of ass thing. I came up with nothing. Not one single thing. But I couldn't risk Lanny not taking my complaint seriously and reassigning me, so I had to get creative.

"He's... little. I might break him or something," I tried.

"Saint, I've seen you defend yourself in hand-to-hand combat while holding a toddler. Are you really trying to tell me you can't teach a grown man self-defense without hurting him?"

"That was different," I said, remembering the case he referred to. "That kid was robust."

"He was a hoss. But he was still a three-year-old. Way more vulnerable than your geek."

"He's not *my* geek," I said. God, did I really sound as childish as I thought I did? Yes. Yes, I did.

Lanny laughed again. "I don't have anyone else stupid enough to get benched, so you're on deck for this, Saint. Figure it out. I have faith in you. Surely you can teach this guy some moves without fucking him. Plus, he has a girlfriend, so I don't think he'd be interested in what you have to offer anyway."

My stomach knotted at the mention of a girlfriend. "You sure?" I asked. "I mean, not that it matters…" Lanny laughed some more and gave me a look that smacked of amused pity.

Was this where I was supposed to admit to having sexual relations with the client?

"Yeah," Lanny said, looking down at some of the work on his desk. "Katrina Duvall. I've met her out with him before at a black-tie thing. Gorgeous woman. She's an anchor for one of the local TV stations."

He had to mention the woman was gorgeous. Either way, it didn't matter. They weren't an item, and Augie was a client. Why couldn't I get that through my head for god's sake?

Lanny looked back up at me from the paperwork in front of him. "What are you still doing here? Conference room, Rex is waiting for you. Go."

I resisted the urge to roll my eyes. "Fine."

"Try not to seduce the client, Saint," he called after me with a chuckle. "Although, to be honest, I'm more worried about your feelings getting hurt from his rejection than him firing us for inappropriate touching. He's a bit out of your league, don't you think?"

I shot him the bird over my shoulder as I walked out.

When I got to the conference room, I was surprised to see a young woman at the table I didn't recognize. She was so young, she looked like she might even still be in high school.

I greeted Rex and lifted a brow in the newcomer's direction.

"Oh!" Rex said. "This is Skipper. She's our new hacker."

Skipper's nostrils flared. "Jesus, Rex. Way to just put it out there. Why don't you call the cops next or the FBI?"

"Hi, Skipper, I'm Saint," I said, holding out my hand to shake.

"Oh, I don't touch people. Sorry."

She went back to tapping on a laptop that seemed more stickers and decals than megabytes of data. I glanced back at Rex. *Where did you find her?* I mouthed.

I wasn't sure, but I thought maybe he replied, *Darth Wem.*

Whatever that meant.

"Have a seat," Rex said out loud. "How much do you know about the Stiel Foundation in terms of where it puts its money?"

"Conservative efforts. Things like Second Amendment defense, anti-abortion campaigns, homes for unwed mothers, veteran rehab efforts, and research for policy change." I listed off the ones I remembered from my short research.

"Right. As well as some great community projects like food banks, job assistance, and low-income housing. And in most cases, it's all very aboveboard. We haven't seen evidence of any of these beneficiary groups involved in any kind of violence or threat of violence. Obviously, you never know. There could be things we don't see, but for the most part, all of the organizations check out. Except this one oddball beneficiary that seems to be a shell for something hinky."

"What do you mean? What is it?"

This time it was Skipper who spoke up. "CSP, which stands for Community Surge Properties, is a registered nonprofit that seems to provide residential housing for low-income families. But when we dug deeper into its actual real estate holdings, we discovered the properties it owns only appear as low-income housing on paper. In reality, they are a combination of high-value development projects and historically important properties. Somehow, the people who run this organization are managing to get around the historic property renovation regulations by having these properties redesignated from historically protected to community beneficial. I don't understand the intricacies of the zoning and shit yet, but it's certainly raising a crap ton of red flags."

Rex looked excited. "Yeah, and then you add the fact that these assholes could be collecting the low-income housing tax credit on top of having nonprofit status already. And they're selling these units for top dollar."

My brain had already made the connection between the fact that both the hinky non-profit CSP and the primary Stiel family business involved real estate investment. Did the Stiels know this was what their money was going toward, or did they think CSP was actually building low-income housing?

"How have they not been caught?" I wondered out loud.

Skipper typed some more without taking her eyes off me. "Most of these properties are located in two distinct areas, which means the housing authority and any other group involved in oversight is limited to these same two districts. One is Dallas County and the other is Cross County."

"Hobie is in Cross County," I said. "Why would this organization care about a county that has two dinky rural towns in it? And what do Dallas and Cross counties have in common besides both being in Texas?"

I knew the town of Valley Cross had some low-income housing in it, but I wasn't as sure about Hobie. It was always understood that the poorer families tended to live in Valley Cross while the wealthier families lived in Hobie.

"Well, both have significant amounts of property owned by CSP," Skipper said. "So like, according to deed records, the Stiel Corporation also owns property in Cross County, including the building next to your brother's pub."

"The antique shop? That would make sense considering Augie Stiel runs it," I said.

"No. That one is managed by a realty holding company, but the building itself is privately owned by a Stiel family trust of some kind. The Stiel Corporation owns the one between the antiques and the pub, and CSP owns the one on the other side of the antique shop."

I thought about the children's toy and gift shop on the other side of Augie's store from the pub. It was definitely not low-income housing. It was an upscale grandma shop with designer baby clothes and handcrafted toys. The vacant space between Augie and the pub, apparently owned by the Stiel Corporation, had been an old-fashioned pizza parlor when I was growing up.

"So the Stiel Corp one is vacant," I began. "But the CSP one is occupied by a specialty gift shop that's been there at least three years, if not longer. As far as I know, they have no plans of moving. Plus, there's no way Hobie would approve low-income housing right on the damned town square."

Rex leaned back in his chair. "Sounds super weird. Like these two groups are connected somehow. Do you think Augie's involved?"

"No! Definitely not," I said. "I can't imagine him involved in something if he knew it was shady or breaking rules. The guy is a rule follower. He won't even jaywalk in our tiny town in the middle of the night."

It didn't escape my notice that I'd claimed Hobie as mine. Even though it had been a long time since I'd made my home there, Hobie had always been a part of me. I'd missed it more and more since my brothers had seemed to be drawn back to it in recent years, and meeting Augie there had made that feeling even stronger.

"Maybe you should ask him about it, Saint," Rex said after the three of us spent quite a bit of time talking it through. "Skipper and I will keep digging tomorrow, but in the meantime you need to have a conversation with the one Stiel who might be willing to shed some light on this."

I let out a sigh. "Okay. I'll talk to him tomorrow at our next session."

I looked at the time and realized it was well into the evening hours. We'd been working longer than I'd expected.

I stretched and stood up. "It's late. You guys should get home. I'm going to go work out my frustration in the gym before I get on the road. Let me know what else you find out, especially who runs CSP and who ultimately benefits from these deals. And thanks, guys."

I was anxious to get back to Hobie to see Augie, but I needed time to think about the best way to approach it. I didn't really know him well enough to point-blank ask if his family was involved in some kind of tax scam or corporate fraud. And I wasn't sure Augie would even know if they were. Maybe I'd begin by asking him about the properties in Hobie and whether or not he knew who owned them.

First, I had to get on the treadmill or lift the hell out of some weights before I thought I'd be calm enough to sit in the truck for a couple of hours. Luckily, the security company had a huge training gym on the premises.

Just as I rounded the corner toward the locker rooms, I looked up and saw Augie. We both stopped and stared at each other. His eyes were stormy behind the lenses of his glasses, and the tic marks of worry were out in full force over his brow.

My heart lurched. "What's wrong?" I asked, instead of my other question, which was why the hell he was at my workplace in Dallas.

He shook his head and clenched his jaw before speaking. "Does this place have a heavy bag I can punch by any chance?"

I blinked at him for a minute before clearing the cobwebs. "Yeah, sure. There are spare workout clothes in the cabinet on the left, and you can change in here."

He nodded and turned into the locker room I indicated without sparing me a second glance. I quickly made my way to one of the supply cubbies in the gym to find us some gloves.

A few minutes later, Augie joined me and gloved up without speaking. We took turns punching and holding the heavy bag for each other until both of us were nice and warm.

When Augie stopped punching just long enough to use the hem of his shirt to wipe his face, I tore my eyes away from his flat stomach and sexy-as-hell happy trail to glance at his face.

"I get the feeling you're not here for another self-defense lesson. You seem to be intent on teaching this bag a lesson."

He dropped the tail of his shirt and looked up at me, sliding his glasses back up his nose with the back of his glove.

"Whatever. It's fine."

I cocked my head at his words. "Augie. What's going on?"

He hesitated before looking away. I stepped closer so no one else in the gym could hear us. "Is this about what happened last night? Is this about us…"

"No," he said firmly. "Not at all. I'm sorry if you thought that."

I couldn't deny the relief I felt in my gut, but he was still clearly upset about something. "Then what happened?"

"Work shit. Family shit."

I waited, knowing that wasn't all of it.

He walked over to where I'd dropped a couple of bottles of water by some towels. After peeling off the gloves, he grabbed a bottle of water and cracked it open. As he swallowed, I enjoyed the movement of the muscles in his neck and the drops of sweat trailing down to the dip in his collarbone. Shit, maybe I enjoyed it a little too much. I shook my head and grabbed the other water, biting the ends of my gloves to yank them off first.

"I think my family is involved in the burglaries," he said.

Despite the information Rex and Skipper had given me, I was surprised at Augie's words.

"What makes you say that?" I asked, gesturing for him to take a seat on a bench near the sparring mat.

"It's going to sound ridiculous," he began, forking his fingers through his damp hair before letting out a breath. "But my great-aunt left me an antique personal letter-writing box, called a slope, in her will. It's something that's been in our family for over two hundred years and holds a packet of love letters written to the woman who owned the box from the man who handcrafted it for her."

"I don't understand. Is it worth a lot of money?" I asked.

"No. I mean, it is, but not the kind of money that would get my family's attention."

"Do they want control of the history inside? Or…" I was trying to figure out what his family could possibly want with an old antique box enough to steal it from his possession. "Did they ask you for it and you refused to give it to them?"

He shook his head. "Not really. Just… just bear with me for a minute and let me talk it through, okay?"

I murmured an apology for interrupting him but forced myself not to take his hand into mine the way I wanted to. Instead, I concentrated on listening.

"First, the home invasion. Three of my slopes were missing from the collection in the large cabinet in the living room. The rest were smashed to pieces. Now that I think back on it, the ones that were taken all bore some resemblance to Melody's slope. Same type of wood, same basic shape and size. They weren't at all the same age, but someone looking based on only the description wouldn't know that."

I wondered how he could tell those three missing boxes weren't part of the broken pile on the floor, but I didn't interrupt to ask. The man knew his antiques, so I trusted he was sure of what he said.

"Another thing that was missing was a jar of old keys. Melody's slope will not open without a key or without bashing the box to pieces. If someone in my family wanted the box, I have to assume they wouldn't want to break it. But that jar of keys didn't hold the key to any of those three slopes or Melody's slope."

Augie twisted the small hand towel with his fingers.

"Then, when my car was left open in Hobie, there was nothing missing because there was nothing of value in the vehicle except the gym clothes you'd given me. And when it was broken into in the parking garage at Grandfather's building, one of the things missing was a box of old keys again."

"The ones that came with the vases," I added. "Not any that would open a slope."

"Right. So here's the part where my family comes in." He took a quick sip of water from the bottle before continuing. There were muffled sounds of people passing in the hallway outside the sparring room, but no one entered.

"The slope came into my possession almost a year ago when Grandfather gave it to me after Melody's death. No one had mentioned it since then until this week. That day you helped me clean up the keys in the shop, my mother asked me to bring the slope to Dallas for dinner. I forgot it in my haste to get to the city, and that's the night my car was broken into. At that dinner, my uncle Eric asked about the slope too. Then the night my grandfather showed up at the farmhouse, he asked to see the slope. I brought it out to him, not even thinking much about it since it had been his sister's. Then tonight I got lured into town supposedly for my aunt's birthday dinner, but when I arrived it was just my cousin Brett. Apparently everyone else had canceled. Then even Brett asked me about the damned slope."

"What the hell is in that box?" I wondered out loud.

"Nothing. I mean, love letters. That's it. I've read them a hundred times, Saint. It's just letters back and forth between two young people in love. There's no mention of buried treasure or hidden gold ingots. No historical significance outside of our family's ancestry."

"Did you tell Brett that?"

"Yes, but… ah… I may have also set a kind of… trap?"

I glanced at him and saw him looking down at his lap where his fingernail was plucking at an edge of the paper water bottle label.

Little Augie Stiel playing private detective? It kinda turned me on, if I was being honest.

"Come again, Five-Oh?"

Augie looked up at me with his typical worry divots front and center. "I told him I sold it. The box, I mean. And when he asked me where I put the papers, I told him they were in a wooden chest above the shop."

"Where is the box itself? I'm assuming you didn't actually sell it?"

"It's at the farmhouse, hidden. But I don't trust that people couldn't find it if they looked hard enough."

It wasn't lost on me that he'd trusted me enough to tell me where it was without hesitation.

"Why don't we go get it and put it in a safe-deposit box at the bank just in case? I don't want anyone coming around to the farmhouse looking for it again."

He shrugged. "I guess so, but I think I'd like another self-defense lesson just in case. This whole situation really gives me a bad feeling. I'm probably being paranoid." Augie laughed and looked down at the bottle he was holding. I put my hand on his elbow to give him a reassuring squeeze, and he flinched. I stared at him before looking down at his elbow and seeing dark red marks like early bruises forming.

"Did he fucking touch you?" I growled, inspecting the marks more closely. Augie yanked his arm away but didn't contradict me.

"Augie, answer me. Did that man hurt you? Who grabbed your elbow like this?"

"It's fine," he said to his feet. The poor man's face was red, and he was clearly embarrassed. "You would have been proud of me actually. I barked at him to stop touching me at the same time I yanked out of his hold and took two giant strides back."

My heart squeezed at the image. "Of course I'm proud of you, but I need you to consider some personal protection," I said.

His eyes came up to search mine, and we locked gazes for a few long beats. Something seemed to pass between us then, but it was fleeting. It was there one moment and gone the next.

"What, like hiring a bodyguard?" he teased. The edges of his mouth were drawn up in a small grin, and I couldn't help but do the same, letting the tone change so the tension would dissipate.

"Perhaps. I hear the good ones are scary and intimidating. Then there are the sleepy-kitten ones. You can probably get that kind at a discount." I'd tried to soften my suggestion with humor, but I was really very serious about it.

He laughed a real laugh and pretended to punch me in the ribs. "Shut the fuck up. Just because you don't scare me doesn't mean you wouldn't scare other people. Just don't let them see you smile. That fucking tooth is too adorable to scare anyone."

The minute the words were out of his mouth his entire face bloomed red, and I knew he regretted what he'd said. Too bad. It was out there, and I wasn't about to let it go.

"What tooth?" I asked with a grin, feeling my cock wake up in the face of a flirty August Stiel.

"Never mind."

"Nope. Too late. The redneck twisty one?"

More red blotches appeared on his neck. And his discomfort only made my dick harder.

"It's cute," he said in a soft voice. "I like it."

My stomach tumbled, and part of me wished Lanny could have been there to see how none of this was really my fault. Augie was irresistible, and it was taking every shred of self-control I had not to throw him down on the mat and lay my body on top of his. I couldn't do that. I was on the clock, and Lanny was still somewhere in the building.

I was completely fucked by this guy. Royally fucked.

"Augie," I murmured. "Let me protect you. It's important to me. More important than anything else right now."

There was an awkward moment where his eyes darted away from me. The skin of his neck turned blotchy, and his cheeks flushed more than before. He was so expressive and reactive. I decided no matter what he said to my suggestion of protection, I would do whatever it took to keep him safe.

He cleared his throat and stood up before looking down at me with a completely neutral expression. "I'll um… I'll think about it. In the meantime, what moves are you teaching me today?"

If he only knew all the ways in which I wanted to answer that question.

CHAPTER 21

AUGIE

"LET'S TALK ABOUT WHAT TO DO IF THERE'S MORE THAN ONE ATTACKER,"
Saint said, switching back into professional mode. When he'd said my
name in that tone of voice, I'd known he was about to shut me down.
I'd made the mistake of flirting with him, and he'd rightly put a stop to
it. It wasn't fair of me to put him in that position after he'd already
told me he'd get in trouble with his boss if anything happened
between us.

He stepped close to me and positioned me by putting his hands on
my hips. "Okay, stand here."

I felt my entire body come alive and all the blood shift south.
There was no way I'd be able to hide the massive hard-on I had for
him if we couldn't find a way to get back to client and trainer only.

I was beginning to realize the inevitability of my feelings for him,
and I'd caught myself spending way too much time going back and
forth about whether those feelings were acceptable or not. I wasn't a
child for god's sake. Why couldn't I be sexually attracted to whomever
I wanted without feeling a rush of guilt and humiliation?

Because I knew that if I ever actually pursued a same-sex relationship, the media would have a field day with it and my mother would
lose her ever-loving shit. I hated the knowledge that the suffocating

environment of my childhood had created those feelings of guilt inside of me. Logically, I knew I should be able to be myself, but I still harbored the feeling of obligation to my family for supporting me with everything I'd ever needed, including the extended education that helped me pursue my dream job. I'd always thought that "ruining" their reputation by coming out would be a shitty way to show my appreciation for all they'd done.

We spent the next hour going through the basics of throwing one attacker into the other, targeting the man in charge first, and other tactics for escaping from a multipronged attack. During our next water break, Saint told me the only thing left to learn was defending against the use of weapons.

Having to fight my physical response to him throughout an entire other session was untenable. I just couldn't do it—couldn't take it anymore. Being near him and not able to run my hands over him the way I wanted to or kiss him when his face was close to mine was just... excruciating.

He looked at me with clear blue-gray eyes. "So we can stop for the day or—"

"No. Let's keep going," I said before he had a chance to finish. "Now that I know there might be more going on here than I thought, I want to be prepared."

He looked at me for a beat before nodding. "Okay. Let me go get some props. Why don't we take five?"

I made my way to the men's room and then stopped to grab another couple of bottles of water. When I returned to the training room, Saint was running his hands through his hair. He looked stressed.

"Water?" I asked, holding out a bottle to him. His face cleared and he smiled his thanks while reaching out to take the offered drink. "Ah, I didn't ask if you were okay to stay. Do you need to go?"

"What? No, not at all. I'm fine. Just got a text from my sister while you were gone, that's all. Sorry." He took a sip of water and then put both of our bottles on the floor by the wall before returning to where I stood.

"Everything all right?" I asked. "Which sister?"

He nodded and picked up some items that had been lying on the floor. "MJ. She's my twin. She's decided to stay in Hobie and take a few days off to take care of Neckie. You know Neckie, the owner of Twist?"

"Yeah, I know Neckie. Is it her pregnancy?"

"I guess her blood pressure is giving her trouble, so they've got her on bed rest. MJ's worried."

"Are they good friends?" I asked, wondering how that worked when MJ was one of the Wildes who lived in Dallas.

Saint's lips widened into a grin. "My grandfather set them up last weekend. Turns out they've both had a crush on each other since middle school. You should have seen the two of them blushing at each other at my grandparents' house last night. No wonder poor Neckie's BP is high."

"I can imagine finally getting together with someone you really like and not being able to jump their bones." As soon as the words were out of my mouth, I froze.

Saint's eyebrows furrowed, and I scrambled to take back my words.

"I... I didn't mean... I'm sorry," I whispered.

He stepped closer and cupped my jaw. "I'm the one who's sorry. You have no idea how sorry I am."

Before I could say anything other than a whimper, two people popped their head into the room, causing us to jump apart.

"We're out of here. Lock up behind yourself, Wilde." The man speaking was someone I didn't recognize, but he had a very military look about him, which indicated he worked there. The second person was a woman dressed in a black business suit and wearing an earwig. I assumed she was one of the bodyguards on staff and had come from or was going to an assignment.

"Will do," Saint called. He turned to me. "What the hell time is it?"

I shrugged since my phone was with my clothes in my locker. Saint grabbed his and cursed. "I didn't realize it was already after five. Should we do a little more and then get a bite to eat?"

"Sounds good."

"Okay, let's work."

We stood and made our way to the center of the mat. When he reached out his hand to give me one of the items he was holding, I realized it was a gun. I almost dropped it on the floor.

"What the fuck?" I cried, bobbling it in my hand until I could get a firm grip on it.

Saint's eyes bugged out, and he started to laugh. "Easy, killer. It's not loaded."

"Shit," I snapped. "You could have fucking warned me you were handing me a weapon."

His large warm hand came down on my shoulder as his other hand took the gun out of my own.

"Augie, this is a prop. It's fake. Well, not fake exactly, but a pellet gun used for recreation. See the orange tip? We use them as dummy weapons sometimes for practice. I promise it's not going to bite you."

I realized my hands were shaking, and I felt cold. "I hate guns."

Those gorgeous eyes studied me as his hand squeezed my shoulder gently. "I can see that," he said gently. "I think maybe we should hold off on the instruction and have a conversation about that first."

"It's not necessary," I assured him with a shake of my head. I had no need to be seen as the coward around him yet again. I didn't want to lose whatever shred of dignity I might still have in his eyes by revealing just how much of a baby I was. "Let's continue."

I reached forward and took the gun out of his hands before looking up at him. If he had any care at all for me, he would let me do this without first having to have a conversation about my feelings. I'd had enough of feeling vulnerable lately to last a lifetime.

Saint hesitated before stepping back. "Okay. Let's begin. Hold the muzzle against my forehead."

I tilted my head, wondering if I'd heard him right. "What? Why?"

"So I can demonstrate how to get out of the position," he explained. "You'll be surprised at how simple this move is. Here, go ahead." He nodded at the weapon in my hand.

I followed his gaze to the gun before looking back up at him.

Nerves knotted in my gut. I had to keep reminding myself that it was fake.

"How do I check to make sure it's empty?" I heard myself ask. My mental voice sounded like it was being spoken through sludge in an echo chamber.

"That's a great question. It never hurts to triple-check." Saint took the gun from me and opened it to show me there was nothing in it. When he handed it back to me, he stood ready for me, arms at his sides.

At that point, my whole face was numb, and I could barely even feel my hands anymore. I wouldn't have been surprised if I'd heard the gun slap to the ground on the mat at my feet. I tried raising it, keeping it pointed at the wall to our right instead of at Saint.

"Right here, my forehead," he reminded me. "Even if it wasn't a prop, it's not loaded. You just saw that for yourself. Thanks for that, by the way," he said with a small smile. "That was kinda sweet if you want to know the truth."

I didn't even register his comment because my brain had started to completely shut down. There was a roaring in my head and a dark fog at the edges of my vision. Saint seemed to still be joking with me, most likely sensing my nerves and trying to put me at ease, but I couldn't hear him.

When he grabbed my hand and swung the gun around to press against his forehead, everything went dark.

CHAPTER 22

SAINT

I HAD STUPIDLY MISREAD THE SIGNS OF AUGIE'S STRESS AS SIMPLE NERVES from being unfamiliar with firearms. But when I'd tried to help him out by pointing the gun at my head to get in position for the maneuver, I'd seen his eyes roll back and was able to catch him before he crumpled to the ground.

"Shit," I muttered. What the hell had come over him? It wasn't even a real gun.

I guided him gently to the mat and was preparing to check his vitals when I sensed him coming around. Thank god—he must have just passed out. While I waited for him to become fully alert, I straightened his glasses and brushed his hair off his forehead.

"Augie," I murmured. "It's okay. You're okay." I continued to stroke the side of his face, running a thumb across the flat of his cheekbone and noticing how smooth his skin looked up close.

"Oh god," he moaned when he opened his eyes and saw me. He immediately closed them and tried rolling away from me, but I reached out to stop him. I used both hands to cup his face.

"Stop. It's okay. Just breathe for a minute."

He brought his own hands up to pull off his glasses, flinging them to the mat before covering his face with his own hands and groaning again.

"Oh my god. How embarrassing."

"What happened?" I asked. "Was it the gun or is something else going on? Have you eaten today?"

He tried to sit up, but I gently held him down.

"I'm fine. It's nothing. Let me up," he said.

"Augie, you're not fine. You just fainted. Talk to me."

"Yeah, maybe I didn't eat enough today," he said. "Do you have any crackers or anything? Oh, maybe one of those chocolate milks would do the trick."

I stared at him. The guy was lying his ass off. His quick answer tipped me off right away. Why would he lie about that? I narrowed my eyes at him but decided to play along. I got up to find him something to eat. By the time I returned with a selection of juices and snacks, Augie seemed to be in a better mood.

"Listen, I'm sorry about all that. I should have stopped us after the first hour and not pushed it. I came straight here from work and didn't eat."

"Get something in your stomach and I'll drive you home," I said. "You still have the rental?"

Augie nodded.

"Okay, we'll leave it and the keys here for one of the Landen guys to turn in tomorrow since I'm sure your SUV will be ready back home."

He pulled the bottle of orange juice away from his mouth. "No need. I'll be fine."

"Sorry. I didn't mean to make it sound like an option," I said. Yes, I was a jackass, but I'd rather that than have him at risk.

He didn't say a word, but I noticed his face flush and his jaw tighten. If he was pissed at me for trying to make sure he got home safely, that was too bad. I wasn't about to let him drive home after fainting.

After he'd had a little bit to eat and drink, I helped him up. We made our way to the locker room, and I had to admit, he seemed to be perking up just fine.

"I'm going to take a shower really quickly," Augie said, walking past me to the shower area. "I don't want to stink up the car for the next two hours."

I didn't hear the rest of what he said as he disappeared around the corner. All I could think about was him alone in a slippery shower room right after he'd fainted earlier. *Maybe I should go in there and keep an eye on him...*

Okay, fine. It wasn't about safety. All I could think about was his body—warm, wet, and naked—right there in the shower room. Every cell in my own body begged to follow him in there, but I knew better.

Didn't I?

Fuck it.

Before the angel could beat the shit out of the devil on my shoulder, I was striding into the shower room, pulling off clothes as I went. To be fair, I didn't do what I really wanted to do, which was jump the guy and hump him to death. Instead, I just made my way to my own showerhead opposite his and turned on the spray.

I faced the wall and tried to mind my own business, reminding myself that just being naked in the same space as August Stiel was plenty exciting.

Oh hell. Who was I kidding?

I turned around to take a peek of Augie and saw him standing under his own spray facing me instead of facing the wall. His cock was half-hard, and he was stroking it with one hand while lathering up his chest and abdomen with the other. My eyes snapped up to his, and all I could see were hazel eyes turned almost deep green. *Ohdeargod.*

I quickly turned back to the wall and leaned my forehead against it, holding my palms against the cool tiled surface and stifling a groan of need. I tightened my palms into fists and tried to distract myself by digging fingernails into my palms. What was I thinking? I'd been a motherfucking idiot to come in this shower room with him.

So I'd leave. Just a quick wash and I'd dash out. I could do this. No problem. I reached out for the pump dispenser of shampoo, but before my hand got there I saw Augie's hand snake around me and pull the lever.

Swirls of white shampoo landed in his palm, and I didn't dare turn around. I closed my eyes and bit my tongue, trying everything I could think of to remind myself what a bad idea this was. But the minute Augie's slender fingers landed in my hair, I was lost.

We didn't say a word. He just washed my hair from where he stood behind me, his long fingers making my insides turn into complete mush and my cock turn into a steel spike. While he massaged my scalp, I couldn't help but feel every movement in my dick. My balls drew up so tight I thought I might come before he finished washing my hair. I didn't. Instead, I simply stood and relished every movement of those magical hands.

"Rinse," he murmured behind my ear before guiding my head a little forward under the spray. His hands helped push the suds out of my hair and down my back until I felt his hands moving all over my back and sides.

"*Augie*," I breathed.

"Is this okay?" he asked. "I just... I couldn't stand not touching you anymore. I'm sorry."

I turned around and came face-to-face with him. He looked so vulnerable without his glasses on, and I felt like I was seeing a part of him no one else got to see. Wet, naked, nothing to hide behind.

I slid my arms around his back and splayed my hands along his warm, wet skin. "Yes," I murmured. "It's okay."

I leaned down and brushed a light kiss across his lips before stepping forward and crouching down until our cocks brushed against one another. Augie's sharp intake of breath reminded me that he didn't necessarily have much experience more than a quick Grindr hookup, and I pulled my hips back away again.

"No," he whispered against my mouth. "More. Again. Please."

I smiled before pulling him closer with my arms until the entire lengths of our bodies were pressed together.

"Better?" I asked, bending my knees slightly to slide our stiff lengths together.

"Oh god," he moaned. "Oh my god."

I moved my mouth down to his neck as his hands tightened around my back. His voice kept making small sounds of pleasure—whimpers and moans barely heard over the sound of the water spray.

All the while I kept kissing him, I moved gently up and down, sliding our shafts together until I realized a couple of squirts of body wash would ease the way. I quickly reached for the other box on the wall and brought my soapy hand back to our cocks, rubbing the slick gel along both lengths until I grasped them both in one large fist and began pumping them together, up and down.

Augie's hands came up to clutch my shoulders, fingertips pressing into the skin so hard I wondered if they'd leave marks. His groans turned to grunts as his cock pulsed in my grip and began thrusting through my fist.

"That's it," I murmured against his wet hair. "Beautiful, sweet Augie."

His head was pressed against my chest, and he began begging. "Saint, please. *Please.* I need to... I need... oh fuck, I'm gonna come..."

The guttural cry that came out of him took us both by surprise, pushing me completely over the edge into my own release. I kept fisting our cocks as I felt his entire body shuddering against mine.

I had one arm around his waist, supporting him on wobbly legs, and when I felt his body go slack against mine, I realized my arm was the only thing keeping him from slipping to the tiles.

I let go of our spent cocks, holding my hand out under the water for a moment before wrapping both arms against him and just holding him. I felt his nose press into my neck, and I brought a hand up to cup the back of his head to keep him tucked there for as long as he needed.

After several long minutes, he began to shift and I pulled back to look at him. His cheek had a red mark from where it had been resting against my warm skin. I rubbed a thumb gently across it.

"Hey," I said with a smile. Nerves tumbled in my stomach as I wondered if he was going to freak out on me. "You good?"

CHAPTER 23

AUGIE

OH MY FUCKING GOD. I'D JUST GOTTEN JACKED OFF BY ANOTHER MAN IN a men's locker room shower like something out of a porn scene. And not just any man. A gargantuan navy SEAL man. With like muscles and ink and... basically the cutest baby face on the planet.

I glanced at the ink wrapped around his upper arm and recognized it as a frog skeleton holding a trident. The reminder of his service in the special forces caused my empty cock to try reviving. God, Saint's body was hot as fuck.

I looked back up at him and saw the concern there. What in the world did he have to be worried about? That I would tell someone? His boss?

For whatever reason, that insecure look on his face convinced me to show him my true feelings for once, without holding back. My entire face broke into an enormous grin before I hopped up against him to crush my lips to his, throwing my arms around his neck to hold on and my legs around his waist.

He made an *oof* sound before his arms tightened around me to hold me against him. My mouth attacked his and demanded entrance; he met me kiss for kiss, and we devoured each other's mouths until we pulled away panting. We stayed crotch to belly until our cocks were hard again and shifted alongside each other as he set me down.

"Not that I'm complaining, but that was a surprise," Saint said with an adorable smile. The twisted tooth was there, and seeing it revealed in his goofy grin loosened something inside of me.

"Do you have any idea what kind of torture it's been to take a shower in the Twist locker room with you naked only a few feet away and not be able to touch you?" I asked.

"Ah, yeah. If it's anything like the kind of torture I've been experiencing with you in there lately, I know exactly how it feels."

I studied his relaxed face and suddenly felt brave. "Come home with me."

WHEN WE WALKED out into the parking lot, it didn't take long for me to put the shower sex out of my mind and replace it with thoughts of getting Saint Wilde's mouth back on mine. Since there was no way to make out with him while he was driving, I had to make do with conversation instead.

"Why did you leave the service?" I asked when we got underway. I'd been curious about his past since he was only thirty or so and already finished with his military career.

Saint looked over at me before putting his eyes back on the road. The dim lights from the dash illuminated the blond beard scruff on his jaw.

"Lots of reasons, really. Otto got into an accident on a ship. I knew he wanted out but was afraid to leave without me. Then my sister Hallie sent me an email telling me about MJ working crazy hours and losing weight. She's always worked really hard anyway, but when you're an attorney trying to prove yourself to the managing partners, it can turn into something really dangerous. But what finally pushed me into leaving was Lanny offering me this job. The ability to work in the security field and still live close to my family was like a dream come true."

"MJ lives in Dallas too, right?"

"Yes. Three of my four sisters live in the city. Sassy is the only one still in Hobie."

I thought about which of the reasons had been the most compelling. "You really love working for Landen, don't you?"

He shrugged. "Lanny was our team leader on some truly epic missions, and he's one of the smartest, bravest men I know. I'd follow that fucker anywhere. Letting him down on the Gemma job gutted me."

It explained so much about the push-pull he seemed to have with me. Honestly, it soothed my nerves a little. I could handle Saint avoiding me out of a sense of honor, respect for Lanny, or his own personal work ethic much more than thinking he just wasn't that into me.

"What happened with the Gemma job? She's a famous singer. I take it you were teaching her self-defense lessons?"

I'd said that on purpose to tease him, but I'd been more successful than I expected with the deadpan delivery.

Saint glanced over at me again with wide eyes. "Are you... are you kidding?"

"Yes, I'm kidding," I said with a laugh. "That spoiled diva wouldn't want to lift a painted nail to defend herself in a fight, so you couldn't have been teaching her self-defense. Were you training her bodyguards or something? Teaching them kickboxing to help them stay in shape?"

He made a huffing sound before giving up trying to be indignant and letting his laughter appear. The man had a damned dimple in his cheek when he laughed, and I ached to press my lips against it. I could feel the phantom stubble against the tender skin of my lips in my mind's eye.

"Jerk," he said with a grin. "I was the lead personal security specialist on her close-protection team."

I ran my palms down the tops of my legs. "Yeah, I may or may not have googled you and seen the media fireworks from that little episode. Sounds like the woman had it coming to her."

"Whether she did or not is immaterial. I should never have lost my cool on a job."

Saint's eyes remained focused on the road, but his smile was gone. I reached over and clasped his hand. "Maybe not, but it's nice to know you're not perfect."

He picked up our joined hands and brought them to his lips, brushing a soft kiss across my knuckles before resting our hands back down on his muscled thigh. The heat of his body permeated his dark jeans, which only made me want to crawl over the center console and curl up in his lap like a kitten.

"What about you?" he murmured. "Tell me about opening the shop."

We spent the rest of the drive talking back and forth about how we'd gotten to where we were today. Both of our stories had been shaped by strong family influences. It had taken the death of my great-aunt and strong encouragement from my sister to leave the auction house where I'd worked in the city and open my own shop, but I told Saint how I already knew in less than a year it was exactly what I was supposed to be doing. And Hobie was exactly where I was supposed to be doing it.

He told me about his shockingly large family. He was the fourth-oldest of ten children, and was especially close to Otto, who'd been born less than a year after Saint and MJ. As he described what it was like growing up basically in chaos, I was struck by just how very differently we'd been raised.

Saint's family had been loud and fun, scrappy and messy. Mine had been elegant and staid, like a delicate flute of Cristal compared to Saint's cardboard carton of chocolate milk.

I'd always craved chocolate milk.

I must have gone off in my head at some point because suddenly the hand I'd been holding was brushing through my hair.

"Augie? Did I lose you?"

His voice was almost as low and soothing as the steady sound of the truck's tires on the highway. The darkness had lulled me into a semi-stupor. There was soft classic country music playing in the background.

"Hm? I think maybe I blinked offline for a minute," I admitted. "Sorry."

His fingers in my hair comforted me. If I hadn't recognized the turnoff to my county lane, I'd have been tempted to let him soothe me right back into a daze.

When we entered the farmhouse, I noticed him looking around at the newly clean space and was doubly grateful Kat and Rory had helped me put the place back to rights while they were in town.

"Do you want something to drink?" I asked, trying desperately to ignore the nervous rolling of my stomach.

"Sure. I'll take a beer if you have it."

"Of course." I tried to calm my breathing for a brief moment as I headed toward the kitchen. After grabbing two bottles out of the fridge, I found a jar of mixed nuts in the pantry and brought everything to the family room off the kitchen area.

Saint took a seat on the sofa, and I set the items on the coffee table in front of him before freezing up. Where the hell did I sit? If I sat next to him on the small sofa, would he think I was desperate? If I sat on the chair next to the sofa, would he think I wasn't interested?

Before I had a chance to decide, he sighed and muttered, "C'mere," before yanking me down onto his lap and grabbing my face for a kiss.

"Stop fucking thinking," he mumbled against my lips. "It's exhausting just watching you struggle with yourself."

I wanted to get defensive—to tell him it wasn't easy to come to terms with the fact I was selfishly putting him in a horrible position with his work. But I was too busy falling into a deep pool of desire where every nerve ending in my body seemed to be alight with shimmering pleasure and all I wanted was more.

"Mm-hmm," I managed to say into his mouth. It was the closest I could come to *"Okay, yes, less thinking and more kissing. Soooo much more kissing."*

I felt his smile against my lips as his large fingers cupped my face. "You taste so fucking sweet," he whispered, almost to himself.

As the kissing deepened and his tongue pushed into my mouth, I turned and straddled his lap, resting my knees and legs on either side of his hips and straightening up to put my arms around his neck. His hands moved to my hips and around to my back. They were strong and firm—possessive in a way I'd never sensed from someone before. I felt sure of his touch in a way I'd never felt with a random hookup, and I realized I fucking loved it. Everything about the encounter was lighting my fire like I'd never imagined.

Saint moved his mouth down to kiss my jaw and neck, shifting just enough to remind me of the giant bulge in his jeans. I groaned without realizing it and brought a hand down his chest and torso to hover over his dick. I wanted so badly to touch it, but I was still nervous and unsure. What if this was all some kind of joke? What if I touched his cock and he beat the shit out of me for it?

Before I could lecture myself about overthinking things again, Saint put his hands back on my face and pulled back from kissing my neck. I snapped my eyes open when I realized he'd stopped.

"What?" I asked.

"If you're not into this, please tell me now," Saint said in a quiet voice. "It's okay, Augie. I'll just head out. You won't hurt my feelings."

Something about that didn't sit right with me, but I didn't take the time to figure out what it was.

"I'm into it, Saint. Jesus, can't you tell I'm into it? What made you say that?"

"You left and went somewhere in your head. I get it. This has to be strange for you, but I don't want to be any part of making you feel uncomfortable."

I moved my hands up to his chest and ran a finger along the side of his Adam's apple. Goose bumps raised behind my touch, and I looked back into his eyes. He seemed to be waiting patiently, and I wanted to kiss him for that.

"You don't make me feel uncomfortable or strange," I said. "You make me feel..." I swallowed and felt tears pricking in my eyes as I realized the truth. "You make me feel more normal than I've ever felt in my life... and *that's* what's strange."

I couldn't look at him, and part of me wanted to run and hide after admitting that to him. Instead, I leaned forward and rested my forehead against his chest and waited. I waited for him to laugh, for him to make fun of me. I waited for him to shove me off him and leave. I knew it was the judgment and bullying in my past that messed with my head in that moment, but it still felt real. Even though he'd never given me reason to expect it from him, rejection was still one of my biggest fears. In truth, I was waiting for him to come to his senses. There were so many things I waited for Saint to do, but he did none of those things.

Instead, he wrapped his arms tightly around me and stood up. Then that hot motherfucker carried me to my bedroom.

CHAPTER 24

SAINT

IF AUGIE HAD ANY IDEA HOW BADLY I WANTED TO FUCK HIM, HE probably would have burst into tears and called the police. My entire body was buzzing with the need to be inside him. I couldn't remember ever wanting someone as much as I wanted him.

I'd been with all kinds of men in my life, but never had I been with one I felt so conflicted about. I wanted to fuck him, I wanted to take care of him, I wanted to lock him up in a tall tower and never let him out into the big bad world. There were other things too. I wanted to ask him more about his childhood, his work, why he was so easily spooked. I wanted to watch him sleep for fuck's sake. And my newfound obsession with him was confusing the hell out of me.

But if there was one thing that Saint Wilde was good at, it was sex. Sex, I could do. Sex, I understood. So sex is what we would do.

As I carried him back to his room, I enjoyed squeezing his round ass cheeks through his pants. "God, your ass," I grumbled against his ear. "I want to get these fucking pants off you."

Augie was trembling in my arms before I dropped him down on his bed and leaned over the top of him. "Talk to me," I said. "I don't want to do anything you don't want to do."

His deer-caught-in-headlights look softened, and his mouth

turned up in a small smile. "You're hot as shit. Do people stop you in public just to tell you that?"

I couldn't help but bark out a laugh. "Not usually, no."

"Liar," he said with a grin.

"It may have happened in a club once or twelve times," I said with a wink. "But beer goggles are common in clubs too, you know?"

Augie shrugged. "No, I don't know. I've never been to a nightclub."

I sat back on my heels and stared at him. "Really? I don't mean just gay clubs. You've never been to any kind of dance club?"

His face flushed. "No. I'm kind of boring, actually."

"Bullshit," I said. "You're not boring just because you haven't been to a club before."

Augie brought his hands up to the hem of my shirt and snuck fingers under it to explore the hair on my belly. His touch sent all thoughts of clubs skittering to the winds and made my dick wake up. Way up.

"Fuck," I breathed. "Baby, what are we doing?" The man literally had ten seconds to tell me to leave before I attacked him.

"Take off your clothes, Saint."

My eyes almost rolled back in my head as I punched out a sigh of relief and reached over my shoulder for a handful of shirt. Once mine was off, I reached for his and stripped it from him, running an appreciative palm up his front to the small, intricate key hanging from a chain around his neck.

"What's this?"

"Key to the—" He sucked in a loud breath as I teased his small nipple with my tongue. "T-the slope. The box thing. Whatever. Keep doing that."

Augie sucked in another sharp breath as the nipple hardened in my mouth, and the sound went straight to my cock. I couldn't help but arch my hips into him and grind, which only made more noises of pleasure escape him.

By the time my mouth moved from his nipples down to the trail of dark hair below his navel, his entire stomach was contracting and his hips were arching up for me. His fingers threaded into my hair, and he whimpered when my hands went to his fly to unfasten his button.

"Saint," he breathed.

"Mmm?" I asked as my mouth followed the open fly down onto his briefs.

"*Saint*," he gasped.

I quickly moved back and grabbed the legs of his pants and yanked them down, revealing small royal blue briefs with a wet spot on them. My mouth watered at the realization he'd been leaking precum already, and I was aching to get that cock down my throat.

I reached back up to the elastic band of the briefs but stopped to tease him a little bit. My mouth landed on the wet spot over his tip, and I mouthed his erection through the fabric. Moans from my own throat mixed with whimpers from his, and both of us seemed consumed in the same haze of lust.

Augie's hips were punching up toward me in a desperate rhythm, and his hands began to clasp my hair tighter. I could tell he was fighting his instinct to force himself into my mouth, and seeing him at war with himself just turned me on even more.

I stripped off his underwear and tossed it on the floor before stalking back up the length of him to hover over his cock.

"*Stop teasing me, motherfucker!*" he cried out. The exclamation took me by surprise so much that I just stared at him with wide eyes. His own eyes widened and his hand clapped over his mouth before his entire body blushed splotchy red. "Oh my god," he gasped.

We just stared at each other for a beat before we both burst out laughing. I tackled him midlaugh and crushed my mouth over his, thrusting my hard cock against his and grinding against him while I kissed the hell out of him. He managed to roll me over until he was on top, and his fingertips landed in my armpits.

"No, stop," I said. "I was getting ready to suck you off before I was so rudely interrupted. Lie back, Mr. Pottymouth." Remembering the sweet, reserved antiques geek calling me *motherfucker* made me laugh again.

Augie peered down at me. "You're even cuter when you laugh. You should do it more often." His face was serious when he spoke, and it sobered me.

"Thank you" was all I said. I rolled him over slowly, all joking gone now, and settled between his legs again. Our eyes locked together and stayed that way for several beats.

Something was happening. There was some kind of *feeling* going on between us, and it was a cross between scary/unknown and inevitable/perfect. I couldn't define it but let it settle there and stay regardless.

Augie took a moment to remove his glasses and set them carefully on the bedside table. When he lay back on the bed, I stared some more. His eyes were filled with intensity, and his pupils were huge. There were no divots of stress on his face.

I started kissing him again, dropping light ones in a trail from his lips, past the old key, and down to his belly again until I was finally ready to take his cock in my mouth.

The crown was purple and lush, and my tongue tested the ridge around it while I waited to hear his reaction. I was rewarded with a whoosh of relief and excitement before I took his entire length into my mouth.

"Holy shit," he cried. "Dear god, don't stop. Please don't fucking stop."

I smiled around his cock before looking up at him and trying to tell him with my eyes that I was nowhere near ready to stop. In fact, quite the opposite. I had half a mind to edge him.

Once he saw the look on my face, he squeezed his eyes closed and dropped his head back onto the bed with a groan. His hands moved slowly from my hair to my cheeks and cupped gently around my jaws as I continued to lavish his gorgeous dick with attention.

I don't know how long it went on for, but every time Augie got close to shooting, I backed off until all that was left of him was the whimpering of my name and a string of whispered pleas repeated over and over again.

I moved my mouth up next to the shell of his ear and brushed my lips over it, setting off a violent shudder in him. "You need to come, baby?" I whispered into his ear as I clasped my large hand around his cock and pulled once.

That's all it took. He came with a strangled cry, hot fluid shooting across his stomach and all over my hand as I kept jacking him off through his release. More shudders racked his body as more spurts coated his abdomen. I'd thought I could hold off my own release until he was finished, but seeing him come apart pushed me over the edge. I reached a hand down to my own cock, using the slick fluid of Augie's release to glide up and down on my shaft until I groaned and came onto his belly as well.

I couldn't help but stare at the combined pools of our semen on his skin and rub it in to somehow cement this moment in time onto his body.

"*Saint*," he breathed at last.

He was watching me from under heavy-lidded eyes, and I could tell he was within seconds of drifting off but was fighting it.

I leaned down to brush a light kiss over his mouth. "It's okay. Let go. I'll get you cleaned up," I said softly.

His lips turned up in a half smile before he closed his eyes and surrendered.

CHAPTER 25

AUGIE

When my phone alarm went off, I woke up alone in my bed, which was surprising in and of itself until a second later when I remembered the large warm body that had been beside me the night before. My arm slid over to test the temperature of the sheets, and I wasn't surprised to find them cold. But I felt the weight of a rock land in my gut all the same.

He hadn't stayed. Of course he hadn't.

Now I knew what it felt like when someone was more than just a Grindr hookup but still ducked out before morning. Empty and cold. Rejected in a way that fucked with my head. Because I knew we didn't have a relationship of any kind. It was a hookup for god's sake. Saint didn't owe me anything.

I rubbed my face and sat up, turning to hang my legs off the edge of the bed before standing. The cool air of the room hit my bare skin, making me shiver, and just as I was getting ready to head to the bathroom to shower, the doorbell rang.

I threw on the clothes I'd grabbed and raced to answer the door. It was Dean from the auto shop. The disappointment I felt at it not being Saint returning from some rom-com jaunt to the bakery for morning-after croissants was palpable.

God, I was pathetic.

"Mr. Wilde asked me to make sure you had your vehicle back this morning, sir," he said with a polite smile. "I figured I'd swing by and give you a ride to the garage since you're on my way. Sorry it took so long to get you all fixed up. That first piece of window glass broke during delivery or we would have had you all fixed up in just a day. Hope you can give Spike's Auto another chance to earn your business."

"Certainly. I understand when things don't go the way you want. Sometimes you just have to roll with it."

After grabbing my phone and wallet and locking up the house, I followed him to his truck.

Rather than go back home to shower and face the bed's rumpled evidence of the night before, I used the bathroom in the upstairs shop apartment. Once put together again, I dragged my depressed, rejected ass downstairs to the shop and tried my best to focus. My cell phone became surgically attached to my palm all day, and I was embarrassed to admit even to myself how often I checked it for a message from Saint, but there was nothing.

Finally, when I got home after seven that night, I broke down and texted him.

Me: *Hi. Thank you for last night. Hope you heard lots of interesting gossip from the soccer mom crowd in your classes today.*

Was that lame? That was probably lame. I groaned and leaned back on the sofa before reaching for the TV remote and mindlessly searching through channels. What was I thinking? I didn't want to watch TV. I didn't want to do anything other than touch Saint's naked body again and feel his mouth on me.

Godfuckingdammit.

My phone rang and I answered it so quickly there was startled silence on the other end. I pulled the screen back to see who it was and felt disappointment flood my system, quickly followed by guilt.

"Hi, Charlie."

"I'm ten minutes away and craving pasta. Do you have any, or do I need to pick some up?"

"Uh... I have the stuff to make it?" What was even happening right now?

"Get on it."

He hung up and left me staring at an empty screen. It took me a minute to get my sorry ass off the sofa and make my way to the kitchen, but I did as he'd asked and put the water on to boil before dumping a jar of sauce in a pan to heat up.

Charlie had always been friendly and open, and once I put away the confusion over the sudden self-invitation to dinner, I was kind of looking forward to the company.

When he arrived, he was all smiles, handing over a cardboard box with a six-pack of beer bottles rattling around inside.

"Thanks. I take it you'd like to have this with the pasta?"

"Hudson's at a family do. And I've been meaning to come over and check in with you since the break-in. You doing all right?"

He followed me into the kitchen and took the bottle out of my hand after I popped the cap off for him.

"My car was broken into also. I'm actually starting to believe it's my crazy family, but honestly, I don't want to talk about it."

I drained the noodles and added it to the pan of sauce, swirling everything together before serving it onto two plates and joining Charlie at the old wooden table that had lived in that spot for a hundred years.

While we ate, Charlie spun a tale about some tourists who'd come into the pub the day before for lunch and couldn't stop complaining to their server about how the small-town pub was a cheap knockoff of the original.

"I finally had to go over there and put them in their place," he said with a grin. "Fuckers. I laid the accent on thick and regaled them with tales of my dad and his dad and his dad before him growing up on that patch of Irish coastline. And how I'd personally come over to open Fig and Bramble in Hobie with my bare hands before taking ownership of it. You should have seen their faces, Augie. Priceless."

His light spirit always managed to boost my mood.

"Thank you for coming over tonight. I needed the company," I admitted. "I think I've been spending so much time on the shop, I've forgotten to have a life outside of work."

Charlie shrugged. "We all do it. Owning your own business isn't for the weak."

That word rattled around in my head the way the beer bottles had rattled in the box. Weakness was always something I'd tried to eradicate, but the older I got, the more I realized that being strong all the time wasn't something I was capable of. And I was so sick and tired of being disappointed in myself.

When I thought about what my dad would have told me about being strong, I realized he'd want me to be human. And humans are fallible. Maybe it was seeing Rory so happy and settled these days with Kat that had begun opening my eyes to the fact I was entering a new chapter in my life. In addition to the move and opening the shop, this past year had also included Rory's own awakening. She was on her own now, working and living as an adult with a great job at a legal aid nonprofit and her very own life partner to take care of her. Perhaps I didn't need to be so brave and strong for my family the way I had for the past fifteen years. Instead, maybe I could reevaluate my own life and start trying to reframe it with my own damned values instead of allowing my grandfather's and mother's voices in my head.

My phone's text alert pinged, and I almost jumped out of my chair to grab the phone, bobbling it in my hands before it went skittering across the kitchen table and onto the floor.

"Fuck," I cried, scrambling after it. When I grabbed it and swiped the screen to unlock it, I saw a text from Landen informing me that my session with Saint for the following night had been canceled and would need to be rescheduled.

My heart dropped into my stomach, and I felt my lips tighten.

So there it was.

Clearly I'd pushed Saint into doing something he didn't want to do, and he couldn't work with me any longer. The guy hadn't even had the decency to contact me himself.

I took a deep breath and held it a few beats before blowing it out. My chest hurt and I felt tired all of a sudden. After powering my phone completely off and shoving it in a kitchen drawer, I returned to my seat at the table and swirled my fork through my spaghetti. There was no way I could put another bite of it past my lips. I'd completely lost my appetite.

Charlie placed a hand on my arm. "What's going on?" he asked in his sexy lilt.

I felt my eyes prickle and clenched my jaw to force the emotion away before speaking.

"I met someone," I said. And it came out sounding like the worst news ever. Because it was.

"Holy shit, Augie. That's fantastic."

I rolled my eyes at him before shaking my head.

"Okay. It's not fantastic," he said with a laugh. A beat later he softened his voice. "Who is it?"

Suddenly the tears sprang past my defenses, and I was powerless to stop them.

"It's Saint," I said in a choked whisper.

"Och, sweetie." Charlie pulled me into a comforting hug.

Thank goodness he was so kind and affectionate. It felt good to be babied for a minute.

"You're not the only one to find himself under the Wilde spell," he said after a while, pulling back with a knowing smile. "Let's open another beer, and then you can tell me all about it."

So I did. And then I told him why none of it mattered anyway. Since I'd fucked it all up.

CHAPTER 26

SAINT

I'D BEEN IN HEAVEN, CURLED UP AROUND AUGIE'S BODY IN HIS BIG BED when one of our phones lit up somewhere in the room. I'd carefully extracted myself from his embrace and got out of bed to find it. It was my phone, and when I reached it, I saw a text from my sister.

MJ: *At Neckie's place. The baby's coming early, but she won't let me call ambulance or go to hospital. Pls call asap.*

I'd flipped my phone on mute earlier, so I realized in addition to the text, I'd also missed some calls from her. Shit.

After slipping my clothes back on, I debated whether or not to wake Augie. He looked so peaceful, and I knew he'd been stressed lately because of work and the break-in. I decided to let him sleep and leave him a note instead.

I leaned over and kissed him on the forehead, keeping my lips pressed against his skin for several long moments so I could inhale the scent of him all warm and sleepy in bed. God, he was beautiful. The selfish part of me wanted to strip down and slide back under the covers with him, but the responsible brother in me knew I needed to go.

MJ was my twin, and she needed me.

Before I left, I found a scrap piece of paper in the kitchen and scribbled a note to Augie, apologizing for leaving without waking him and explaining that I was going to help MJ and Neckie. I slipped into the master bathroom and set the note on the mirror behind the sink faucet so he'd see it first thing.

Once I got on the road, I called MJ to get an update on Neckie. She'd gone into premature labor, and the baby was coming whether it was ready or not. But because Neckie was all new age and natural, she insisted on maintaining her home birthing plan.

The woman lived in one of the most secluded cabins on the far side of the lake. It was closer to Oklahoma than to Hobie, and I'd never understood why she'd never chosen to move closer since she owned a business in Hobie.

When I got to Neckie's little treehouse in the woods, there were already half a dozen vehicles there I recognized. Thankfully, I saw West's truck as well as Hudson's ex-girlfriend Darci's car. Having a doctor and nurse on site helped me let out a breath.

Doc and Grandpa opened the door, but instead of letting me in, they hustled me right back outside.

"You don't want to go in there," Grandpa said. "MJ is in the zone as Neckie's coach, and if she sees you, she's going to lose her focus and let her worry overtake her."

"How's Neckie doing?"

"She's having a tough time of it, but Darci brought a labor and delivery nurse friend of hers who's helping. I can tell West is trying his hardest not to be a doctor in there."

"Why not? She needs a doctor, doesn't she? I thought she had high blood pressure?"

Doc reached for Grandpa's hand as they walked farther away from the front door. "She does, but Elena is more experienced with birth complications than West is. He and I are both here in case Elena needs assistance, but Neckie really wanted to do this at home without medical intervention. We have to respect her birth plan."

I knew he was right, but I worried about Neckie and the baby, my brother and Nico, and most of all my sister's heart. If something happened to Neckie this soon after coming together with MJ, I wasn't sure if my sister could take it.

"What can I do to help?" I asked.

Doc's face widened into a grin. "Make us a big stack of grilled cheese sandwiches. I brought groceries."

So I went to work. As the hours of Neckie's labor passed, I made myself as useful as possible. I cooked and cleaned, ran laundry, and even drove Grandpa's truck out to fill it with gas. At one point I realized I'd never brought up the real estate mystery to Augie in my haste to get him in bed. I spent time trying to figure out the best way to tackle the tricky subject without making his family out to be scammers. One thing was for sure: I'd have to tread lightly.

By the time my new niece came into the world, it was after dark and half my family was huddled around a makeshift fire ring next to Neckie's driveway.

"She's here!" Darci called from the front door. "She's tiny but strong as hell. Gonna be just fine. West wanted me to get Doc and Grandpa."

Doc and Grandpa were in the midst of a tight hug of relief when they heard that. Doc pulled away but not before leaning in to place a soft kiss on his husband's lips. I couldn't hear their whispers from across the fire, but I could see the words of love on their lips.

It was the most selfish thought in the world considering the timing, but I couldn't help but want that. I wanted what the two of them had shared for the past forty-something years.

I couldn't help but think of Augie and wonder if he'd ever allow himself to have that kind of love—open and free for everyone around him to see.

There was one thing I knew for sure regardless of how Augie felt about finding love.

I, Saint Wilde, was finally ready for it.

MJ HAD BEEN A STAR. She'd mastered the balance between soothing and encouraging Neckie to keep going when she'd wanted to give up. As soon as I had a turn to go in and see them, I noticed the way Neckie looked at MJ.

Like MJ was a frigid waterfall in the middle of a desert, offering sweet relief for Neckie's parched and tired soul.

All around me were shining examples of partners loving and supporting each other. How in the world I'd managed to make it to thirty-one without realizing I was missing something huge was beyond me.

I spent a few minutes examining the tiniest toes on the planet as Nico and West sat huddled together on the papasan chair in Neckie's front room staring at their new baby.

"We already asked Neckie's permission to use her name," Nico announced.

The room fell silent.

Neckie and MJ were still in the bedroom with the nurses, but the Wilde family in the front room were careful not to make a single disparaging noise. All ten of us siblings could attest to the sheer frustration at having an unusual name. Our Canadian mother had been fucking insane when she'd named us all after towns in her beloved home country.

"Um..." My sister Sassy looked worried. "Can I just tell you from personal experience that..."

West cut in. "Relax, everyone. We're going to call her Reenie. Her full name is Adriana Nectarine Wilde after Nico's sister too."

Sassy sat back with a smile. "Reenie. I like that."

Nico's tears overflowed, and West leaned over to thumb them away before replacing the dampness on Nico's cheeks with kisses. "I love you so much," he murmured with a choked voice.

I heard Grandpa turn to Doc and call him "Great-Grand Doc," which set all of us off laughing.

After a few more moments spent celebrating the new Wilde

among us, it was time to clear out and let Neckie get some peace and quiet. I poked my head in long enough to blow Neckie a kiss and thank her for giving my family an amazing gift. MJ walked me out to the car.

"You were incredible today, Em," I told her. "She obviously loves you as much as you love her."

"Isn't she amazing?"

I pulled my sister into a hug. "You both are. She's going to need your quiet company in the days to come, I'm sure. Please tell me if I can help in any way. I know West and Nico will not just ditch her, but it might be easier for me to help than them. I'm sure looking after a two-year-old and newborn is going to be a challenge."

MJ nodded. "If you can keep helping at the gym, that'll be the biggest worry off her shoulders. She has good staff, but I'm sure she can use all the help over there she can get."

"I'm on it," I promised. "Get some sleep."

It was midnight before I got back to my grandfathers' ranch and the bunkhouse. I was exhausted from the emotional upheaval of the day, but I could finally rest easy now that I'd seen how healthy the baby was and had been able to witness the pure love and support radiating from my sister toward Neckie.

When I finally slid between the sheets, I checked my phone. It's not that I hadn't thought of Augie all day—I had. But I'd had no way of calling him since my phone hadn't charged while I slept at Augie's and there was little to no reception where Neckie lived. I'd finally used Hudson's phone to text Lanny at the office and make sure they told Augie not to show up for our lesson the following day. But I didn't have his number to call him directly.

When my phone powered up back at the bunkhouse, there was a missed text.

Augie: *Hi. Thank you for last night. Hope you heard lots of interesting gossip from the soccer mom crowd in your classes today.*

Work? Why did he think I'd gone to Twist when my note said I was going to Neckie's? Despite the late hour, I typed in a response.

Me: *Sorry it's so late. Didn't you get my note? Neckie had the baby.*

I fought sleep as long as I could, waiting for a response, but it never came. The minute my eyes popped open the next morning, I knew what I needed to do. I threw on the same clothes from the night before and bolted out the door.

CHAPTER 27

AUGIE

I awoke very early on Wednesday morning to the sound of my doorbell ringing and wondered where the hell I was. There were empty beer bottles on the coffee table in front of me, and my feet were tangled in the knitted afghan I kept on the family room sofa. I'd fallen asleep there after Hudson had come and carted off a drunken Charlie. The confusion of being half-asleep and half-hungover didn't clear until I was standing at the front door in nothing but boxer briefs looking through the peephole at Saint Wilde.

My stomach started flipping over like an excited puppy, and I felt its betrayal like a knife in the back. *Don't get excited over someone who obviously doesn't give a shit about you, idiot.*

I opened the door carefully and gave him my best attempt at a glare. It failed.

He rushed into my arms and grabbed me into a bear hug, squeezing me so tightly I squeaked. My anger disappeared in a puff of smoke. Before I could think about it, I was hugging him back. I felt his entire body trembling in mine, and I started to worry.

"Saint?" I asked in a strangled voice. "What happened? You're scaring me."

He loosened his hold just a little bit but kept his face tucked against my shoulder. "Did you get my text?" he asked. The words were muffled against my bare skin, and the warmth from his breath made me shiver.

"No. My phone is turned off. Come inside."

The frigid morning air was blowing past him through the open door, and I felt goose bumps prickling up everywhere on my exposed skin.

"Come on. I'll fix us some coffee. It's freezing," I murmured as he pulled away from me.

He quickly dashed at his eyes and looked away. It happened so quickly, I almost didn't believe I'd seen it.

I grabbed his hand and pulled him toward the kitchen, parking him on a stool while I rounded the corner to start the coffee. The entire time I filled the pot, I could feel his eyes on my bare back like an intimate touch. Just his presence in the room was enough to make me breathless, but knowing he was tracking me made me stupidly horny on top of it.

Once the coffee was going, I rinsed out my cotton mouth in the sink and turned to face him. His eyes snapped down to the tent in my shorts, and I felt my skin flush. Okay, so he knew I wanted him. Big deal. Surely by now that wasn't a surprise.

When his eyes locked on mine, they were as deep blue gray as the center of a storm. I closed the distance between us and stepped between his legs before asking him one question.

"I just need to know if you're okay first," I said.

He nodded. "I am now."

And that was all I needed to hear. My mouth landed on his, and his hands instantly came around to grab my ass and pull me closer. My own hands wrapped around the back of his neck to hold his mouth against mine while I devoured him. Desperate moans were leaking out of me, and he made growling noises as he took ownership of my mouth.

Before long, his hands had made it inside my underwear and were splitting my cheeks open; long fingers took turns rubbing over my hole, and my moans turned to whimpers. It defied all logic, but I knew without a shadow of a doubt that I wanted that man to fuck me. I wanted his fingers, his tongue, his anyfuckingthing in my ass, and I didn't want to wait another minute.

"Fuck me," I begged. "Please, please fuck me."

Saint sucked in a breath and stared at me with wide eyes. "Augie..." he began.

"No," I said with fingers over his lips. "Don't say no. Don't ask me if I'm sure. Don't make me wait one more minute to feel you. Please, Saint."

I honestly didn't care why he'd left me the morning before or why he'd shown up all emotional on my doorstep practically before dawn. There would be time for those things later. The time now was for touching, and I wanted him with every fiber of my being.

He stood up and moved me in front of him, placing his hands on my hips and propelling me down the hallway to my bedroom. When I entered the room, I headed straight for the bed, which was still rumpled from our previous time together.

Saint's hands were already pushing at my underwear, and I turned around to start removing his own clothes. His mouth crushed down on mine, and I struggled to catch my breath. It was hot and fast. Fingers were everywhere, and my heart banged so hard I thought it was going to bruise my chest.

I pulled off his shirt and started fumbling with his jeans before getting them undone and shoving my hands inside. His cock was poking out of the top of his underwear, and that was when I realized he was wearing the same clothes he'd been wearing two nights before at my house.

"Saint?" I asked. "Haven't you been home since you were here last?"

He both nodded and shook his head before chasing my mouth again with his own. I pulled back. "Where have you been?"

"Neckie's. With MJ. The baby," he said before grabbing the back of my neck and covering my mouth with his again. I let him kiss me deeply while I pushed at his pants and underwear. Just before his jeans slipped to the floor, he grabbed them and fished his wallet out of his pocket to retrieve something from it.

He stepped closer to me until I was practically bending backward over the bed.

"You gonna lie down, or are you waiting for me to push you down?" Saint asked with a sexy-as-hell grin. I swear to fucking god, I almost swallowed my tongue.

"Your call," I challenged. I watched as his pupils overtook the stormy irises. His large hands brushed up my sides until he grabbed me under the arms and tossed me effortlessly onto the bed.

My stomach was tumbling at this point, and I thought my cock was going to shoot clear off my body. When that man climbed onto the bed and stalked his way up my body, a part of me realized I'd never be the same after what was about to happen.

"Turn over," he said. "And show me that gorgeous fucking ass."

CHAPTER 28

SAINT

I worried Augie wasn't really as ready for anal sex as maybe he thought, so I'd decided to push him a little to see if he backed down from the idea.

He did not back down.

The man flipped to his belly without hesitation, and when I grabbed his hips to pull them into the air, his cock began dripping precum like a faucet.

"Oh fuck," I muttered, pushing his hip back over until he was on his back again. I needed his sweet taste in my mouth first. Translucent strings glistened from his belly to the tip of his cock, and full beads of fluid spilled over the edge of his crown. My mouth watered at the sight.

I dropped my lips onto his cock and sucked it down quickly before hollowing out my cheeks and pulling back to swirl my tongue in that sticky sweetness at the tip.

"Jesusfuckingchrist," he gasped, clutching fingers into my hair with one hand and scrabbling to hold on to the sheets with the other. "Saint. *Saint.*"

I loved it when he chanted my name. It made my entire chest feel tight, and I knew I could listen to it my entire life, especially the way

Augie said it in the throes of pleasure.

My mouth continued bathing his shaft in licks and sucks while my hands explored his thighs and abdomen. His hips pulsed up to meet my mouth, and I smoothed my hand back down his stomach to cup around his balls. Augie's hand tightened in my hair.

"Stop, stop, or I'm going to finish before we even start," he warned.

"Have you forgotten being edged the other night?" I asked. "You think I'd let you come this soon? Are you out of your mind?"

He groaned and threw an arm over his face, punching his hips up again until his wet cock was nudging my chin. I took it back into my mouth and down my throat, tamping down my gag reflex as much as I could and humming around his length.

The sounds coming out of his mouth were garbled and incoherent. My tongue traveled down past the wrinkled skin of his sac to the tight flat strip below. I pressed against it with my tongue before continuing down to his tiny pink hole.

Fuck, I wanted in that hole. It was calling to me, and the idea it had never taken a cock before had me harder than I'd ever been. I reached my tongue out to tease it lightly, and Augie shouted.

"Oh god, oh god!"

I couldn't help but smile before stiffening my tongue to poke inside a little. His opening was so small, I knew it would take lots of time and attention to get him ready for me. The last thing I wanted to do was hurt him.

"What are you—?" he gasped. "That feels... oh my god."

Augie's entire body was pulsing with need, and his cock continued to leak clear fluid all over the hair leading to his navel. The man was beautifully responsive to everything I did to him, and it encouraged me to keep trying different things.

I reached my hand up to stick my index finger in his mouth.

"Get it wet," I demanded. "*Very* wet."

He did as I said, rolling my finger around with his tongue until it was coated in saliva. I brought it back down to his hole and began alternating finger and tongue until he was looser and babbling. Once

I'd opened the lube and introduced more than one finger, his erection had begun to flag.

"It's okay," I whispered in his ear after climbing back up his body. "Stop me anytime, sweetheart."

His wide eyes locked on mine. "I trust you."

I pressed my mouth down on his and kissed him deeply, feeling his tongue come out tentatively in search of forbidden flavors. I rewarded him by running the tip of my tongue over his lips and then pulling his bottom lip into my mouth and sucking hard until he groaned.

By the time I pulled back from the kiss, his dick was hard again, and I decided if I waited any longer to enter him, I wouldn't be able to do it gently.

After grabbing a condom and lube packet and suiting up, I returned to the bed and pushed his knees up toward his shoulders, opening him up in the very best way. My cock head brushed his hole, and I saw him clench tightly. I leaned back down to murmur in his ear.

"Shhh, it's okay. Deep breath. Open for me. That's it... Let me in, Augie. I want to be inside you."

He threw his head back with a gasp as I breached him, exposing the long column of his throat above the chain he wore, and I took the opportunity to latch my mouth on that creamy skin and suck. I kept the pulses of my hips shallow while his body got used to the invasion. His face was flushed and tight, so I whispered more words of reassurance in his ears to relax him.

When he seemed to finally be more comfortable, he let out a long groan before clutching his fingers into the skin of my shoulders. "God, your cock is fucking enormous," he muttered. "How do you walk around with that thing—*oh my fucking god, do that again!*"

I must have brushed his prostate because his eyes flew open, and he stared wide-eyed at me.

"Again, Saint," he begged. "Please."

I kept the same angle and thrust again. And again, and again, until all that was left of him was wide eyes and short breaths interspersed with whimpers.

Something about introducing him to that kind of pleasure was intoxicating, and I wanted to keep stroking into him forever. But his channel was so hot and so tight, I couldn't last one more minute. My hand grasped his cock and jacked it to the rhythm of my thrusts until both of us were shouting each other's names and coming at the same time.

My dick was clamped in a vise as it pulsed inside of the condom, and Augie's entire abdomen was coated in spurts of fluid as aftershocks kept hitting him one after the other. I noticed his legs were wrapped around my back and crossed at the ankles to keep me from leaving him.

Fine by me. I leaned down to press small kisses on his cheeks and neck and ears while he caught his breath. I felt his body relax around mine until he seemed to sink into the mattress in a daze.

Finally I pulled out of him and strode to the bathroom, coming back after a moment with a damp towel for him. He was almost asleep and gazing at me through half-closed eyes and a goofy grin.

"You are so damned cute right now," I said quietly as I reached out to wash him off. "Go to sleep. I'm not going anywhere."

"That's what I thought last time," he said.

"Neckie had the baby," I said. "I had to leave. MJ needed me. I didn't want to wake you up, so I left a note."

Augie studied me for a beat before speaking again. "You did?"

"Yes. It's still in there, on the sink. You didn't see it?"

He put his hands over his face and groaned before smiling. "The mechanic came yesterday before I had a chance to shower, so I didn't see it. Then I fell asleep downstairs last night. Oh my god."

After tossing the towel on the floor, I crawled back into bed until we were lying on our sides facing each other. "You thought I just left with no note?" I asked.

"Well, yeah. What else was I supposed to think? When I woke up, you were gone."

He had a point.

I reached out to run my fingers through his hair. "I'm sorry. I wouldn't have done that to you, Augie."

He leaned forward to kiss me sweetly before pulling back and settling on the pillow again. I reached out to trace the antique key resting in the hollow of his throat with my finger.

Augie's voice was sleepy and relaxed. "Tell me about the baby. What happened? Why were you so upset?"

I told him everything that had happened at Neckie's since I'd left his bed the previous morning. When I got to the part about the baby being West and Nico's, his eyes widened in surprise.

"Did you know?"

"I found out the other night. I didn't know before that. Poor MJ. But I think it's going to work out for the two of them."

Augie reached out to take my hand, threading our fingers together lightly. "How do you feel about it?"

The worry lines reappeared over his brow, and I leaned forward to kiss them. "These damned quotation marks," I murmured. His skin tasted like the perfect mix of sweet Augie and salty skin, and I wanted more. But I also needed to ask him about his family foundation and their association with Community Surge Properties.

"I have mixed feelings," I explained, putting off the topic change because I was a coward. "I empathize with MJ, but I'm also thrilled for West and Nico."

"I hope Rory and Kat have kids one day," Augie said. "I'd like to be an uncle at least."

"Do you want kids?"

"Mmm. Well, kind of."

I reached out to caress his cheek. "Explain kind of."

His eyes met mine before glancing away. "I want to give a child the love my dad gave me. Make their childhood safe and warm and... easy. Tell them they could do or be anything they wanted and I'd support them."

"I think you'd make an amazing father, Augie," I said softly.

"I'd fuck it up."

I scooted even closer to him and kissed his cheek. "You'd nail it."

"You'd be better at it," he said. "You'd be a fun dad. You'd make them laugh and take them on adventures."

"You'd be loving and understanding. The dad who reads interesting stories at night and has the patience to listen to a twenty-minute monologue about playground politics."

Augie's eyes locked on mine, which had the usual effect of making my heart take up more space in my chest.

"Sounds like a good combination," he murmured before blushing deep down to the roots of his hair. "I mean... I didn't mean..."

I leaned in and kissed him again, letting my gentle laughter escape into his mouth. "I know you weren't suggesting getting me pregnant, Augie."

He lost himself in the kiss until pulling back. "Not that I would mind trying. I can just imagine you with Neckie's big belly." His grin was adorable, and I hated to spoil the mood. But I really needed to ask him about his family.

"Do you do any work with your family foundation?"

His smile dropped. "Other than volunteer with some of the beneficiaries, no. I'm not even on the board."

"Do you know a company called CSP? It stands for Community Surge Properties."

His forehead crinkled. "No. What's this about?"

I propped myself up on my elbow. "The Stiel Foundation contributes to CSP. It's a nonprofit that's supposed to be creating low-income housing. But records show it's actually doing the opposite. It's taking historic properties, getting them approved for the designation change to low-income community-beneficial housing, and then selling them on to commercial developers."

Augie sat up and moved back until he was sitting against the headboard. I pulled the thick bedding up to cover him from the chilly room air.

"How are they getting away with that?" he asked.

I shrugged. "It's buried fairly deeply behind legal entities, but it seems like there'd still need to be someone at the county level aware of what's going on. I'm not sure."

"How do you know all this?"

"I had Landen look into it."

"Why?"

This was the tough part.

"I was worried after everything that's been happening to you. Thought maybe it was due to your family name or some of the controversial issues the foundation supports. When I asked Rex to look into it, he and an associate of ours discovered this anomaly in the foundation's beneficiaries."

"But what does this have to do with me? With my great-aunt's writing slope? It doesn't make sense."

I sat up and faced him so I could tick off points on my fingers as I explained. "So, right now, there is a strip of buildings surrounding your shop. The vacant place between you and the pub is owned by Stiel Corp. Then your building is owned by your grandfather."

"Wait. What?"

"You know that, right?"

"No. I pay rent to a company called Cross County Leasing," Augie explained. "My shop doesn't have anything to do with my family."

I stared at him. "But Cross County Leasing is just the management company. The building is owned by Jonathan Stiel."

Augie's face went pale. "That can't be right. When I chose the location, I met the owner. His name is John Gravely."

I knew John was a local man who, like my grandfathers, had invested plenty of money in Hobie property to help keep Hobie's charm from being washed away by big commercial developers.

"Your grandfather purchased the property about ten months ago. I didn't realize Mr. Gravely owned it before that, but he's the type of man who would have made a fair deal as long as your grandfather reassured him it would be well cared for."

"Grandfather would have told me if he bought the property my shop is on. I think? Why would he have bought it in the first place?"

"To contribute to your future security?" I asked. "Maybe he thought he was looking out for you."

"He doesn't make financial decisions based on sentiment," Augie said with a tight jaw. "He makes them based on profit and returns."

"Regardless, it doesn't explain why he wouldn't have told you."

"So, wait a minute," Augie said, turning to face me and drawing his legs up to hug his knees around the thick blankets. "If the family business owns the vacant shop, and Grandfather owns my shop... what does that have to do with this CSP company you're talking about?"

"CSP owns the building on the other side of you. Jen's shop."

"Apple Dots," Augie added under his breath. "It's the furthest thing from low-income housing you can get."

"Right."

"So, three historic buildings on the edge of the Hobie square all basically owned by my family or associates of my family. And all three entities are into commercial real estate development."

We sat in silence for a few minutes, each of us pondering the long game of this setup.

"Do you think your grandfather or CSP has plans to bundle all three properties and sell to a developer?" I asked.

He seemed to think about it. "My grandfather is cold and old-fashioned in many ways, but I can't really picture him deliberately targeting my business like that. He wasn't the best father figure while I was growing up, but I've always felt like he loves me in his own way. Granted, his way is hands-off and distant, but it's there. He was the one who encouraged me to spend time with Melody. And he was the one who suggested I pursue a graduate degree in art history if I wanted to go into the appraisal business. If it had been up to him, I would have joined the family company as an attorney or accountant. But when I clearly didn't want to do that, he supported my crazy choice to work with antiques."

"Any idea what the connection could be to the writing slope? Could there be property deeds or schematics inside the box that have something to do with this? Didn't you say your grandfather gave you the box after Melody passed?"

"Yes, but it's just love letters. I've looked at them since then."

"Let's look again now that we know there might be something to look for," I suggested.

Augie nodded and moved off the bed. As he made his way toward his closet door, I watched the pale, slender expanse of his back and ass in the faded sunlight streaming from a nearby window. He moved with a quiet elegance, which only added to the allure of his beautiful body.

"I can feel your eyeballs on my butt," he said over his shoulder. "It's making me self-conscious."

"You have a stunning butt," I assured him. "In case I haven't made that clear."

"It's too skinny."

"It's perfect."

"I have toothpick legs and razor-blade hips," he griped.

"Then you won't mind if I sink my teeth into your legs and rub my face across your hips."

He turned to face me. "What are you even talking about right now?"

"Stop disparaging the man I like," I said in a firm voice. "It's insulting to me as a connoisseur of fine male forms."

Augie's jaw dropped. "It's like I want to be both jealous and proud. You're so fucking confusing. And weird."

I felt myself smirk. "You're not the first to say it."

He stepped into the closet, moved clothes to either side along the hanging bar, and began to climb.

"What the hell?" I stood and followed him toward the closet.

"Stay back!" he barked. "Don't come in here."

I stopped halfway there and watched as his entire body disappeared into the ceiling of his closet, leaving a clear view of the ladder rungs built into the back wall.

After making his way back down, he turned and presented me with a wooden box about the size of my sock drawer. We settled back down next to each other on the bed with the warm covers pulled up. He pulled off his necklace so he could use the key to open it.

As he pulled the lid open, he explained. "I already checked it after Grandfather asked about it last week. I didn't see anything besides the love letter packet."

The box opened on a slant, creating a sloped writing surface covered in a thin smooth layer of tan leather surrounded by shiny gold-leaf details. There were a few visible drawers and sections that I imagined were for ink pots and quills as well as paper, but I was surprised when Augie unlatched the leather-covered writing surface and lifted it up to reveal a storage space underneath.

There, bound in old ribbon, was the stack of love letters.

"See?"

"Wow," I murmured. "If I think that's amazing, I can't imagine how much it interests you with your love of antiques and history."

"Right? It's so cool. To have something this special that's actually attached to my own family's history."

"Are there any other hidden compartments? Someplace your grandfather could have hidden information."

"Nothing big enough to hide a letter or paper," he said. "There's a spot, but it's only big enough to hold a tiny pocket portrait or locket— something like that."

He closed the writing surface and opened up the equivalent panel on the other end. Nothing was in that side of the large storage area, but then Augie reached a finger deep inside the space under the hinge and did something that made a click sound.

A tiny panel door popped open below one of the ink pot cubbies, revealing a dark space with the barest glint of something silver in it.

We both leaned in closer to see what it was, fully expecting an old key or piece of jewelry.

It was neither of those things, but I recognized it right away.

Jackpot.

CHAPTER 29

AUGIE

IT WAS A USB DRIVE.

Seeing something so modern inside the two-hundred-year-old box was jarring. Just when I wanted to sputter out, "What the hell?" Saint was reaching for the little device with an excited grunt.

His fingers were too big to get a good hold on it, so I batted his hand away. "Skinny comes in handy sometimes," I muttered, reaching for the little thing. "I never even thought to look in here earlier. Just glanced in the main storage areas in case someone had shoved in... I don't even know. Papers? It didn't occur to me anyone else really knew about this tiny spot. I'm an idiot."

I handed the drive to him and peered into the tiny space to make sure nothing else was lurking there.

"Do you have a computer here?" Saint asked.

I stood up and grabbed my bathrobe from the back of the bathroom door. "Yeah, let me grab it. It's brand-new, so I haven't had a chance to set it up yet."

After retrieving the new MacBook from the box on the kitchen counter, I returned to the bedroom and plugged it in. It took a while to load and process my credentials, but then we were in.

Saint inserted the USB drive into the side of the machine and clicked a few buttons. Suddenly, my grandfather's face appeared on screen in a video.

"There's a video file, some photo files, and a few documents. I figured the video file might be a good place to start," Saint explained.

He hit the Play function to begin.

My grandfather appeared in his study, and I recognized his long-time friend and attorney, Nathan Olsen, moving around in the background, setting paperwork in front of him.

"The purpose of this video is to document my true wishes for property disbursement after my death." Grandfather's voice was its typical clipped business style, but Mr. Olsen interrupted to state the date and time into the camera. The video had been taken ten months previously.

"Upon the death of my sister Melody, I inherited her portion of a string of commercial property in Hobie, Texas. I assume she left it to me since I'm the real estate investor, but now that Augie has decided to open an antique shop, the building should belong to him. I have established this property at 820 West Vine Street into a trust for my grandson August Bailey Stiel to ensure the future security of his business in Hobie. This string of three properties was originally owned by our parents. Upon their deaths, one parcel went to Melody, one to me, and the third went to the family business. In the process of creating Augie's trust, my attorney discovered the parcel owned by the Stiel Corporation had been donated through the Stiel Foundation to a community housing non-profit organization.

"I will not go into the details of this situation other than to say that it is my intent to safeguard the property located at 820 West Vine Street for my grandson August Stiel. At no time shall a property transaction related to the Stiel family, the Stiel Corporation, or the foundation negatively affect Augie's business. My wishes in this matter have been recorded in the proper legal instruments, copies of which can be found in the attached files. My attorney is privy to all of these dealings but is bound by privilege to keep them quiet until after my death.

"Other files included in the documentation are cognitive testing and assessment reports by two doctors attesting to my ability to make this informed decision and to sign in good faith my current Last Will and Testament."

Grandfather took a deep breath and seemed to deflate a little.

"Augie, if you're watching this, I need you to understand why I didn't say anything to you about it while I was alive."

It was spooky watching this now, knowing full well that the man was still alive.

"Nathan has left the room now. I suspect he has some loyalty to your mother, Eric, and Brett. I have been struggling with some memory issues lately. My biggest fear is being easily influenced by others in this family, various board members, or even Nathan himself. Any of those people might cause me to change my mind and dissolve this trust if I'm in a vulnerable state. I've written personal letters to each of you to be delivered upon my death. As you know by now, your letter has instructions on where to find this documentation in Melody's box in case you need to defend your claim. Now, don't worry, son. The doctors have done everything possible to back up this legal decision with the proper documentation, and it's my hope I'll be around for a very long time to help support your business directly."

I felt my eyes fill.

"I want you to have your dream, but I can't abide this decision splitting our family apart. I'm sure you can understand I don't want to spend any of my remaining time arguing over property rights when I feel like I've spent my entire life doing that."

Saint's arm reached out to pull me against his side. Soft lips pressed on top of my hair as Grandfather continued.

"Be happy in your life in Hobie. Remember money isn't everything. Find someone to love and love him well."

The image blacked out, leaving me slack-jawed and staring at a blank screen.

"Rewind that last part," I whispered, swiping at my eyes.

"He said *him*."

"No. He couldn't have. He said *them*."

"No, baby," Saint insisted gently. "He said *him*. It was clear."

I turned to him in shock. "But… he almost sounded okay with it."

"You said something at one point about coming out to your family *again*. Doesn't that mean they already know?"

"Well, yes, when I was a teen and couldn't hide it, but it wasn't acceptable. They made it very clear."

Saint sighed. "Well, that's bullshit. No one gets to say whether or not your sexuality is acceptable or not. Maybe he's mellowed? A lot has changed in the past decade."

I set the computer on the nightstand and leaned into Saint's chest, wrapping my arms around his warm back. His own arms came around to hold me tight. I wanted to tell him how grateful I was for his strong, supportive presence. I wanted to tell him to stay forever.

But more than anything, I wanted to forget everything I'd just learned, if only for a few moments.

I reached out my lips to suck a path along his collarbone and down to his nipple. Without saying a word, he knew exactly what I needed. He turned us around to lay me down on the bed beneath him where he began mapping my body with his tongue.

A desperate choking noise escaped my throat.

Losing myself in Saint's ministrations was the closest I may have ever come to the true feeling of freedom.

I forced all rational thought out of my head and let go. As his tongue and teeth bathed, nipped, and explored every inch of my body, I thought I'd happily died and gone to heaven. He was so attentive, so possessive in a way no one had ever been with me. I let myself fantasize that he was claiming my body for his own, claiming *me* for his own.

If only I could have taken a mental snapshot and sent it back in time to a young teenaged Augie. *This is something that's going to happen to you, and it's going to blow your mind.*

A laugh bubbled up from my chest.

Saint's tongue froze halfway out of his mouth, the tip barely grazing my nipple. Every hair on my body was at rigid attention awaiting the next commands by the sensual drill sergeant.

"Something funny, baby?" Saint asked with a grin. "Ticklish?"

"No, I just imagined what my young, scrawny self would have thought if he knew one day he'd be naked in bed with the big man on campus."

"Mm, no. That would have been my sister. I was her sidekick—she bossed me around, and I followed her like a puppy."

I laughed some more. "I can't picture anyone bossing you around. You're pretty dominant."

Saint's eyes intensified. "That a good or bad thing?"

His fingers trailed down over my breastbone, past my navel, and into the wiry hair at the base of my cock. I sucked in a breath. "Saint," I gasped as the fingers continued their trajectory. "*Good...* it's a very good thing. Please."

I wasn't quite sure what I was asking for since my ass was still plenty sore from its debut performance in The Taking of Saint's Megacock. I'd played with dildos and fingers plenty of times but nothing that big and nothing that pounded into me with the force of a former navy SEAL behind it.

The more I thought about the megacock, the more I realized my mouth had begun to water.

"I want to taste you," I said in a breathless admission. "Suck you."

Saint's lovely luminous gaze met mine. "I don't like to receive oral sex."

I stared at him in surprise, the heat of embarrassment beginning to crawl up my neck, when I noticed a twitch in the corner of his lips.

"Asshole!" I cried, smacking at him. "I believed you. Just for that, forget it. I revoke my offer."

Saint's chuckle vibrated against my chest as he hugged me tightly. "I'm sorry, but you're so damned cute. It's making me feel a little giddy. Forgive me. Maybe I can make it up to you by being the one to go down on you."

He began to slither down my body, but I stopped him by clamping my legs around his waist.

"Lie back," I said. "And take your punishment like a man."

Before sliding off me, he leaned up and kissed me slowly on the lips. I let out a moan at the gentle pace of the kiss and marveled at how someone could be so strong and yet soft at the same time. He was a study in contradiction.

When he was finally on his back with his hands behind his head, I took a moment to drink in his naked form. It was ridiculous, really. How I even had the confidence to be naked in front of a man like this was hard to fathom.

"You have a V," I said, rolling my eyes. "Who even has that shit in real life?"

"I assure you, it's a P," he cracked.

"Shut up." I traced the iliac furrow from above one hip down to his pelvis and up again. His cock jumped. "It's the kind of thing you see on marble statues of Apollo. And male models who eat zero carbohydrates. I've seen you swallow a giant croissant in one bite."

I felt my face heat at the admission since the pastry-stalking incident had been the other day on the town square when I'd looked back to see my sister handing over my own pastries to the man.

"What can I say? I have good genes."

I thought about the Wilde siblings I'd met. They were all stupidly beautiful.

"Truer words," I murmured, leaning down to take the pearl of precum at the head of his dick onto the tip of my tongue. The salty taste was overshadowed by the shock of having Saint's cock head against my lips.

His abdominal muscles clenched and rippled, and he sucked in a breath. I teased the smooth skin of his shaft with a light trail of open-mouthed kisses before nuzzling my nose into the dark blond nest of curls at the base and inhaling his musky scent. God he smelled incredible.

I was so gay. How could there be anyone on earth who didn't get off on this smell of a man? Who didn't want to suck a cock and feel the wrinkled skin of a ball sac tighten up under their fingers in anticipation of making someone come? It was heady stuff, and I took every opportunity to enjoy myself with his sexy body on display for me. To be honest, I was attempting to edge him the way he'd done to me before.

By the fourth time I'd pulled him back from the edge, he was harder than ever and leaking all over his happy trail.

"You're killing me," he muttered. "Fuck this, I can't take it."

Suddenly I was on my back with Saint's giant cock hanging over my face and a hot, wet throat inhaling my own erection.

Sixty-nine was my new favorite number.

"Fuck!" I cried. "Oh fuck."

I tried sucking Saint off while he did the same to me, but I was blowing my load down his throat within seconds, screaming and clenching his butt cheeks with my hands. The top of my skull had flown off, and I was barely able to open my eyes in time to see Saint kneeling over me jacking off frantically until his cum shot all over my chest and shoulder.

"Oh god, Augie." He gasped. "Fuck, look at you."

Lord only knew how I looked, but I *felt* utterly debauched. Surely my hair was a rat's nest, the pale skin of my face raw from his beard scruff, and my lips dry and chapped from all the kissing. The wet splatters across my skin felt cool in the open air, and I shivered.

Saint's blond hair was sticking out everywhere like a mad scientist, and his face turned smiley like a kid with a giant lollypop.

"You look pleased with yourself," I pointed out. "And you proved my point about being dominant. I stood no chance."

His smile dropped. "Thank you for trusting me, Augie."

My confusion must have showed because he hurried to continue.

"With... I mean... your first time... doing anal. Are you... was it okay?"

His hand came down from where he still knelt beside me to brush through my hair. It was a sweet, affectionate gesture that changed the entire tone of the conversation.

"More than okay," I confessed. "Thank you for caring."

"Of course I care. I don't want to ever hurt you or do anything to make you feel uncomfortable. There's a difference between being dominant and being an asshole."

"You're not an asshole."

"You're biased. Besides, you haven't known me very long."

The comment stung because it was the truth. But I wasn't about to let him disparage the guy I'd come to... care about. Respect. *Like.*

"True. But I'd like to," I admitted. The heat infusing my face revealed just how true those words were.

"Ask me anything," Saint said, shifting off the bed before reaching a hand out for me. He pulled me off the bed and led me to the bathroom.

I felt put on the spot, so I distracted myself with surreptitious glances at Saint's blessedly tight ass.

It was enough to make me believe in god. Someone big and powerful had to have created that shit.

"You coming?"

My eyes shot up to catch Saint grinning at me. Clearly he could read my mind and see what kind of thoughts I was having about his bare body.

"Huh?"

"Shower time. Come on."

He reached out an arm from the large walk-in shower space and gently pulled me toward the warm spray. I immediately walked into his embrace and leaned my head on his chest while his strong arms wrapped around me.

"You were going to ask me something," he rumbled against the top of my head.

"You have a really nice butt," I admitted. "I forgot what I was going to ask."

His chuckle vibrated between us.

"You should take the USB key to the bank. Put it in a safe-deposit box."

I pulled my head back to meet Saint's eyes. "Do you really think I need to do that? It's hidden pretty well here. Or I could put it in the ground safe on the property."

Saint's hands came up to cup my face, and worry marred his expression. "Augie, I'd rather it not be on the property if it's the reason you're in danger."

My stomach tightened at the concern he had for me. I wasn't sure the last time anyone had looked out for my safety because they cared about *me*. Sure, my mom and grandfather had cared about my safety, but it had always seemed to be more about protecting my family's reputation than myself.

I stood on my toes to press a kiss of gratitude to his lips. "Okay," I murmured against his soft mouth. "Thank you for caring."

Suddenly, Saint's face hardened into a scowl. My heart skipped a beat—something inside me worried I'd misstepped.

"Finish washing up and get back in that bed," he said in a gruff voice. "We need to get a few things straight."

CHAPTER 30

SAINT

Hearing Augie thank me for the second time in a row for basic human decency set off all my warning bells. It made me fucking crazy. Clearly, no one had treated him well enough in his life for him to expect that as his due. And that needed to change.

Once we got showered and dried, I led him back to bed, pulling back the thick stack of covers to let him slide between the soft sheets in front of me. I moved in beside him and pulled him around until we were lying on our sides, face-to-face. A slice of bright daylight landed across his shoulder from a nearby window, reminding me it was still morning.

His dark hair was wet, and a few thick strands were sticking up like a rooster's comb from where I'd rubbed a dry towel through it in the bathroom. His clean face looked young and smooth despite the two-day beard on his cheeks. I reached a finger out to brush across the softening stubble.

"You're beautiful," I said softly. "If I haven't told you that already, I'm an idiot."

Augie's eyes widened and his throat bobbed with a swallow. Before he could say anything, I continued.

"You deserve to be cared for. You deserve to be looked after and protected, Augie. When you thank me for caring for you, it hurts my heart. Everyone should care for you. Everyone should treat you with kindness, tenderness, respect." My voice was coming out rougher than I'd intended. "I don't want you to ever think for a minute you don't deserve the best."

His chin wobbled a bit so I moved my hand to cup it and leaned in to kiss the corner edge of his lips. "You deserve to be adored," I whispered against his dark whiskers. "To be pampered..." More kisses along the edge of his jaw to his earlobe. "To feel like the center of the universe."

A small whimper escaped his lips as he turned to brush his lips against my own face. "Why are you saying these things?" he asked. "You don't need to... I don't need..."

I distracted him with nibbles to his earlobe, causing him to suck in a breath and arch into me.

"You *do* need," I grumbled against his ear. I wanted him to feel amazing, to know how incredibly lucky I felt to be naked in bed with him. "Let me show you."

"No."

I pulled back to study him. It had been a long time since someone had rejected my offer to give them physical pleasure, and it had certainly never pinched in my gut the way it did coming from him.

"I... I mean, can I... can I show *you?*" Augie stammered. "I want to touch you. Explore."

His hazel eyes met mine with an unspoken plea. This was important to him for some reason. I lay back, kicking the covers down until I was spread out bare for his perusal.

"Anything you want, handsome. I'm yours."

Augie licked his lips before scraping his bottom one with his top teeth as if trying to decide where to begin. His eyes skittered down my naked body before glancing back to my face.

"Anything?"

My cock went from semi to fully erect at the catalog of options available to him.

"Mm-hmm... anything at all."

Augie's face turned mischievous, which was cuter than anything. He reached out a ring finger and just barely grazed a nipple before drawing the finger down my sternum to my navel. Every hair on my body stood on end, and my cock bounced. He was playing with fire, and he knew it.

His finger ghosted down my shaft, and we both watched as my eager dick jumped up to meet his touch.

"Hm," he murmured. "That's good?"

"Augie..." I warned. "Don't you dare think about edging me."

He flashed a fake innocent smile at me. "I would never do that to you. Can you imagine what that would feel like? If I got you harder and harder but didn't push you over the edge?"

I growled low in my throat as his delicate finger continued to tease me.

"You're more devious than you appear," I croaked as he gently cupped and tugged my sac for only the briefest second. I arched up into his grasp searching for more. "Fuck me. Please."

The words might have even surprised me more than him. Maybe I was desperate to get this show on the road, or maybe I wanted to be at his mercy—to give him power over me and let him take me in every way.

Augie froze above me.

"Is that what you want?" he asked carefully.

"Yes."

"Me inside of you?"

The words spoken in his tentative voice were even hotter than the image in my head of him pounding his slender body into me.

"Yes," I repeated, meeting his eyes. They were molten hot with lust but still held a sliver of insecurity. "Please, Augie."

He cleared his throat and stepped off the bed. "Turn over."

I did as he said while he grabbed what he needed from the nightstand. A cool hand held one of my ass cheeks as a slick finger teased my hole.

"I've never done this. Is it... okay?"

I turned my head to gaze at him, enjoying the sensations of his tentative touch. "Mm-hm. Very okay. Feels good."

His smile was shy, and a pink bloom washed across his cheeks. "You have the hottest ass of anyone. I kind of want to bite it."

The sassy words coming out of my shy Augie surprised a bark of laughter out of me. His blush deepened.

"What's so funny? It's true."

"You're welcome to bite it, sweetheart. Just be gentle about it."

Instead of biting it, he leaned down and sucked a patch of skin hard enough to leave a mark. I closed my eyes and enjoyed the feeling of him taking ownership of our encounter. His wet mouth moved across my skin, licking, sucking, and nipping as he went. All the while his slick fingers and thumb teased my entrance and drove me fucking crazy.

I thought back to the last time someone had fucked me. It hadn't happened more than a few times before I'd determined I much preferred topping. But in the beginning, when I'd first started sleeping with men, I'd tried it. One guy in particular had been insistent on topping me, but he'd been aggressive and rough. After that, I'd vowed to give a shit about the person I topped by reading body language cues and being considerate of how they were feeling and what they were experiencing.

Augie was a dream when he took charge of prepping me.

His mouth distracted me while his fingers began to invade. With every stroke of a tongue or finger, his movements became more confident, more demanding. Nothing shocked me more than when Augie's lust-gruff voice began to command me.

"Put your knees under you. Ass in the air."

Precum flowed out of me as I did what he said. But then his command turned quickly into adorable babble.

"God, this ass," Augie muttered, almost to himself. "Can't believe you're going to let me do this to you. I'm going to blow as soon as I get inside you." His hands smoothed over my butt and lower back before he reached for the condom he'd chucked on the bed. "So sexy. You're blind. You're crazy. I think you don't know what you're doing letting me top you. It's a pity top. Oh wait, you're going to top from the bottom. Probably. That makes more sense. But still. I'll take it. Fuck. This ass. I swear, I—"

"Baby, it's okay," I said, biting back a chuckle. "Believe me, I know exactly what I'm doing. I want you to feel good, to feel what it's like to fuck someone."

"More muscles than brains," he said, leaning up and pressing his lips to the back of my neck. "You could be reading me the instruction manual for a lawn mower and I'd feel good right now. I don't need to put my dick in you to feel good naked in bed with you."

"You changing your mind?" I asked breathlessly. Augie's cock slid through the cleft between my cheeks, lighting up the nerves in my entire groin with need. "Because I didn't figure you for a tease, August Stiel."

"Mpfh," he grunted, flexing his hips to grind into me harder. "Definitely not changing my mind."

He pulled back and maneuvered his cock to my hole. For a split second, I felt like turning around so I could see his face when he entered me. But then I had a strange sense of fear. That it would be too intimate, too close. That I would see things in his eyes I couldn't fix or needs I couldn't fulfill. It was better this way. Doing my best to relax my body, I buried my face in the bedding as he pushed into me.

"Oh god. Saint. Oh fuck." His voice had a hint of sob behind it, which only made me want to turn around more and take him into my arms.

The pinch and burn I felt in my ass was nothing compared to the now-familiar tightening in my chest when I thought about the man in bed with me. Even as he pressed into me, his hands continued their gentle caress of my skin like he wanted to memorize the dips and planes of my body while he had the chance. Every time he touched me, there was tender affection behind it. I wondered if he realized how much emotion he projected with his movements?

I wonder if he realized how much emotion his affection brought up in *me*?

When he was finally fully inside me and still, I took a deep breath.

"Move, please," I said. "Want to feel you."

"Saint," he croaked, pulling back a little before pushing in again. "Not gonna last. Christ, *so tight.*"

I reached a hand back to squeeze his hip. My cock throbbed against the bedding beneath me. "'S'okay, baby. Me neither."

He stroked in and out of me, lighting up my channel while picking up the pace. Suddenly he pulled out with a grunt and tugged at my hip.

"Over. Want to see you."

I scrambled to my back and pulled my knees up, watching the flushed heat of his face and the giant pupils in his eyes. Augie concentrated on finding his way back inside me before leaning over me and locking eyes.

"Better," he said softly, searching my eyes with his typical look of vulnerable insecurity. I reached my hands up to hold his face and draw it down to kiss him.

As soon as our bodies were connected from mouth to cock, everything felt perfect and right.

We kissed like we couldn't get enough. His body slammed into mine like he was frantic to crawl inside me. My arms tightened around his back like thick bands of *never fucking leave me.*

When I felt the rough hair of his happy trail tug at my cock, it was enough to have me scrambling a hand between us to finish myself. His movements sped up and his eyes widened. We stared at each other until I tumbled first, crying out a curse and arching up as my release shot over my stomach and chest.

I felt myself tighten around him in pulses of pleasure. He thrust into me two more times before calling out my name in a gasp. After he collapsed on top of me, I ran greedy but lazy hands all over every inch of his skin I could reach. He felt perfect against me despite the sweat and fluids between us.

"I need to get up," he grumbled against my neck. "Can't move."

"Do you have to go into work today?" I asked.

"Not till late afternoon. I just have to close."

"Tell you what," I said, gently moving him off me. "Let's shower again and grab the box. We'll take it to the bank, then I'll treat you to brunch at the Pinecone."

Once we were in the shower doing a quick wash, Augie looked up at me bashfully through wet lashes.

"Did we seriously just have sex three times in one morning?"

His cheeks were already pink from the hot water, but they deepened to a darker shade.

"If you don't stop looking at me like that, I'm going to make it four," I promised.

CHAPTER 31

AUGIE

THE NEXT COUPLE OF DAYS WERE A DREAMSCAPE OF FLIRTING WITH Saint Wilde during impromptu "self-defense lessons" and daydreaming of him during my time at the shop. He was busy covering extra classes at Twist for Neckie and visiting his new niece on the side.

Our time at Twist in the evenings was more touching and horny wrestling than actual self-defense, but somehow those sessions left me feeling stronger and lighter at the same time. Simply being around the baby-faced SEAL made me feel alive in a way I never had before. It may have been corny and cheesy, but it was still true.

With the USB drive tucked safely away in a secure cubby at Hobie First National and the writing slope itself locked in Melody's ground safe in the barn, I finally had a sense of peace I hadn't had before, and the couple of nights Saint stayed over at the farmhouse with me had gone a long way toward helping me get used to sleeping in my own bed again.

We'd had a conversation about what to do regarding the infor-mation inside the box, but ultimately I'd decided to take a few days to think on it. The last thing I wanted to do was rush into confronting my family directly against my grandfather's wishes. And now that Brett thought I no longer had the box, maybe I was safe after all.

As for Saint, I wasn't quite sure what was happening.

There were two sides of myself at war. Part of me fantasized that Saint and I were in the early stages of an actual relationship. When he was around, he showered me with attention and treated me like a unique treasure. We talked for hours about anything and everything— his time in the navy, my time in school and working at the auction house, our families, our favorite movies and music. But then there was the part of me that knew the truth. Saint Wilde couldn't possibly be the type of guy to settle for one man, and if he was, that man certainly wouldn't be a small nerd with a penchant for spewing obscure facts about seventeenth century table leg shapes. Someone like Saint would want a beautiful international fashion model or a strong, brave soldier type like himself. Regardless, he'd choose someone with confidence and poise, not a man who was scared of his own shadow and who thought rifling through dusty estate sales was the best thing ever.

The "fantasy boyfriend Augie" waited for calls and texts, swooned when Saint stopped by the shop with a mocha and biscotti from Sugar Britches "just because," and felt unsteady cardiac rhythms when awaking in the warm protective circle of Saint's arms.

The "lame-ass geek Augie" hid behind a giant plastic pumpkin to avoid running into Saint when he was spotted with his grandfathers outside of Ritches Hardware, idly wondered what other gay men in Hobie Saint was hooking up with when he wasn't with me, and felt absolute certainty this whole thing was a mental fabrication and proof my mental capacity was slowly but definitively running off the rails.

It wasn't until Friday morning that Geek Augie began to wonder if Boyfriend Augie might actually become a reality.

"Will you please come to the ranch for dinner with my family tomorrow night?" Saint asked from his spot next to the Edwardian stand mirror behind my checkout counter. He'd stopped in after finishing an early kickboxing class that had left him deliciously flushed and sweaty.

"What?" I asked. The sight of him was so distracting, I thought he'd invited me to meet the family.

"Family dinner tomorrow. Will you please come?"

Huh? I tilted my head at him. Surely, he hadn't meant to ask me that. I needed to stall him to give my brain time to process.

"I thought the Halloween bonfire was tomorrow?"

Saint nodded, a lock of his blond hair falling over one eyebrow. "No, that's next weekend. Grandpa always runs a chili test night the weekend before, but we do have our own Wilde bonfire at the ranch on chili night."

My pulse sped up. "Are you... are you asking me to..."

I couldn't finish the question. My eyes skittered here, there, everywhere but made damned sure not to catch Saint's own gray-blue gaze.

A throaty chuckle came from his chest. "Babe. You've already met my family around town. Why are you being strange about this?"

I snuck a glance at him and swallowed hard. "What will they think I'm there for?"

Saint's eyes narrowed. "Chili. They'll think you're there for dinner, Augie."

I turned to punch random numbers into my cash register tablet as if I was busy ringing up twelve customers at once instead of the zero customers who were in my store at the moment.

"I'm not hungry," I said lamely. "I never really liked chili. And also, bonfires are the leading cause of forest fires."

My entire body broke out in a sweat, and my stomach lurched. What was I doing? And why couldn't I shut up?

I heard him shift and stalk closer to me. Warm hands slid from my hips to my stomach, pulling me gently until my back rested against Saint's chest and his chin nudged my hair.

"You're not hungry because you just had lunch. This is tomorrow night's dinner we're talking about. You have plenty of time to get hungry for it. There will be other things there besides chili. And the forest fire thing is complete bullshit, not to mention the fact my brother Otto will be there. And he's an actual firefighter."

I clenched my teeth.

"Augie, if you don't want to go out with me, you can just say so."

The disappointment in his voice surprised me. Maybe this actually meant something to him.

"It's not that," I admitted, turning to look at him. "I've just never... um. I've never been introduced to a family as somebody's *something* before. And I didn't know whether you... I mean, are we... that is to say, I don't need to be somebody's *something*. I don't want to assume that there's anything going on that needs to be defined or... labeled. Because that's just unnecessariness—"

Unnecessariness? Stop talking, you idiot.

I felt like I was probably going to vomit and shit myself simultaneously, which would explain Saint's attraction to me.

If he was insane.

"I would love to introduce you to my family as someone I'm currently seeing, but if that's uncomfortable for you, I could always introduce you as a friend. Which is silly, honestly, considering they already know you and you won't need to be introduced to anyone anyway."

Currently seeing.

That sounded both wonderful and temporary. I silently debated what would happen if anyone in my family found out I was officially "seeing" a man.

"Yeah, okay," I kind of squeaked. "That's good. Food, family, and fire. Did you know those ancient rituals have remained the same for tens of thousands of years?"

Fuck. Not historical facts. Not now.

I continued for the sake of clarification. "Longer than that, really. Evidence shows humans have been controlling fire for around a million years. Or, more accurately, 700,000 years according to evidence found in Wonderwerk Cave in South Africa." I cleared my throat to continue when I saw Saint's lips pressed together and his eyes dancing with suppressed laughter. I let out a noisy breath. "Asshole," I muttered.

"Don't be nervous," he said with a sweet smile. "And that's not easy for me to say considering you're cute as hell when you're nervous."

"Shut up."

"Even though we've established its *unnecessariness*, is it okay with you that I call you my date?"

"Why do I even give you the time of day?"

I pretended to rearrange the pair of large bronze candelabra on a nearby table. Saint stalked me again, pulling me into his embrace and bending over to nip at the spot on my neck he knew drove me crazy.

"Oh god," I whispered as a shiver ran through me. "Cheater."

"Holy mother of *pearl*, what is happening in here?" The familiar high-pitched screech of Stevie Devore shot through the room from the shop doorway. Saint and I jumped apart—me with my hand on my heart and Saint with a hand at his side where I'd sometimes seen him carrying a weapon in a holster. Today there was no weapon.

"Jesus, Stevie," I called out. "You scared the shit out of me."

"Looks like Mr. Wilde here was scaring the *spit* out of you, more like," Stevie said with a wink as he sauntered over toward me. "You two trying something on? Not that I can blame you—Saint here is hot stuff. Not that I'd notice, mind you. I have a hot fire chief at home."

"Damned straight," Chief Paige muttered from the doorway. "Can you stop racing ahead? I swear you move at the speed of actual speed."

Stevie looked back over his shoulder at the older man. "Keep up, Daddy, or I'll have to trade you in for a younger model."

"Don't call me that."

"Gramps?"

"Mpfh." The sexy fire chief leaned over to scoop up Milo from his spot in an overstuffed armchair. "Hiya, cutest. Give me some love."

"In a minute," Stevie said, oblivious to the fact his man had been addressing the cat. "I'm here for the..." His eyes caught on the vintage gramophone that was playing Van Morrison's "Into the Mystic." "What's with the loud flower?"

"That is an Edison phonograph from 1902," I explained. Stevie looked at the big petal-shaped bell speaker with a blank stare.

"A record player, sweetheart," Chief Paige added, slipping an arm around Stevie.

"You mean, like those old CDs? This thing plays those?"

The older man narrowed his eyes at his younger boyfriend. "You damned well know what a record player is. Don't fuck with me. Remember what happened earlier this morning when you asked if I wanted Metamucil in my coffee?"

Stevie's face turned bright red. "I, uh, got a spanking."

"Damned straight you got a spanking. You want to see what happens to that pink ass when you get another one on the same day?"

Now *my* face turned bright red. I lectured my eyeballs not to even think about turning Saint's way, but they disobeyed me. Saint's gaze burned a hole into me and filled my dick in about two seconds. If Saint Wilde laid a hand on my butt, I would probably orgasm instantly. Even the idea of it was doing unsettling things to every single cell in my body.

"Ahem, well, that's... something," I managed to squeak out. "But no. This thing plays vinyl records which were the de facto format for playing music for over eighty years. Then there were eight-track tapes, then cassette tapes, then CDs, then MP3, then streaming. This particular record player is over a hundred years old."

I could see Stevie contemplating whether or not to make another age joke at the chief. All it took was one steaming-hot glance from the fire chief to change Stevie's mind.

"Hm. Well, it's pretty at least," he said instead. "Where's my dress?"

Stevie had asked me to source a lookalike Marilyn Monroe dress for his Halloween costume and a formal top hat for the chief's. I wasn't quite sure how the two of them went together, but it wasn't my place to ask.

"It's upstairs. Let me grab it."

As I passed Saint, he reached out a finger to graze the back of my hand. A flock of feral butterflies banged every which way inside my stomach, and I thought my heart might hammer straight out of my chest. Once I got upstairs to the apartment where I stored some of my overflow items, I took a minute to close my eyes and catch my breath.

When I opened my eyes again, I noticed the wooden chest. Something about it didn't look right. The lid wasn't fully seated, and there was a large scrap of fabric hanging out of one side. I would have never left it like that. Fabric snagged against old wood was a pet peeve of mine. And my part-time employee wouldn't have had any reason to be up here in that part of the space at all.

"Saint!" I yelled downstairs before I had a chance to stop myself. I tried to calm myself down. "Um, Saint?"

The sound of his heavy footfalls taking the stairs two at a time kept me from turning tail and running. He hit the top of the stairs at a dead run and almost ran into me before skidding to a stop. "What is it?"

I pointed to the chest. "Someone's been in here. That's not how I left it."

He looked around and quickly moved to investigate all the potential hiding spots in the room before approaching the chest. Saint knew from my description days before that I'd mentioned this chest to my cousin. He also knew that the chest was full of Melody's vintage clothes and photo albums, which meant it didn't have enough space left in it for a person to hide. Had there been room for a body in there, I might have already been passed out in a puddle of my own piss from fear.

Saint lifted the lid. Everything inside the chest had been tossed around. A few books and photos were scattered in heaps and rucked up to one side tangled among sequins and feathers. Somewhere in the mix, I spotted my original copy of the Hot Wheels Collectors Guide. It was a book I'd had for years since Rory had given it to me for my birthday one year. After pulling it from the debris, I was grateful to see it was undamaged. I held the slim volume to my chest.

"It's him, isn't it?" I asked in a shaky voice. "Brett."

Saint's arm came around my waist as we both peered into the mess. "Looks like it. I'm sorry, Augie."

"But why? I just don't understand it. How does he know Grandfather put that USB in there?"

He pulled me around in front of him and held my chin gently between his thumb and forefinger. "I think we should go to Dallas and meet with your grandfather. Find out what's going on. Until we get to the bottom of this, you're never going to feel safe."

He was right, of course, but the idea of confronting my family about anything made me sick.

"They're going to accuse me of stirring up drama. They're going to think I'm greedy."

"They're wrong."

"You guys okay up there?" It was Chief Paige's voice, booming in his no-nonsense work voice.

"All clear, Chief," Saint called down. "Be there in a second."

His hand cupped my cheek. "Will you let me take the lead on this? Please?"

"What do you mean?"

"I think we should arrange a meeting with your grandfather at the Landen offices."

"Why? We can just go to my aunt's birthday dinner tonight and stay after?" I'd forgotten all about Prima's birthday celebration that night, but Saint's mention of his own family dinner the following night had reminded me.

Saint's face widened in a grin.

"What?" I asked. "Why do you look like you just pulled one over on me?"

"You said we. You invited me to dinner with your family."

Fuck.

"No," I said, trying desperately to backtrack. The very idea of taking Saint to a family event where surely everyone would be able to see me giving him heart eyes made my stomach butterflies manic. "I meant me and... Milo."

He pulled me in close until our chests were pressed together. "No you didn't."

"Saint, I..." How did I tell him I wasn't ready to come out to my family while all this other shit was going on?

"Baby, relax. I'm not going to be anything other than your security presence if that's what's most comfortable for you. But I'm sure as hell not allowing you around your cousin without protection."

Maybe I should have been annoyed at his bossiness, but I totally wasn't. I loved every fucking minute of him wanting to protect me.

"Will it bother you if I don't introduce you as... something else?"

Great, now I was talking in prude code. I needed to grow the hell up.

"Augie, it will bother me more to see you upset. Whatever you need is fine with me. You forget that I lived plenty of years under Don't Ask, Don't Tell, and even when it ended, I still understood many people's choice to stick with it. When, how, and if you decide to come out to your family is completely up to you. I support whatever is best for you."

Of course he did. It only really mattered in a long-term relationship, and he wasn't planning on sticking around. The man lived in Dallas and traveled all over the world with his job. Once this assignment was over, he'd be back in some pop star's world getting lusted after by thousands of rabid fans.

"Fine," I muttered, seriously depressed all of a sudden at the reminder this was all temporary. As soon as we solved the danger I was in, there would be no reason for Saint to stick around in Hobie. "Whatever. Let's go to Dallas."

Saint's smile faltered and he looked at me with concern. Before he had a chance to ask me about my sudden mood shift, I faked a smile and leaned up for a kiss. "Sorry, just stressed about seeing my family if they're the ones behind this."

Lie.

I'd face a thousand jackass Stiels if it meant I could keep one baby-faced Wilde.

CHAPTER 32

SAINT

AUGIE WAS LYING. OF COURSE HE WAS STRESSED ABOUT HIS FAMILY, BUT there was something else going on with him too. When the two of us were alone at his house, things were easy and perfect. But for some reason when we were in public, his insecurity came screaming in at breakneck speed. I had to assume it was because he wasn't fully out yet, but he'd told me he was out in Hobie. Was this moodiness just a symptom of his trying to get used to being out? Or did he have another reason to get uncomfortable around me?

I'd tried hard to reassure him of my feelings for him. We'd even talked about the trouble I was in if Lanny found out the two of us were sleeping together. I'd explained Lanny was a good man who would be able to understand this wasn't the same thing as a quick fuck with a personal security client. Augie meant something to me, and Lanny wouldn't have a problem with me finding someone special, even if it was a client. Augie seemed to relax a little bit about it, but I knew he still had insecurities about my feelings for him. I didn't blame him. It wasn't like I had a history of commitment to relationships. Unfortunately, before Charlie realized Augie meant something to me, he'd told Augie I had a history of sleeping around. It would take time to prove myself to him. I hoped to start by proving myself to his family whether they knew we were an item or not.

I left Augie at the shop with a promise to pick him up later that afternoon for the drive to Dallas. I headed back to the ranch to shower and change in order to help Doc and Grandpa prep for the chili dinner the following night. When I pulled in to the drive, I recognized MJ's car, which surprised me. She'd been spending almost all her time at Neckie's house since the baby was born three days before. I entered the big house and heard chatter coming from the direction of the kitchen as usual.

A pack of three dogs had greeted me noisily at the front door and accompanied me with bouncing yips to the back of the house.

"Who's that?" Doc called out.

"Saint," I said, almost tripping over Grump the coonhound.

When I entered the big open space, I saw Doc at the island dumping muffins out of a tin and onto a cooling rack. MJ and Neckie were both snuggled on one of the sofas under a blanket, and a fire was going in the stone fireplace. Neckie looked pale and tired, but she had a soft smile on her face when she looked toward my sister.

"How are you feeling?" I asked, making my way over to give each of the women a quick kiss on the cheek.

"Like I gave birth to a fat Wilde," Neckie teased. "You people have big heads. Be glad you're not a woman. When I have my own kids, my wife is going to have to do the hard part while I watch from a safe distance."

She shot a wink at MJ, which caused my normally nonplussed sister to blush and look down at her lap.

Neckie leaned over and pressed a kiss on MJ's jaw, murmuring she was just teasing. MJ glanced up at me with the most contented look on her face. It opened something inside of me that made me feel like I could suddenly breathe more deeply for the first time in my life. MJ was in love. She was being adored. My twin would be okay.

"How'd the kickboxing go?" Doc asked. "Neckie told us the rumor is you're getting better at it."

"Yeah, actually I really like that one. And I did a spin class earlier this morning too. A few of the guys from the firehouse stopped by to ask me if you offered some of the CrossFit-type classes. I said I'd ask you about it," I said, turning to Neckie.

"God, Saint," Neckie said. "It would be a dream come true if you'd come in halfs with me and run the hard-core stuff while I did the yoga and stretching part. Twist has grown so much, it's hard to manage with just one person now."

I tilted my head and studied her, wondering if she truly did want a business partner.

MJ cut in. "She means it, Saint. She never intended to work around the clock like this. She does classes at five in the morning and eight at night some days."

"I already have a job," I told them. "But I can certainly ask around. I know a ton of former SEALs who'd be great at it."

The idea of someone else in there taking my place at Twist kind of didn't feel right. I'd enjoyed joking around with the clients before kicking their asses. When the guys from the station had asked about tougher workouts, I'd already started thinking about putting together some of the stuff my team had done as part of our routine daily PT. Building lung capacity and endurance was just as important for a firefighter as it was for a SEAL. I could talk about that stuff for hours.

"He's thinking about it," Grandpa said quietly to Neckie. I looked up in time to catch him shooting her a wink.

"I... well, I can't say I'd mind living back here in Hobie," I admitted.

The room went quiet.

"I feel the same way," MJ admitted.

Our eyes met across the room. "Are you thinking about making a big move, sis?"

Neckie looked down where her fingers were tangled with MJ's over the blanket. The corner of her lip was turned up, but she stayed quiet.

MJ raised both eyebrows. "Seth told me Honovi Baptiste is looking for a law partner now that the real estate side of his firm has exploded. He wants to hand off litigation."

"Hon is a good man," I said with a nod. "I could see you thriving in that situation."

The room crackled with change.

"I'm not sure how I feel about living in a different city from my other half," MJ said. Everyone in the room knew she meant me. "It sure would be amazing if you were here too."

I thought about going back to Dallas and away from Augie. My brain couldn't even wrap around moving forward without him.

Not to mention being sent back on the road to protect someone else like Gemma. Or being sent to northern Africa again to protect wealthy oil executives. Neither job sounded nearly as fun as teaching people how to be healthy and fit and then seeing my family every day.

"I'll think about it," I said. "I hadn't ever really thought living in Hobie was an option, but then again, I never thought I'd actually make it through BUD/S training either."

Doc and Grandpa chuckled. "You were the only one, then," Grandpa explained. "The rest of us knew you were stubborn enough to make it happen."

"He means determined," Doc said.

"Sure he does," I said, walking past Grandpa and squeezing his shoulder. "Now, I came over here to help cut onions for the chili. Who's ready to cry like a baby?"

We began prepping for the two types of chili Grandpa planned to make and were halfway through burning our eyeballs out with onion vapors when the doorbell rang. The three dogs declared Armageddon and took off scorched earth style to bring down the insurgents.

When I got to the door, I could see the outline of a man about my age through the windows in the door. He twisted around looking behind himself before facing the door again. His arm came out like he was going to ring the bell a second time, but then he dropped his arm and shook his head.

"May I help you?" I asked once I got the dogs under control and pulled the door open.

The man's head snapped up, and his eyes widened. He was cute, but I definitely hadn't ever seen him before.

"Oh, ah… sorry, I… I'm looking for Weston Marian. Does he live here?"

The guy was plenty nervous and actually wrung his hands in front of himself while he waited for me to answer. Grandpa's first name was Weston, but he'd been a Wilde for decades.

"May I tell him who's asking?"

I rubbed the tears away from my eyes, which seemed to get his attention.

"Oh god, oh no. I'm so sorry. This must be a bad time. I didn't mean to—"

"Saint, who is it?" Grandpa asked, coming up behind me to see who was at the door. His eyes were even redder than mine were, and he'd removed his glasses to rub at them.

"He's asking for you," I told him before turning back to the stranger. "Why don't you come in."

The poor guy looked horrified, glancing back and forth between Grandpa and me and clearly getting the wrong idea.

"I've clearly interrupted something," he stammered. "I'm so, so sorry. I'll come back."

He turned and began hurrying to his car, which I could see was a rental.

"Wait," I called to him with a laugh. "We were cutting onions. Come back."

The man spun around, but now he was the one with red eyes. "I shouldn't have come here. I'm sorry."

I turned to look at Grandpa, who seemed just as confused as I was. "He asked for Weston Marian," I murmured. "Not Wilde."

Grandpa's entire body stiffened. "Get Doc," he said quietly before taking a step off the porch. "Tell him I need him."

I didn't second-guess him. Instead, I raced into the house and quickly explained what was going on to Doc.

"Shit," he muttered, wiping his hands off with a kitchen towel. "I knew this was coming. Your grandfather would live in denial if given half a chance. Stubborn bastard."

"What's going on?"

"Old chickens coming home to roost. Stay here with your sister."

I finished prepping the chili fixings before cleaning up our mess. By the time I was done, Doc and Grandpa came back in, looking emotional.

"Grandpa?" MJ asked, unfolding herself from the sofa. "Who was that?"

"Sit down, sweetheart. I'll tell you everything. Doc already called in the troops so I only need to tell it once."

While we waited for my siblings, I put on another pot of coffee and set Doc's muffins on a tray. There was fruit cut up in tubs in the fridge, so I set that out too. My aunt Gina arrived first, still wearing pajamas and her bathrobe. She kissed her dads on their cheeks before heading straight to the coffee.

"Carmen's coming. She wanted to take a shower first."

"You could have waited for your wife, Gina," Grandpa chastised. "It's hardly worth leaving the house looking like a slumber party runaway."

We all stared at Grandpa. He was the least judgmental man of our acquaintance. He winced and looked at Doc.

"I'm sorry," he said in a low voice. Then to Gina, "Forgive me, sweetheart."

Gina's forehead creased with worry, but she didn't say anything.

Hudson and Charlie got here next, followed by West. Nico, Pippa, and baby Reenie were conspicuously absent, which I decided was probably for the best since Neckie was there. Otto and Seth appeared with Sassy in tow. That was about as good as we were going to get from my side. King was somewhere off doing secret squirrel stuff for his secret squirrel job. Hallie and Winnie were in Dallas. My parents were in Singapore, and Cal was on a boat somewhere in the Caribbean getting his captain's license.

My cousin Katie turned up with her brother Web, which surprised me since neither of them lived in Hobie. But then I saw my aunt Brenda come in behind them already spewing out guilt trips about how their one trip to the family lake house in six months was already being interrupted by family drama.

"Shut your piehole, Brenda," Doc snapped. "You can turn right around and go back to the lake house if you don't want to be here. No one said it was mandatory."

Brenda's eyes widened in surprise, and she sat down in the nearest chair. "No. I want to be here. Sorry, Dad."

"I'm here!" Carmen came flying in, long wet hair in a messy bun on top of her head. "Sorry. I smelled like manure after gardening this morning."

She tossed a quick kiss on Gina's cheek. "Sorry, babe. I brought you some clothes if you want to change later."

"Thanks."

"Okay," Doc said. "Sit down, everyone." He glanced at Grandpa for some kind of married-person silent communication.

Once we all settled down, Doc opened his mouth, but Grandpa cut him off.

"I've got it, hon. Thank you." He reached out his hand for Doc's and pulled him down in the big chair beside him before turning to the rest of us. "The short version is, my family kicked me out when I was a teen after my dad caught me with another boy. I didn't have anywhere else to go, so I lied my way into the army where I eventually met Doc. After that, Doc and all of you guys were my family. I put my biological family behind me and tried not to spend time thinking about the past."

He took a deep breath. "Two years ago, someone related to my biological family showed up in Hobie. It was a complete coincidence, but we realized Nico's best friend Griff's father is actually my nephew. Griff's grandfather was my brother, Walter Marian, but he passed away years ago."

We all stared at him. West was as confused as the rest of us. "Griff is related to you? That's not possible. Nico never said a word to me. We don't keep secrets from each other."

"He doesn't know. I asked Griff's mother, Rebecca, not to tell anyone until I knew how I wanted to handle it. And then I chickened out and pretended like it had never happened. That was two years ago."

Aunt Brenda leaned forward with her elbows on her knees. "Who's the guy who came to the door today? Someone from that family?"

Doc chuckled. "Fate. Fate came to the door and told him to get his head out of his ass."

Grandpa pretended to elbow him. "No, that was someone I didn't know existed. His name is Miller Hobbs. He did one of those ancestry DNA kits and discovered he's a close match to me and a closer match to a Matilda Marian in San Francisco. My sister. Since I've never had biological children, I explained it either had to be through my brother, Walter, or my sister, Matilda. It looks more like a match to Tilly."

Doc cut in. "There are no records of Tilly ever marrying or changing her name. Miller's mother was born to an anonymous unwed mother in a home in California. Tilly would have been eighteen at the time."

"Has Miller met her yet?" I asked.

Grandpa sat up straight. "She refuses to meet him or acknowledge him. He came here in hopes I could help get through to her." He paused for a moment. "His mother is dying. She wants to meet her biological mother if possible before she goes. Miller wants to do this for her."

Silence descended again.

"Well, shit," MJ said. "What are you going to do?"

"Go to California to see my sister," Grandpa said. "And try and figure out how the hell to say 'sorry I disappeared, hey can you do this kid a favor' when I get there."

"Wow," West said. "You know Nico and I will come with you to help any way we can."

Grandpa nodded at him. "I think that would be great. We'll need all the help we can get. If Tilly is anything like she was as a girl..." He sighed and then smiled fondly to himself. "I might need to wear a suit of armor and bring a fire hose."

CHAPTER 33

AUGIE

Saint was quiet in the car on the way to Dallas Friday night. He seemed to be in another world, so I left him to his thoughts. I may or may not have snuck a few glances over to appreciate the navy man in a french-blue button-down shirt and black dress pants. He looked downright edible, if a bit distracted.

After an hour in the truck, he finally blinked and turned to me, reaching across the center console for my hand.

"I'm sorry, Augie. I didn't mean to sink into my head like that. Something happened this afternoon at the ranch."

"Is everyone all right? Doc and Grandpa? Neckie?"

"Oh, yeah. Yes. Everyone is fine." He continued to tell me about his grandfather's long-lost-relative situation. Then he updated me on his siblings and the baby. "She's so freaking sweet, Augie. So tiny."

"Yeah," I teased. "They make 'em small, don't they?"

"Neckie said she had a big fat Wilde head. I wonder if I had a baby... if it would have a big head."

I looked over at him. His *everything* was big.

"Yes," I said before clearing my throat. "But don't forget big heads hold big brains."

Saint's smile faded a bit, and he glanced at me. "Neckie asked if I might want to go into business with her."

The sound of the tires on the road filled the spacious cab, and flat plains whizzed by outside the windshield on either side of us. I told my galloping heart to calm the hell down.

"Like, at Twist?" I asked.

"Yeah. She said it's grown so much, she wishes she had an equal partner. MJ told me later she thinks Neckie actually wants to sell it eventually when she starts her own family."

My breath came quickly, as if I'd been jogging well past a comfortable pace.

"And, that would mean... what? You'd work there? Live there? In Hobie, I mean?"

The idea of seeing him regularly and not being able to touch him made me feel dizzy. I could just imagine walking to Sugar Britches for coffee and running into Saint Wilde and his beautiful new boyfriend. Because he would have one. He'd have a damned string of them.

Saint opened the center console to grab a pack of gum stashed inside. I caught sight of his handgun in its holster and spotted a box of bullets underneath in the dark recesses of the storage compartment.

He had his gun.

Gun.

My breathing came even faster.

"Yes. Move back to Hobie. Quit my job and help run the gym full-time."

He glanced over at me again, so I turned my head to look out the window. "Oh. Yeah. That's... y-your f-family would l-love that."

Awkward silence fell in the cab, and I struggled to catch my breath.

I would have to move away. There was no way I could see Saint with someone else in my little town. No fucking way. Oh god. Who was I kidding? I was a scrawny-ass geek. This was a lark for him. He was a big, highly skilled tough guy. I was a weakling. A coward. Hell, I couldn't even convince *myself* I deserved a relationship. How the hell did I think I could convince someone else?

"Augie?"

"Gngh?"

He looked over again, but I turned my shoulder so he couldn't see me struggling for breath.

"Baby, shit."

"No, I'm fuh... fuh... *fine*." I sucked in a loud breath and grabbed at my chest. "Just breathed something wrong," I gasped and tried not to let any part of my body touch the center console where the gun was. What if I accidentally set it off? What if I knocked it with my elbow and...

I couldn't breathe. My fingers searched frantically for the window button.

"Fuck," he bit out as he yanked the car off the highway onto a side road. He scrambled around to the passenger side, but I was already out and stumbling across the dried grass into the nearby field.

"No, 's f-fine," I tried reassuring him. "S... Sorry." My knees wobbled until I decided I might be better off on the ground. I went down hard and would have landed on my face if Saint hadn't grabbed me and kept me from pitching forward.

He moved me around until I was cradled on his lap in his arms.

"Do you need an ambulance? Is it a panic attack?"

I met his eyes and shook my head before nodding. "The gun," I whispered.

Realization dawned. "You're afraid of guns. When you fainted at Landen—it wasn't blood sugar. It was the gun?"

I tried nodding as I let out a slow breath.

"Oh, honey. Oh, Augie. Christ, I'm so sorry. Why didn't you tell me? Never mind. I know now."

"I..." I heaved in another breath and tried to slow down. "My d-dad was shot in an armed robbery. I w-was there."

He held me even tighter, cursing softly under his breath. Saint's neck smelled like heaven. The familiar scent of him went a long way toward helping me calm down.

"Augie, I knew that but didn't think about it. I didn't ever even... shit. I never even asked you about it. When I read the article about the robbery, it was before I knew you. Before... I'm so fucking sorry I never even asked. Of course you get nervous around guns. It's completely understandable. I'm so stupid."

"Not stupid."

The adrenaline spike was fading quickly, and I began to shiver violently in the cold October air despite Saint's warm body against mine.

"Let's get you back in the truck."

He made me wait by the hood while he moved the gun around to a locked tool box in the bed of the truck. He'd told me to look up the traffic on his phone to see if there was anything we needed to avoid on the route, but I knew what he was doing. It was thoughtful as hell, and I felt myself falling even faster for him. The idea of this ending between us broke my fucking heart.

Saint helped me get back in the truck before hopping in and getting us back on the highway. His large hand clasped mine the rest of the way to Dallas and didn't let go until we were pulling through the large metal gates at Grandfather's house. Once we were parked in the forecourt between the giant fountain and the overly large front doors, I panicked all over again as I realized I was about to stand in front of my family and deny this man was mine. What if that would somehow make it true?

"I don't want you to have a gorgeous boyfriend!"

Saint slow-panned toward me. "What?"

"I… I don't… It'll be too hard to see you with someone beautiful and perfect and… please." Okay, I was completely off the rails and might as well shoot for the moon. "Please, um… just don't… or, ah, maybe just give me a chance? I mean, if you're looking. For someone. To date."

Both of Saint's hands landed on my shoulders and gripped firmly enough to get my attention.

"Remember what I said about not disparaging my judgment in men?"

Fuck.

I nodded.

"I happen to already have the most beautiful boyfriend ever. And I don't really understand what's happening right now, but—"

"Who? Who?" There was an owl nearby, perhaps. Either that or I'd had a complete break with reality.

"You, you idiot. Why do you want me to give you a chance? I don't get it. Aren't we already dating? I mean, I know it's been fast, and we haven't really put a label on it yet, but—"

"Me?" I squeaked, à la Stevie Devore. "Me?"

It wasn't an owl, it was a parrot. And the damned thing wouldn't shut up.

Saint's eyes glanced toward the front door of the house where I could see my grandfather's valet standing and waiting. It was a good thing my sister had warned me she wasn't going to make it until later, or I was sure she'd already be out here watching me make a fool of myself through the truck window.

"Yes, you," Saint said softly, as if Salvatore could hear us from inside the truck. "Surely you realize the main reason I'm considering Neckie's offer is the hope you'd be willing to put up with me a little longer."

"Little longer?" Again with the parrot act. I was losing it.

One of his hands lowered to my hip where Sal wouldn't be able to see it. Saint's thumb rubbed a small but intimate circle just above my waistline.

"As long as you'll have me? Maybe until you realize I'm a big dumb jock and you deserve better." His voice stayed low, and it washed through me like a deep, romantic Randy Travis ballad.

"You're too good for me," I admitted. "I don't deserve you."

"You have it the wrong way around," he whispered back, eyes boring into me with an intimacy I'd never before experienced. He was stunning in his intensity. "You're everything that's good in the world."

"*Saint,*" I whispered.

I felt like I was half a breath away from hearing words I'd never heard before when the sound of my mother's heels clip-clopped across the slate walkway toward the car. I pulled back, feeling Saint's missing touch above my hip like a brand. He cleared his throat before murmuring for me to hold still while he got the door.

No way in hell.

As he climbed out of his side, I did the same, turning and pasting on a fake smile for my mother.

"What in the world is taking so long out here? Did you bring your aunt Prima the Screaming Eagle?"

"Two bottles of 2006 Screaming Eagle Cabernet. If I see her drink them both in one sitting, I might have to have words with her," I warned. "It was a thousand dollars a bottle."

"Oh, stop complaining. You can afford it, and you know it's her favorite."

Mother leaned in for a kiss, so I aimed an air kiss somewhere near her right cheek. "Who's this?" she asked rudely when Saint came around the truck.

"Mother, this is Saint Wilde. Saint, this is Diane Stiel, but she goes by Di."

My mother narrowed her eyes the tiniest bit. "You may call me Mrs. Stiel."

Saint snorted, quickly covering his mouth and pretending to cough. I thought back on the night in the gym I'd told him he didn't have permission to use my first name. How embarrassing to learn that the apple didn't fall far from the tree.

After my mother sniffed and turned to walk back in the house, I finally had the guts to meet Saint's eye with a smirk and mouth, *I'm sorry.*

I could have fucking sworn he mouthed back, *I love you.*

And so I tripped up the stairs and lost my footing.

It seemed when I was in the presence of Saint Wilde, I was always falling.

And he was always there to catch me.

CHAPTER 34

SAINT

AUGIE'S FAMILY WAS A BUNCH OF ELITIST BASTARDS. WHICH ONLY served to make him seem more sweet and humble and perfect by comparison. I tried desperately to school myself so I didn't look at him with a lovesick puppy face. It was bad enough I'd finally come to the realization August Stiel was my person right when I couldn't tell him that out loud, but I'd make a big mess of things if I couldn't find my game face somewhere.

You're a navy SEAL. This is a mission. Get your shit together, sailor.

I gave a polite nod to each of them. Augie's aunt Prima was hands down the friendliest person there, but it was a bit like going to the mean girls' table in the lunchroom and picking the least bitchy of the bunch.

"And you are...?" she asked with a big smile. I noticed her hand had gone limp from the sheer weight of the diamond ring on her finger. The man I assumed was Augie's uncle Eric stood a few feet behind her looking bored.

Augie's jaw ticked. "I just told you who he is. His name is Saint Wilde. He works for Landen Safekeeping, who I hired for security."

A younger version of Augie's uncle Eric scoffed. "Pfft. Little cuz has himself a bodyguard? It's about time. You could have used one of those back in school, eh, Augustine?"

I turned to face the jackass spewing schoolyard bully crap. Thank fuck I was at least five inches taller than he was and a good forty pounds of muscle stronger.

"I beg your pardon?" I asked in a low voice through my teeth. Without thinking, I'd stepped between the asshole and Augie.

Augie reached out to squeeze my arm. "Ignore him, please." His voice was soft enough for me to hear it but barely.

"His name is August," I corrected. "Or Augie. Or even Mr. Stiel."

Instead of getting angry at me for not keeping my cool, Augie puffed out a laugh. "That's okay, Saint. Brett's not really one to talk. His name stands for—"

"Fine! You win," Brett snapped. "Tell your babysitter to stand down for god's sake. It was just a joke."

"Where's Grandfather?" Augie asked his asshole cousin.

"In his study. He'll be out for dinner."

"I'm going to go say hello," Augie said, nudging me toward an archway that led to a quiet hallway. I knew he was anxious to speak to his grandfather about the information we'd found in the box.

We wandered past a few open doorways until coming to the door to a dark-paneled study.

"Brett, is that you?" The old man's voice sounded weaker than I expected.

"No, it's August," Augie called out, knocking a knuckle against the doorjamb before walking in. Augie took a seat in an armchair in front of Mr. Stiel's desk while I stayed back by the door. As soon as Augie realized I wasn't in the chair next to him, he looked back at me in frustration. "Get over here."

I quickly joined him in front of the desk but didn't sit yet. "Saint Wilde, sir. Nice to see you again," I said to Augie's grandfather. He looked at me in confusion.

"Have we met?"

"Yes, sir, briefly in Augie's driveway."

"Oh, sorry. Are you Augie's... ahem, *boyfriend?*"

He looked like he was trying his hardest to be cool with the term, but he clearly wasn't.

"Uh…" I looked at Augie for help. He was busy studying his grandfather as if seeing him with new eyes.

"Yes, Grandfather. Saint and I are dating."

I could hear the tremor in his voice, but his words were sure. I was so fucking proud of him, I wanted to grab him and squeeze him before whisking him away to do sexy things to his naked body.

"Navy man, am I right?"

"Yes, sir. Ten years. I'm in personal security now."

For a brief moment, he seemed more lucid. He locked eyes with me and pointed a shaky index finger at me. "You take care of my boy. He deserves the best."

Augie's soft inhalation of surprise broke my heart. Those shouldn't have been words that surprised him.

"I agree completely. I won't let you down," I promised in a rough voice. "He's an incredible person."

Jonathan Stiel seemed to deflate. "My sister told me to take special care of him. I miss her."

Augie glanced at me with devastation on his face. I took the risk of reaching for his hand, slowly and without bringing attention to it. Mr. Stiel wouldn't have been able to see below the level of his desk even if he'd been completely lucid.

"I miss her too, Grandfather. She was something special. Remember when she made you hang that pinecone wind chime?" he asked with a smile.

"She didn't make me hang it. You made it, so I hung it. Didn't make pretty noise, but it seemed to put a smile on your face anyway."

Augie's lips froze partway open. This wasn't the cold grandfather he'd described to me. Clearly his dementia had brought about changes in his personality or perhaps lowered his inhibitions.

I leaned forward. "How did Augie get into antiques? Was that because of Melody?"

He tapped his chin with a finger. "I took him to something at the Majestic… what was it? The symphony?"

"*Mamma Mia,*" Augie murmured.

"He was enraptured by the music and the historical surroundings. I remember he saw…"

"The giant chandelier," Augie added. "And all the gilt everywhere."

"Yes," Mr. Stiel said with a nod. "That's it. His eyes were like saucers."

Augie looked at me. "It was twelve days after my father died and the first time I felt the magic of stepping into the past."

I stared at him—this brave man who'd made his way through a childhood trauma with little support, who'd found a way to self-soothe and escape. I was in awe of him. He was the most gentle soul I knew.

After squeezing his hand, I let go and stood. "May we escort you into dinner, sir?"

Augie met my eye and nodded. We both knew there was no helpful information to be had by bringing up the property puzzle with him tonight. He was stuck somewhere in the past at the moment, and I could tell Augie wanted to leave him there as long as he seemed calm and settled.

"Dinner. Yes. I believe Melody has instructed the chef to make stroganoff. She knows I despise it," Mr. Stiel grumbled. "Do you have a sister, Mr. Wilde?"

"Please call me Saint, sir. And yes. I have a twin sister and three others. I'm one of ten, if you can believe it."

He came around to the front of the desk to join us by the door. "Ah, your parents are Catholic maybe. Or simply gluttons for punishment."

As we walked out toward the main part of the house, I chuckled. "A little of both, I think. My father traveled quite a bit for his job, so I think they took advantage of his visits home. Luckily my grandfathers lived on the same property. They helped my mother raise us."

"And were your grandfathers navy men as well?"

"No, sir. Army. But I try not to give them hell about it too much."

That got a smile out of him. "They must be proud of you, Saint."

I felt a kind of validation that was rarely put into words. There was no doubt my family loved me and supported me, but hearing this important, powerful man imply I was worthy gave me a sudden sense of relief. Maybe I was worthy of his grandson after all.

"I hope so," I said.

He studied me for a long moment. "Yes. Yes indeed. I want you to take this." He reached into the collar of his shirt and pulled out a chain identical to the one Augie wore. It even had the same tiny antique key.

"Grandfather?" Augie asked in surprise.

"Keep him safe," he said to me.

"With my life," I said roughly.

Mr. Stiel took the necklace off and placed it around my neck, tucking it under the collar of my dress shirt. I wasn't sure whether or not to accept it, so I looked to Augie. His eyes were shiny, and he nodded at me.

"Thank you, sir."

"Mm. That will do nicely. If only Melody were here to see what a fine man our August has grown into, yes?"

I nodded while Augie looked down at his hands clasped in front of him.

As we exited the hallway into the foyer, the older man's brows creased. "Do you know my grandsons?"

I glanced at Augie. "Yes, sir. I'm here tonight with August. I met Brett a few minutes ago in the living room."

"Mmpf. Well, we'll not talk business at the table tonight, do you understand?"

"Yes... sir..."

Augie stepped around me to place a hand on his grandfather's back. We were almost to the living room where I could hear quiet chatter.

Mr. Stiel turned to him. "Brett is going to bring up that housing project again. He's like a bulldog, that one. Won't let it go."

Augie glanced over his shoulder at me before turning back to his grandfather. "What housing project?"

"Wants me to donate another building to his pet charity. I told him

I'd consider it, but I refuse to talk business at the table. Do you understand?"

Augie cleared his throat. "Yes, sir."

Once we entered the room, the rest of the occupants made comments about holding dinner back while we took our sweet time. The Stiels were a lovely bunch.

After Augie helped Mr. Stiel to the head of the long table in the formal dining room and got him situated, he turned to gesture to where he wanted me to sit.

"You've got to be kidding," Brett drawled. "He's not eating at the table with us. Shouldn't he be standing against the wall or something?"

I could see Augie take a breath. It took everything I had not to manage this situation for him, but I somehow kept my mouth shut.

"Brett, Saint is here as my guest. He is not being paid to be here. He will sit next to me at our table."

I did as he said after making sure Augie's seat was pushed in to his liking and helping his Aunt Prima with the same. Eric helped Augie's mom with her chair at the foot of the table before taking his own seat opposite his wife. Brett landed heavily in his own chair next to his dad without a care in the world for the two women at the table. Doc would have nudged his leg under the table and given him A Look for forgetting basic manners.

An attractive young woman in a waitress uniform came out from a door in the corner of the room and began to serve wine. This was quickly followed by a salad course during which there was little to no talking.

It was the complete opposite of dinner at my own grandfathers' house.

Finally, when the salad plates were being removed, Diane Stiel spoke up. "August, did you wish your aunt Prima a happy birthday?"

Everyone at the table looked from mother to son.

"Ah, yes. When I came in. Did you have a nice time at your charity dinner, Aunt Prima? A fashion show, right?"

Prima finished wiping the sides of her mouth with the delicate cloth napkin before tucking it back in her lap. "Yes, thank you. The Dallas Women's Society raised over a hundred thousand dollars for the Dallas Afterschool programs, the Texas Hunger Initiative, and... oh, something else. Orphans or something, I don't remember. But the best part of the night were the gowns. You should have seen how beautiful they were."

I was grateful there hadn't been any food or drink in my mouth when I snorted. At first, I thought she was joking, but I could see by the looks on everyone else's faces she wasn't.

"Oh, tell me about them," Diane exclaimed. "Also, Laura told me to ask you what Beverly Sitton was wearing. All I heard is that she looked like a bloated banana."

Prima's eyebrows lifted. "A *bunch* of bananas, maybe. That tummy tuck didn't take. And did you hear about Savannah Hews? She dropped her clutch in the center of the grand foyer and out spilled every kind of narcotic known to man."

The two ladies tittered over that poor woman's bad luck while I sympathized with the woman who needed prescription courage to make it through a Dallas society event like that. It made complete sense why she needed to be medicated.

"Mother," Augie urged, sitting back to allow his dinner to be set in front of him. He murmured a quick thank-you to the server before focusing back on his mother. "You don't know the woman's story. Maybe she has chronic pain."

Diane Stiel shot her son a look. "Her chronic pain's name is Lowell, and if she didn't want it, she should have divorced him years ago."

"Can't argue with that," Mr. Stiel added from the head of the table. "One good side effect of having retired—not having to see that putz in the office anymore."

Augie's fork clattered to his plate. "Since when are you retired?"

"August," Eric snapped. "Mind your manners."

"Since the diagnosis three months ago," Diane said with a sniff. "We didn't want to tell you."

We both turned to Augie's grandfather at the end of the table, but he was looking down at his plate.

"Diagnosis?" Augie asked in a strangled voice. "Is it... is it Alzheimer's?"

"Vascular dementia, dear," Prima said, reaching over to pat Augie's hand. His other hand shot out under the table to grab for mine. I caught it and held tight, letting him know he wasn't alone. Even though he'd known about the dementia, hearing an official diagnosis somehow made it more real. "He's had some mini strokes in the past six months. That's how they discovered it."

"Complete nonsense," the elder Mr. Stiel added in a stern voice. It was the kind of voice he'd probably used hundreds of times in boardrooms over the years. "I'm fine. It was simply time. And Eric has been in charge for many years anyway. What do they need an old man around for? I've served my time."

His voice softened as he mumbled something about playing more golf, but everyone seemed to ignore him after that.

Diane sat forward. "Augie, there's something I'd like to discuss with you since we have you here."

I kept a hold of Augie's hand under the table, resting our joined hands on my leg.

"Is it about Grandfather? Do you want me to move back and help?"

My heart jumped at the suggestion. Just when I thought I was moving to Hobie to be near him, he might move back to Dallas? Well, I guessed I could stay in Dallas and continue my work for Lanny. But that would mean travel again. Time away from Augie.

I didn't want that.

But I would do whatever he needed me to do to support him.

"No, no. It's... well, yes. It's a little bit about Dad, I guess." Diane glanced at her brother Eric, who nodded encouragingly. "Eric and I would like to help you purchase a better retail space for your antique shop."

"That's awfully nice of you," Mr. Stiel added. "Of course I'll help any way I can. You know I support you, August."

Augie looked from his grandfather back to his mother. "But I don't need a better retail space. I'm happy where I am. I love my shop."

"Oh, honey, it's a dusty old place," Diane said. "Don't you want a nice, modern..." She seemed to catch herself. "I mean, wouldn't it be better if you had a larger space with plenty of sunlight to show off your treasures?"

Even I knew antiques didn't fare well in sunlight. Augie's current shop had special film on the window glass to protect the antiques inside from harmful UV light.

"What's this really about?" I asked.

Eric sighed. "This doesn't concern you, son."

"If it concerns Augie, it concerns me. I think it's time to get everything out on the table here."

"Who is this bozo?" Brett said with a laugh. "Dude, none of this is your business. You're a fucking fitness instructor."

I felt Augie's hand go rigid in my grasp. He yanked it out and stood, placing both hands on the table and leaning in. "He's a personal security specialist and happens to also be my boyfriend! That's right. Saint is my boyfriend, and he deserves respect. He's right. If it concerns me, it concerns him. I have no secrets from Saint, and I trust him with my life. Now tell me what the hell is going on with my shop."

Diane sighed and shook her head. Eric and Prima stared openmouthed. Brett's face twisted into something ugly, and Mr. Stiel seemed more interested in his roasted potatoes than the fact his grandson had just bolted out of the closet and into the light.

I reached out slowly to place a hand on his back. He turned to me with an exasperated expression. "What the hell, Saint? Has the whole world gone mad? Why am I still part of this ridiculous family?"

"Because you're loyal and kind. You want to think the best of everyone," I said calmly.

"I'm an idiot."

"You're a star," I said with a smile. "A brave, beautiful star."

He chuckled at that. "You're blind."

"Maybe."

"I've always wanted a gay friend," Prima said with a grin. "Does this mean we can go shopping together? I'll bet you'd never have put Beverly Sitton in yellow neoprene. What would you have picked? She has red hair and god-awful freckles."

Augie was right—his family was ridiculous.

"Can we skip this nonsense and talk business?" Eric asked, exasperated. "This deal needs to get done. I have people crawling all over me to make this happen."

A fist slammed down on the table. The elder Mr. Stiel's face was purple with rage.

"I said no talk of business at the table!"

The rest of the meal was spent in silence. I'd never spent so much time mentally thanking my family for being batshit fucking crazy.

It was after we'd moved to the living room that the truth finally came out.

CHAPTER 35

AUGIE

AFTER COMING OUT IN A BLAZE OF GLORY AT THE TABLE, I SPENT THE rest of the meal shaking like Jell-O in an earthquake. Brett shot me snide looks from across the table, Uncle Eric's jaw tightened to the point of cracking teeth, and my mother let out a put-upon sigh every few minutes.

Thankfully, Prima asked the server to move dessert and coffee into the living room so we could cut the painful portion of the meal short.

It still took fucking forever.

Through it all, Saint was so calm and settled I wondered if he was raking a Zen sand garden in his mind. How the hell could he be so chill when I was about to vomit across the table from nerves? There'd been absolutely no fallout yet from my big announcement. I waited for the judgment from my mother and uncle, not to mention the awful teasing Brett was sure to do when he got me alone.

When we moved to the living room, I chose a small love seat next to the big gas fireplace. I remembered spending hours in front of the mesmerizing flames when I was fifteen and home from school for Christmas break. It had been so soothing to stare into the fire and daydream about another life, another time. That was the same winter I'd discovered my grandfather's set of Agatha Christie's mystery novels. I devoured as many as I could get my hands on and then watched the movies too.

"Want me to ask if they have chocolate syrup in the kitchen?" Saint murmured next to my ear. I looked up to see the same server from before pouring coffee. "I could mix it in and make a mocha?"

My heart nearly toppled out of my chest.

"I love you," I whispered.

Saint's eyes widened in surprise. He wasn't the only one. That hadn't been the way I'd imagined telling him.

"I'm sorry," I spluttered.

"Why are you sorry, sweetheart?" His voice was still low enough that no one could hear what he was saying.

"I didn't mean to tell you for the first time here... where I can't... where..."

"Tell you what," he said with a growing smile. The little twisted tooth grounded me and reminded me that he wasn't some perfect untouchable model. He was *real*. "I'll save mine until we're somewhere by ourselves. Then we can do whatever it is you want to do right now but can't."

The look on his face made my heart stutter even worse. He was so sexy and so thoughtful. It was a lethal combination. "Yes. Good. Please. Yes."

Saint pressed his lips together to keep from laughing.

"Shut up," I mumbled. "The kitchen is through there. Go tell that woman you'll do anything for chocolate."

"Anything?" he asked with a raised brow.

He was so damned cute. Before I could growl a warning at him, I heard my sister's laughter from the direction of the front door.

"We're here!" she called.

"Who's 'we,' darling?" Mother called out before catching sight of Saint making his escape toward the kitchen. "Tonight must be the night for uninvited guests."

"Aurora and Kat," Rory called back, rushing into the room in front of her girlfriend. "I, ah, figured since Augie was going to be here, I'd swing by and pick up—"

HIS SAINT

"Rory," I said, interrupting. "I brought Saint. And, ah..."

"He told us he's a fag," Brett said. "Big surprise."

Rory's nostrils flared and she lurched toward our cousin with her claws extended. "You little—"

"Rory!" Kat caught her around her waist and kept her from attacking Brett.

"Let me go! He can't say things like that. He can't, Kat."

"I know, dear. But I'd rather not have to visit you in jail. The optics on that would be terrible."

"Aurora Stiel, sit down," my mother insisted from her spot on a nearby arm chair. "We were just getting ready to discuss an important business matter with your brother."

I noticed Saint race back into the room quickly, looking around to assess the situation. He must have heard the yelling.

"Katrina, Rory, nice to see you again," he said when he didn't detect a foreign invasion. He returned to the spot next to me and pulled a little white packet from his trouser pocket. Hot cocoa mix.

"Best I could do," he said softly, handing it to me. "I have chocolate syrup at my apartment, so you can have a true mocha in the morning."

I swallowed. He'd mentioned us staying over at his apartment downtown rather than driving back to Hobie, but I'd told him I usually stayed here at the house in my old room.

I kind of loved him mentioning his apartment again as if the decision was out of my hands. I'd begun to notice his bossiness usually centered on protecting me or giving me pleasure in bed, both of which I was absolutely on board with.

"Perfect," I said. "Thank you."

After accepting his own coffee from the server, Uncle Eric sat back in his chair. "August, we'd like your help convincing Dad to donate the building your shop is currently in to a charity project Brett and I have been working on. One of the foundation's beneficiaries—"

"I know about CSP," I said.

Eric looked surprised. "Oh, well, yes. CSP creates low-income housing which is—"

At this, Saint was the one who interrupted. "I'm going to stop you

251

right there, Eric. There's no way the powers that be in Hobie are going to let anyone put low-income housing right on the town square."

"That's as may be, but we'd like to give them a chance to try. Until we can get the property under their ownership, they can't even attempt it."

Saint sounded annoyed. "So you want Augie to find a new space, sign a lease with another location, and move everything out of his shop on the off chance Hobie's town planners will approve a ridiculous plan for low-income housing on the square?"

Brett jumped in. "This is really none of your damned business. Do you even have a college degree? Because we're talking about complex real estate investment deals and not how many steel plates you managed to bench-press at the gym."

Saint took a breath to remain calm. The smile on his face was glacial and his voice was smooth as silk. "My father is the global director of Winstone Capital. He manages $500 *billion* dollars worth of 'complex real estate investment deals' all over the world and also had a hand in facilitating my grandfathers' multimillion-dollar investment specifically into Hobie real estate. I'd say I have a passing knowledge of what we're talking about here."

Mr. Stiel chuckled from where he stood by the fireplace. "Brett, Saint here was a navy SEAL. Takes more than a big lung capacity to pass those tests. Stop being an ass."

Rory moved around to give Grandfather a quick hug before leading him to a chair so he could sit. She proceeded to fix him a coffee and piece of cake from the tray on the side table.

I looked to my uncle. "Eric, why this particular piece of property? Why not look for something more affordable and appropriate to donate to CSP? Maybe even something in a location near the elementary school or the hospital?"

"We already own all three properties in question," Eric explained.

"Not true," Grandfather muttered. "The company owns one, I own one, and CSP owns one. Three different owners."

"Yes, but my dad is in charge of the company's assets," Brett said, gesturing to Eric. "Grandfather, you can sign over the one you own, and CSP already has the third."

I wondered if I should just agree. Was my current building worth fighting for? I loved it, but shouldn't I love my family more? Why not just step away, move my shop, and be done with this whole family conflict?

But did I love my family enough to support such a massive fraud on the taxpayers of Hobie? Could I abide a quasi-charity taking a donation from my family foundation and using it to take advantage of tax loopholes? The answer was no.

"Why in the world would I support the efforts of a fraudulent nonprofit?" I asked Eric. "And why, specifically, do you want our family foundation to support this particular charity with such a high-value donation?"

"Dammit, Augie, we don't have to explain this shit to you. You're a tenant for Christ's sake," Brett said. "We just need you to convince Grandfather you're willing to move your shop."

Saint sat still next to me with his hands clasped together in his lap. I wanted to ask him what I should do or simply lay my head on his shoulder and have him take over for me. I was tired of being the odd man out in my family. I hated making important decisions on my own. Moreover, I'd always disliked being in charge of anything.

But I also hated being *bullied* by anyone, especially my own family.

"I'm not willing to move my shop." There, I'd said it.

Everyone stared at me, presumably trying to work out how quickly I'd cave under pressure.

"But darling," Mother said. "Think of all the people who would be helped by this project."

"What people?" Saint asked. "Hobie's poverty rate is less than 8 percent. That's unheard of in rural Texas. It's an affluent town because of the lake property, whereas the people who need low-income housing live in nearby Valley Cross. Why not do this project there? I'll tell you why—there's no low-income housing project. It's a sham."

Eric chimed in. "Hardly. Besides, we don't determine the best places. CSP does that. We're just the benefactors."

"Why is this particular project so important?" I asked. I wanted to hear them say it.

Eric clenched his teeth and looked away. Brett took over.

"Look, Augie. We made a commitment to this nonprofit to assist them in putting together this package. How does it look to the nonprofit community if we fail to deliver on that commitment?"

"Why this building in particular?"

"Because CSP's plan involves combining all three lots for their housing project," Brett explained.

"So they plan to raze the Depot?" I asked incredulously. Jen's shop was in the town's original train station. The charm was half of what made Apple Dots so special. "That's even older than the Huddler building." My shop's building had been originally built by Cletus Huddler to house his construction business in Hobie. I even had two of the original drafting tables left from the original business assets in the third-floor storage space.

The warmth of Saint's body came through the leg of my pants as he moved a little closer to me.

"The Depot?" Grandfather asked in surprise. "Eric, you didn't tell me they planned to tear down that historic station."

"They don't even provide low-income housing," I snapped. "They're a sham. They're a front for a commercial developer. Did you know that?"

"That's not true, son," Eric stated immediately. "I don't know what information you think you have, but CSP is a registered nonprofit that specializes in low-income housing."

"That's what they say," Saint added. "But their actual property transactions show a full history of putting together commercial development packages for strip malls. Eight of their last ten projects included a Health Plus drug store, a Ship and Save mailing center, and a Starbucks."

"What?" My mother suddenly looked confused. "Is that true?"

"Dammit, Eric!" Grandfather barked. "What the hell are you thinking?"

"Dad, it's a multimillion-dollar property deal. It's a low-income housing project to help those in need, and we need the Huddler building to make it happen. Augie, I'm ashamed of you. Since when are you so goddamned selfish?"

I sat there with my mouth open, but Saint didn't have the same problem.

"How dare you call him selfish," Saint boomed, standing up from his seat. "Do you have any idea the lengths this man has gone to in order to accommodate this family? You say jump, he asks how high. You say don't be gay, he keeps his whole life in shadow. You say dinner's on, he drops everything to get here for it just to find out it's canceled and no one bothered to say. He lost his father!" He looked at Rory. "They both did. They lost their father, and you all told them to stop fucking crying. Who does that?"

He turned to me with utter anguish in his eyes. "Augie, we're leaving. I can't let you stay here a minute longer. I can't."

I stood up and took his hand, turning to my grandfather with an apologetic look. "Thank you for dinner." I turned to Aunt Prima. "Happy Birthday." And finally to my mother. "Goodnight, Mother."

Then I followed Saint to where Rory sat next to Kat and gave them each a hug after Saint dropped a kiss on each of their cheeks.

My sister whispered hoarsely in my ear. "Tie him down if you have to, brother of mine. That man's a keeper."

She had no idea.

CHAPTER 36

SAINT

Brett followed us into the driveway, begging us to come back in and listen. After getting Augie seated in the truck, I turned to Brett.

"Listen, asshole. We know about your scam. You're in this bullshit up to your ears, and you're going to get caught. Leave Augie alone, or both of us are going to the police to give them the evidence we have about CSP and Stiel. Got it?"

Brett stared at me in surprise before stammering out a reply. "I d-don't know what you think you have on me, but I've done nothing wrong!"

"I have a little USB drive of my own that says otherwise," I lied. Really it was information Rex and Skipper had at Landen. "So stay the hell away from Augie and find another property to fuck up with your illegal schemes."

He didn't say anything, so I leaned closer, meeting his eyes so he got the message loud and clear. "And that USB drive lives on my person. Come for it, Brett. I dare you."

I turned around and stormed to the driver's side before pulling out of the iron gates.

During most of the drive back to Hobie, I simmered with rage. I knew if I opened my mouth, I'd lash out at the nearest target which unfortunately was the person who least deserved it. When I finally got my head out of my ass, I pulled onto the side of the quiet highway and got out of the truck to walk around to the passenger side.

I opened the door and unclipped Augie's seat belt before pulling him out of the truck and into my arms. Augie buried his face in my neck and breathed in. Just the feel of him in my embrace calmed me immediately. How had I ever thought I could live without someone to love? How had I ever believed it was better to avoid relationships than to risk loss? Even if I only got minutes with Augie, they'd be worth any amount of pain at losing him.

I pulled back and cupped his cheeks.

"I love you so much," I said. "I am so fucking proud of you. And I'm sorry."

"Why are you sorry?"

I felt my face light up in a smile just for him. "Because I didn't do much better than you. I dropped the L-bomb in a cow pasture for god's sake."

Now it was his turn to grin. "It's perfect. Just you and me. And the giant piles of pungent poop. What man can ask for more?"

I leaned in and kissed him softly before pulling back again. His lips were so soft, I could have kept my mouth against them all night. "Are you angry with me?"

"Christ, no. What for?"

"For dragging you out of there by your hair while I might as well have been brandishing a club in my other hand," I admitted. "It wasn't very elegant."

Augie swallowed and turned us around, nudging me until I sat down on the passenger seat and he could stand between my open legs. He kept his arms around my neck.

"No one has ever stood up for me like that to my family," he said. "Or made me believe I deserved better than being treated that way. I felt so loved and cared for when you did that, Saint."

"I didn't want to stay in the city after that," I admitted. "I hope you're okay with us going home to Hobie."

His smile grew. "Only if we're going to the same place and sleeping in the same bed."

My heart soared. "Damned skippy. Your place okay? If we go to the bunkhouse, my family is going to be all up in our business before the rooster crows."

He nodded. "But maybe… maybe we could still go to the ranch for the chili thing tomorrow night?"

I smirked at him. "You sure you're going to be hungry? You're not really a chili fan. And bonfires are hella dangerous."

Augie pinched me under the arm.

"Yeow! What was that for?" I asked through the laughter.

"I was nervous before. I didn't know what you thought about me. I felt… I felt temporary."

I let the laughter die. "Not if I have anything to say about it. I'm through with temporary things. It's time for both of us to settle in. What do you say? I know it's soon, Augie, but… I'm ready."

"Are you really going to consider running Twist with Neckie?"

The familiar tumble of nerves returned to my stomach, but I recognized it for the excitement that comes with change. "I am. Did I ever tell you that I was in charge of PT on my team when I was in the navy? I fucking loved being on the Grinder."

"I don't know what any of those words mean," Augie said. "But I guess it has something to do with being a frogger?"

I snorted. "Frogman. And now I'm going to have to put you in my pocket because you're so fucking cute."

He rolled his eyes but simultaneously crawled onto my lap and ground his erection into my belly. "Talk navy to me, frogman."

"That's not sexy," I said, wrapping my arms around him and cupping his butt. "But your little ass in my hands sure is. And while we're on the subject of this hot body, I need you to promise me no more Grindr hookups. The app stays in the app trash. Got it?"

"Why would I need Grindr when I have you?" he asked in my ear before latching his teeth onto my lobe. "Saint… I want you to fuck me. I want to squeeze myself around your cock and see if I can make you scream."

Dear god.

"Sss-sounds acceptable," I hissed. His hands had pulled my shirt tail out and snuck up inside to pluck my nipples with cold hands. All of the nearby skin puckered in response. "Baby, let's... I don't know if I can..."

I'd intended to tell him we should continue on to his house where we would be more comfortable, but the *whoop-whoop* of a law enforcement vehicle split the night and blue-and-white lights began strobing everywhere. I stood up and set Augie behind me before peering toward the vehicle behind us.

"Saint-Michel-des-Saints Cupcake Wilde, spread your legs and—"

I recognized my brother Otto's voice immediately.

"Asshole!" I yelled. I couldn't see him or Seth past the headlights of Seth's sheriff SUV, but I knew the two of them were getting a kick out of coming across us on the side of the road.

"Public indecency," came the cry from the opening passenger door. "Vehicular necking. Contributing to the delinquency of a minor."

"Hey!" Augie scoffed. "Take that back. I'm only three years younger than Cupcake here."

"You know that's not my real middle name, right?" I asked, putting my arm around him and pulling him into my side.

"It is now," he said, grinning up at me.

Seth came around from the driver's side and reached out a hand to shake. "Forgive me. He's a little tipsy. We went to dinner at Sweet Boy's in Bowie for meatloaf and cobbler, but then he talked me into stopping at the pool hall for some pitchers of beer."

Otto flashed a shit-eating grin. "Guess who got to drink the pitchers?"

"I'm guessing not the law enforcement officer?" I said with a laugh.

"You guessed right. It was me," Otto said a smidge too loudly. "And now he said I can fuck him and be really noisy when we get home since Tishie's at her mom's."

Seth smacked his chest with a laugh. "Shut the fuck up, Wilde Man. Or the offer gets rescinded."

"You wouldn't dare."

"Get in the car, Otto," Seth said. "If you haven't passed out by the time we get home, you can try your best to show me what you got." He winked at us and mouthed *too drunk to fuck.*

I smiled and chuckled as Otto did an about-face and got his ass back into the SUV.

"Be safe, brother," Seth said, making my heart feel full. Seth Walker had felt like family since he and Otto had become best friends in elementary or middle school. Now that they were actually married, it was finally legal. "Augie, take care."

After waving them off, we got back in the truck and headed the rest of the way to Augie's in comfortable silence.

It wasn't until two hours after falling asleep curled around Augie that Skipper's text came through on my phone. The *ping* woke me up out of a dead sleep because I'd forgotten to put my phone on night mode.

Skipper: *Sorry it took so long. Owners of CSP shell corp are listed as Duvall and Kohli. That was a shifty maze of shit. Emailing you deets.*

The names rang a bell, but I couldn't place them for a few seconds until my brain fully came online.

Duvall.

As in Katrina Duvall? Was it her father or a brother? Or could it be a coincidence?

Augie shifted in his sleep and snuggled closer. I guided his head onto my shoulder and wrapped my arm around him before playing with his hair with my fingers.

Could Kat be involved in this? Could Rory? No. No way would Rory do anything to harm Augie.

I debated whether or not to wake him up so I could ask him about Marco. But he'd had a rough night, so I decided to let him sleep.

～

I came awake again to the sound of breaking glass. It was muffled, but I'd spent way too many hours on special forces missions to sleep through a sound like that.

"Augie," I whispered, shaking him. "Baby, wake up. I think someone's breaking in again."

"Wha? Saint?" He looked adorably confused, but I needed him alert and on the move. I reached for my trousers and slipped them on. I was pretty sure my shoes were in the living room or kitchen.

"Babe, I need you to find a place to hide while I get my weapon. It's in the truck. Can you do that? Take your phone and call 911. I'll call Seth."

"Saint? Fuck. I don't…" He shook his head to clear it. "Yeah, go."

"Remember what I taught you. The best way to stay alive is to stay away."

He was already stumbling out of bed but turned to me and nodded before heading to the closet. I knew he had an attic space above since that's where he'd hidden the writing slope earlier. If I'd known what or who was outside, I would have forced him out the bedroom window with me. But for all I knew, they were still out there while we were in here. I locked the bedroom door closed and jammed some kind of decorative metal crab under the jamb as a kind of doorstop. It wouldn't stop them, but it might slow them down enough for me to get there with my weapon.

I made my way out the window into the freezing night air. It wasn't like me to leave my truck unlocked with the weapon inside. Hell, it wasn't like me to leave the weapon inside either. But we were in the middle of nowhere, and Augie was terrified of guns. I'd planned on coming back out to get it after he was asleep. So much for that plan.

Scattered rocks in the lawn poked hard into my bare feet. I noticed a white sedan in the drive behind my truck, and the front door of the house was hanging wide open. Why hadn't the damned alarm gone off? Had we forgotten to set it? Had we seriously been that horny? I deserved to be fucking fired.

I tried not to worry about Augie alone and scared in the closet. Just the thought of him at anyone's mercy made me see red.

This was all my fault. If the intruder was Brett, I might as well have waved a red cape in front of him before we left.

After making sure the coast was clear, I raced to the passenger-side door of my truck and eased it open. The dome light went on, so I lurched up to click it off as soon as I could.

I reached for the Glock 19, anxious to feel the familiar comfort of the pistol grip in my hand. It wasn't there. The memory of stashing it in the locked box in the bed of the truck came rushing back. I quickly grabbed the extra magazines of ammo deep in the storage bin before sneaking around to get the gun out of the tool box. Once I'd checked the chamber and pocketed the two extra magazines, I squat-ran across to the front door and peeked in. I could hear someone moving around, but I couldn't swear it was only one person inside.

Quick decisions were something I'd learned had to come from your gut. I took two steps away from the front door and pulled my phone out of my pocket before pressing the speed dial button for Otto.

"Don't say anything," I hissed before he had a chance to bitch me out for the middle-of-the-night call. "Burglary at Augie's."

I heard a quick grunt which I assumed was him hitting Seth awake. After quickly setting the phone on the ground so the light wouldn't come on inside the dark house and rat me out, I slipped back to the door.

Suddenly the loud sound of someone banging on a door cut through the night. I rushed in on quiet feet and followed the sounds to the bedroom door.

Two men stood outside the door. One was Brett and the other one was a darker-haired man with olive skin.

Both men had weapons held at their side. The hallway was dark, but it looked like one of the men held a phone out using its flashlight function.

Brett took a kick at the door, bouncing back and almost stumbling into the wall opposite.

Stupid bastard had obviously never done this before. He was a paper pusher for god's sake. These guys were idiots. I took aim on the one who wasn't Brett. Augie had told me a story about Brett being a terrible shot, so I made a calculated decision to worry more about the unknown gunman. This wasn't a covert mission where I could shoot at will or snap someone's neck. I was a private citizen. And one of the intruders was a blood relative of the homeowner.

"Drop your weapon," I said in a clear voice. "The sheriff is on his way."

Brett jumped and turned, firing immediately without even looking where he was shooting. I managed to duck back out of the hallway and hit the floor as bullets slammed into the wall and ceiling in the general area of where I'd been standing. Part of my brain scrambled to figure out where Augie was up there. Could he have been hit? Surely we would have heard a scream. I forced myself to focus.

"Drop your fucking weapon, asshole!" I yelled. "This doesn't end with you getting what you want. Too many people know. My boss at Landen knows all about Marco and CSP!"

I needed them to leave, to get far away from Augie. Obviously I wanted them arrested, but it was way more important to get them out of the house right now and away from the man trapped in the attic.

"Go now before the sheriff arrives," I suggested. "I won't follow you."

"He's lying, Marco," Brett said. "He's the only one with the proof. He told me so himself. We need that drive."

The other man spoke up, his words directed at me. "I'll shoot you now, claim you're the intruder, and then take the drive from your cold, dead body. Then I'll shoot Augie to get rid of the last witness."

I was such a fucking idiot telling him I had a USB drive. If I lived long enough to see Augie again, I'd have to tell him to dump my ass. No one deserved to be stuck with someone as reckless as I had been that night.

"Give us the drive," Marco barked. "Slide it over here and no one gets hurt."

I tucked in my chin and squeezed my eyes closed while silently cursing myself. Where the hell was there a USB drive in this house? Could I get to one in time to fake it? No. What the fuck could I do to get them away from Augie?

When I opened my eyes, the glint of metal reminded me of the key I now wore. It was the second key to the writing slope which was tucked safely away in the old floor safe.

"It's in a safe in the barn," I called out. My brain rushed to catch up with my mouth. "I have the key. I'll take you out there."

It didn't have a key. It had a combination, and I didn't know it. I'd politely looked away when Augie had stashed the box in there earlier in the week. I just needed them out of the fucking house.

"Prove it," Marco called out.

I slipped the key from around my neck and held it out in front of the open doorway to the hall. "The key. Brett probably knows about the safe in the barn. It's pink."

Brett mumbled sounds of agreement to his buddy.

"Go get it," the man shouted. "Go get it and come back."

"No deal," I ground out. "I'm not leaving you in here alone." We all knew the words I hadn't said.

Alone with Augie.

"Go get the goddamned drive!" the man shouted. "Or I'll bust this fucking door down and yank that scrawny ass out of his fucking bed and hold this gun to his head."

"He went out the window," I said, hopefully loudly enough for Augie to hear and make his way out of the damned house. "I'm sure he's intercepted the sheriff by now."

A gunshot rang out, and I hit the floor. I scrambled to the open doorway and peered around. There Marco stood aiming high into the bedroom door before taking another shot.

Brett screamed for him to stop. "You'll kill him!"

Now that he'd opened fire, I had no qualms shooting the fucker. I aimed at his right shoulder and took the shot. He screamed like a holy terror and dropped his weapon before crumpling to the ground in shock.

Brett turned and fired at me out of reflex, shooting wildly again into the walls and ceiling. I waited for his magazine to empty before rushing him and tackling him to the ground.

Footsteps thundered toward us from behind me. "Cross County Sheriff—drop your weapons!"

I recognized Seth's voice. "Two handguns not including mine. Both on the ground. Unsure of other weapons."

Until I was sure both guns were secured, I wasn't taking my hands off Brett Stiel's wrists where I had them pinned to his lower back.

As soon as Seth leaned over me to clip handcuffs on Brett, I jumped up and backed off. One of the sheriff deputies was dealing with Marco, who continued to scream in pain.

"He fucking shot me," he yelled. "Arrest him."

Seth gave me a look. "You know you have to come in and help us sort this shit out."

I was already trying to shoulder my way through the bedroom door when I grunted in agreement. The wood was splintered where bullet holes had torn chunks out of the thing, but it still stayed strong.

"Augie!" I called. "You can open the door now. It's safe."

I heard a muffled whimper and almost lost my damned mind.

"Shit," I muttered, turning to race out the front door and around to the window.

"Where's he going? He's getting away!" I heard Marco call from behind me.

I climbed into the window and scrambled to the closet. As soon as my first hand was on the rung, a dark splash of crimson fell on the back of it.

Blood.

"Augie," I cried up the ladder. "Are you hit?"

I climbed as fast as I could and pushed open the hatch. There, in the absolute farthest corner of the tiny nook, huddled my Augie in a tiny, trembling ball.

He lifted his head up to look at me.

His face was ice white and punctuated with huge, dark pupils. In the tiny space lit only by a few fairy lights glinting off golden keys, the bright red river of blood pouring down one side of his head stood out like a lit flare.

Augie blinked once, and then he hit the deck.

CHAPTER 37

AUGIE

Surviving gun violence wasn't something I'd expected to do more than once in my lifetime. When the first loud shots sounded through the house, my blood turned to sludge and darkness nudged the edge of my vision. The familiar loud *whoosh* sound roared through my ears again, and I felt myself shutting down.

Guns.

There were guns and gunmen in my house.

And Saint was out there somewhere with his own deadly weapon. What if they turned it against him? What if they outnumbered him?

My brain went to another place while I pressed myself into the corner of my hiding spot so firmly, I didn't even notice the exposed roofing nail by my head. As soon as the staccato pops of the second round of gunfire erupted, I threw my head to the side to get away from the sound and gouged my scalp with the nail. The pain was blinding—so much that I began to black out. I quickly sank to the floor so I wouldn't bump my head when I fainted. While I tried to get my brain jumpstarted, I watched the blood trickle down to the rough-hewn floorboards of the attic space over the closet.

It wasn't until I heard noises directly below me that I was able to scramble back to the corner and hide my face in my knees.

For some reason I didn't realize it was Saint at first. I stared at him blankly, trying to place the reason my heart felt tender and raw. The lights went out, and I tumbled forward. I vaguely recalled later that something about me losing my balance seemed to spur him into action. He lurched for me, bumping his head on the low roof before gathering me to him.

Everything ran together after that. There were murmured words of love and reassurance whispered into my ear, soft kisses pressed into the side of my face that didn't hurt like a bitch, and bright lights of a hospital corridor shooting daggers in my skull. Through it all, I was aware of a large, warm hand in mine. It never left my grip, no matter what harsh words were spoken or soft instructions given.

At one point I tried to swat at someone tugging on my scalp, but Saint's voice soothed me back to a place I could let the medicine take over. I drifted in and out until waking up fully to a hospital room filled with sunlight.

"Blinds," I croaked.

"You're blind?" Stevie's screech pierced my eardrums and caused me to wince, which shot arrows of pain into my skull.

"Get him out of here." Saint's voice wasn't happy. "He promised to be quiet."

"Steven," the fire chief warned in a low tone.

"Fuck," Stevie muttered. "Look at him though. He looks like Harry Potter. No amount of concealer is going to…" Someone must have shot him a look. "Anyway, could be worse I guess. At least it's not Mad-Eye Moody."

Charlie's soothing lilt came from the other side of the room. "Blinds as in window coverings. Hudson, love, pull those curtains closed. The man's head must be splitting wide open."

I winced again but tried opening my eyes slowly as the brightness behind my lids dimmed significantly. Saint's beautiful baby face was right in front of me, peering worriedly with his blue-gray eyes.

"Thank fuck," he breathed. "I missed you." He carefully moved to bury his face in my neck and inhale. I recognized it as a self-soothing gesture and hoped we had many years ahead of him finding comfort in me.

I brought my hands up to his shoulders, careful to watch the one with the IV in it. "You okay?" I asked. "I didn't do a good job of…" I paused to catch my breath. Saint leaned back to look at me. His fingers brushed my hair off my forehead. "I didn't protect you."

Saint huffed out a laugh. "You did perfect. You did exactly as I asked and trusted me to handle it. That was the best gift you could have given me. I'm the one who failed."

"You scraped the nail across my head?" I asked with a weak smile. "Funny, I thought that was me."

His big hand cupped the side of my face. "I thought you'd been shot. You scared me to death."

"Not shot. Allergic to guns, remember? My boyfriend told me to stay away from them. They're hazardous to your health." I tried smiling, but the short conversation had already worn me out. "Why so tired?" I asked under my breath.

"Shock," West said from the other side of the room. "You were pretty shocky when they brought you in. That's why we kept you overnight. You can go home this afternoon as long as someone keeps an eye on you for a couple of days. Don't underestimate the mental and emotional toll something like this takes on you, Augie."

"I'm not leaving his side," Saint said. "We're going to stay at Doc and Grandpa's until they're done fixing Augie's house. Doc's desperate to take care of him, and Grandpa is cooking everything except chili now. He even quizzed me on Augie's favorite foods so he could go grocery shopping before we get home."

I let myself drift off to the sound of Saint and our friends and family chatting about whether or not to still hold their chili dinner that night. I didn't have the energy to participate, but I was relieved when Charlie spoke up and said I'd be horrified if they changed their plans for me.

"He can stay snug as a tick in a back bedroom and doesn't need to spend any more time with you lot than necessary," he explained. "Best of both worlds, yeah?"

I woke up again to a room empty of everyone except Saint and my sister Rory. They were talking quietly next to the bed. Rory sat in the visitor chair with her legs drawn up beneath her while Saint crouched next to her with his arms folded on the arm of the chair.

They were talking about Marco.

I cleared my throat. "Water?"

Both of their gazes snapped up to me. "Hey, sleepyhead, how are you feeling?" Saint asked, moving toward me with an affectionate smile. He grabbed a cup from somewhere and held a straw to my mouth.

"Headache," I mumbled around the straw. "Itchy."

Rory straightened up and leaned toward me. "I get itchy from heavy pain meds. That's probably what it is."

"Or the stitches in your scalp," Saint added. "Gonna have a hot-as-hell scar there. My very own bad boy."

I reached up to feel where the bandage was. It covered the edge of my hairline and part of my forehead. I hoped it didn't leave an ugly bald spot in my hair.

Saint leaned in close and grabbed the hand messing with the bandage. "I'm kidding, babe. It's deep but small. West thinks at most you'll have a half-inch line on the very edge of your forehead. It'll be fine. And since you're not in the market for picking up guys anymore..." He winked at me before dropping a kiss on the unbandaged side of my forehead.

"Tell me about Marco," I said when he pulled back.

Rory stood and came closer to the bed so she could reach for my hand. Saint moved around to the other side and slid onto the bed beside me, lying on his side with an arm around my waist so he could face Rory. Feeling him so close to me was soothing. I thought maybe I was finally beginning to trust he was really in this with me.

"I'm so sorry, Augie," Rory said. "I promise I didn't know."

Saint twisted around and came back with my glasses, slipping them gently onto my face. Suddenly, I could see my sister's red-rimmed eyes and tear tracks down her face.

"Of course you didn't," I said. "Why are you so upset? Where's Kat?"

"She was in on it," she said in a shaky voice. Tears spilled over and washed down her cheeks. "She was using me. Using us."

I reached out a hand to her and grabbed onto her own cold fingers. "Shit. Oh god. Rory, I'm so sorry. Are you sure?"

Saint's grunt of disgusted confirmation was all I needed to hear to know it was true.

"Their father started CSP and brought Marco on right after graduation. I remember hearing he was working for a nonprofit, but I guess I just assumed it was... I don't know. I remember when Kat started suggesting beneficiaries for foundation donations. It started off with obvious ones like the Children's Cancer Initiative, but then she suggested an organization that specialized in low-income housing. I finally put her in touch with Brett and Uncle Eric since they worked with the foundation more directly. I had no idea CSP was her family. Or that they were not a true nonprofit."

"But why? I don't understand what Brett and Eric had to gain. Don't they already have enough money? Why get involved in this?"

My throat felt dry, so I gestured to the water cup on the table again. Rory handed it to me and helped keep it steady.

Saint was the one who answered. "It's early still, but thankfully Brett couldn't keep his mouth shut. Apparently, Marco and his dad have Eric and Brett over a barrel. The Duvalls threatened Eric and Brett to make this deal happen or he'd expose them for their involvement in CSP."

My head hurt just thinking about the complexity of the situation. I gingerly laid my head back on Saint's shoulder. "But wouldn't Uncle Eric have been able to expose them too? They're the ones running a fraudulent non-profit."

"The Duvall's brought Eric and Brett into CSP eighteen months ago. According to the researcher at Landen, Community Surge Properties is joint owned by Marco, Katrina, and David Duvall along with Eric and Brett Kohli. I didn't get that tidbit till earlier today."

I locked eyes with Rory. Kohli was Aunt Prima's maiden name.

"Shit."

"Yup," Rory said with an exhausted sigh. "And before you ask, Mother didn't know anything about it. She just thought they needed her help making an important deal for the foundation."

"Well, that's something," I muttered. "I guess."

Saint pressed a kiss to my head. "Brett is in Cross County lockup for the armed B&E, and Marco is in custody here at the hospital for the same. He had to get his shoulder stitched up. Seth is handing over the CSP stuff to the IRS and FBI since it involves tax fraud. It'll be up to the US Attorneys Office to determine whether or not to indict Eric, Kat and David. Meanwhile, your grandfather was lucid enough to contact the chairman of the board to have Eric removed and a temporary CEO put in place. They'll order an external audit of the company to help defend Stiel Corp from any blowback."

I wanted to pass out again and bury my head in the sand. The entire situation was so fucking ugly.

Rory sighed. "We're not sure if this is what happened exactly, but Mother recalled a conversation Grandfather had one night when he was kind of out of it. He told her that he'd set aside your building for you in his will and put all the supporting documents, *including the actual deed*, into Melody's writing slope."

"No. Not the deed," I said.

"Right. But that's why she wanted to get her hands on the box. To recover the deed and whatever other evidence of his dementia before you had a chance to realize he intended to gift you the building. She thought his decision to give you the building was something he'd decided *after* his diagnosis. She didn't want to get your hopes up just to have the will blocked after they realized he had compromised cognitive ability."

"Pfft. Not sure I believe that," I muttered. "That's awfully kind of her."

Saint let out an *mmpfh*. The supportive suspicion made me smile.

"Well, we'll see what happens. In the meantime, let's get you out of here and back to the ranch. Saint said there's room for me to stay over if you don't mind me leeching onto you two. I don't want to go back to Dallas right now."

"I don't blame you," said Saint. "You're welcome to stay with us as long as you want. Hell, you can move to Hobie and come work for us at Twist if you want. Your brother told me the self-defense lessons were your idea in the first place. You could learn how to teach them."

Rory smiled for the first time that day. "Don't tempt me, Saint Wilde. Living away from my brother this past year hasn't exactly been a cake walk."

"She's a paralegal," I added. "Has a really good job in the city."

Saint snickered softly. "My sister MJ is an attorney starting at a practice here in Hobie. I'm sure she'll need some help…"

My heart was so fucking full that seeing Rory's face light up with possibility made me spring a leak from my eyeballs.

I thought maybe I'd made the best decision ever when I decided to stick with Saint Wilde as my self-defense instructor. I'd agreed to Rory's suggestion of the self-defense class to feel empowered and strong. I'd thought the lessons themselves would bring that about, but they hadn't. Instead, they'd brought me friends and a new place to belong.

And that was what made me feel empowered and strong.

Saint shifted off the bed and reached for the button to lift me to a sitting position. He reached his hand out to help me stand up.

"Come on, slowpoke. It's time to get you out of here. Let me help you up."

So I did. And I always would.

EPILOGUE

SAINT

There was someone in the house, and it wasn't any of the Wildes. The sound was completely different from the usual creaks and groans of Doc and Grandpa's ancient rambling farmhouse, and I felt in my gut it was an intruder.

Of the sexy variety.

"They sent me in to find out what's taking so long," Augie said with a grin. "Little did they know I was headed in here anyway to steal some kisses."

His face held a slight blush since being sexually confident was still a very new thing for him.

"C'mere," I grumbled low in my throat. "I almost tackled you outside a minute ago. Those jeans and cowboy boots are doing things to me."

He'd gone all in on the western look for the Halloween bonfire. The snap-button shirt tucked into tight Wranglers was topped by a bandana and my own Stetson that we'd uncovered in Doc and Grandpa's attic. I'd worn that thing the whole time I was in high school. As soon as Augie'd gotten his hands on it, I knew it was joining the vintage Rolling Stones T-shirt and oversized rescue diver hoodie in the collection of things he'd stolen from his boyfriend and was never giving back.

Of course every single one of those things looked better on him than me.

"Giddyup," he said with a shy smile. "Ride 'em—"

I cut him off with a laugh. "No. Those words sound wrong coming out of your blue-blooded mouth."

"I beg your pardon," he said in his hoity-toity highbrow voice. "I do not know of what you speak, sirrah."

"That's better," I said, pulling him in for a kiss. The sound of horns honking outside interrupted us. "We should skip it and go back to your place. I think you'd feel better if you were naked."

"No way. I've been too chicken to go to a famous Hobie bonfire since moving here. We are going."

He glanced at me through dark eyelashes. The stitches on the very edge of his forehead were still dark in contrast to his pale skin. "But, ah, afterward? Maybe we can do the naked thing? I mean... if you're staying over again?"

I hadn't slept apart from him since the incident. We'd gone back to his place two nights before, grateful beyond measure to my brothers Otto and Hudson who'd replaced sheetrock, window glass, and doors. Even Sassy had come over to help paint.

I ran a thumb along his jaw. "Baby, if it were up to me, I would stay over every night."

His eyes opened wider. "Really?"

I nodded. "Of course. But I'm not in a hurry and don't want to rush you. I know you've been through so much shit with your family. It's a lot of change at once."

We were interrupted by MJ's shout from the front door. "Put your dick in your pants and let's go!"

After grabbing the grocery bag Doc had left behind with the marshmallows, graham crackers, and chocolate bars, I followed Augie out the door and to the truck.

Once we were at Walnut Farm, enjoying the giant bonfire with half the town of Hobie, Augie brought the subject up again. I was sitting with my back against one of the giant coolers we'd brought.

Augie was sitting between my legs with his back against my front. My fingers had stolen under his jacket to stay warm against his chest.

I could feel his heart pounding.

"Would you consider... I mean, if not, it's completely fine... but, maybe would you think about..." He took a deep breath and tried again. His face was toward the orange light of the fire, so I couldn't see his expression.

"Saint, would you move in with me?"

Doc must have heard the words from his camp chair right next to us. He turned his head with a big catlike grin.

"I would fucking love to, baby," I said before reaching up to tilt his chin so I could kiss him. "Thought you'd never ask."

"What? But I..."

"He's kidding, Augie," Doc said with a chuckle. "It's what he does when he doesn't know what else to say."

I cut in. "I know exactly what to say. I'd love to move in with you. And I love you so much, I might explode into heart-shaped confetti right now if I get too close to the fire."

"I'd like to see that." The deadpan comment came from over my shoulder. I turned back to see my long-lost brother King standing with his hands in the pockets of a trench coat.

I kissed Augie on the top of his head and untangled myself from him so I could stand up and give King a hug.

"Where the hell have you been?" I asked. "We haven't seen you in months."

He looked awful. There were dark smudges under his eyes, and the angles of his face were more pronounced in the warm light of the fire.

"Here and there. On a job."

"What are you doing here?" Hudson asked as he walked over and bear-hugged our brother. "I thought you were in the Middle East or something."

"I came back for the wedding."

The rest of our siblings wandered over as Doc and Grandpa looked at King with arched eyebrows. "Whose wedding?" Doc asked.

"Yours," MJ said to our grandfathers. Her arm was around Neckie who held little Reenie asleep on her shoulder. She'd finally recovered enough from the emotional delivery to decide she wanted to be an auntie to the baby she'd carried for Nico and West. Every time the two of them were together, I thought my grandfathers would break their phone cameras with overuse.

"What?" Grandpa asked.

"You haven't told them yet?" King asked.

"We're already married," Doc said with a frown.

"You are, but as you also know, your forty-five-year anniversary is in a few weeks," West said. "And, well..."

"You're going to renew your vows," Aunt Gina cut in. "In Napa. And we're all coming."

Sassy nudged Hudson out of the way to get to the front of the group. "It's going to be epic!"

Doc and Grandpa exchanged a look. "A family trip sounds nice, but—"

"It's already arranged," MJ cut in. "You just have to show up."

"Why Napa?" Grandpa asked.

MJ and I exchanged glances. The idea had only come about a few days before, but Nico had managed to pull it all together after calling Rebecca Marian. The vineyard hosting us was owned by Matilda Marian's family. The vow renewal ceremony was the perfect excuse to get grandpa there without him coming up with another excuse to avoid seeing his sister.

Nico fielded the question. "I know the people who own the vineyard. They're giving us a great deal."

I thought about traveling to California with Augie to celebrate my grandfathers' unofficial but very real forty-five-year marriage. The idea that one day he and I might be able to do the same brought tears to my eyes. The past forty-five years in Doc and Grandpa's lives had brought love and pain, joy and grief. They'd raised children and lost friends. They'd been to war and come out of it changed forever. They'd ranched and practiced medicine and watched over their small town with affectionate pride, even when the people there didn't support their union.

But most of all, they helped raise two generations of Wildes to help change things. The Hobie we lived in now was very different from the Hobie they'd raised my father in and the one I'd grown up in. And it would be different from the Hobie I hoped to raise Augie's children in.

Augie turned to look at me with an excited smile. *Can I go too?* he mouthed.

"Always," I whispered past the lump in my throat. "You're one of us now."

"An honorary Wilde?" he asked with a chuckle.

"Yes," I said.

And in my mind, I took the word "honorary" and chucked it right out the door.

∼

Continue reading for a bonus scene.

BONUS SCENE

AUGIE - NEW YEAR'S EVE

I was late getting home from a client's house where I'd spent way too many hours indulging a young Westlake society wife on how best to set a table for her "authentic Downton Abbey" murder mystery evening. Let's just say it involved last-minute sourcing of twenty sets of Royal Worcester dinner plates to replace the Wedgewood Gillman ones she'd discovered had been sold in the US instead of the UK in 1915.

"Regardless of her American daughter-in-law, Lady Crawley wouldn't have allowed such things on her table," Ashley had insisted with a sniff. "As soon as I discovered the mistake, I about lost my shit."

It had taken every ounce of self-control not to point out that she may need to work on her vulgar language before slipping into her corset and evening gown later. But it was honestly none of my business.

And I had a hottie waiting at home for me.

"Anyone home?" I called out when I entered the front door to the farmhouse. Milo let out a *mrrp* before trotting toward the back of the house. Saint had a fairly new habit of stopping by the shop to grab him before coming home so Milo wouldn't be lonely overnight. The jury was still out on how Milo felt about the daily commute back and forth. As I watched him go, I noticed two things: the interior of the house was lit by only candles, and there was a trail of scattered keys on the floor leading toward the bedroom.

"Saint?" I called, setting down my own keys and wallet on the table by the door. I kicked off my shoes and tossed my coat over the back of a nearby chair before following the trail of keys deeper into the house. "Sorry I'm late. Ashley kept asking me how to make pin curls and whether or not to choose the Lotus clip or the Vever comb. Remind me never to carry women's hair jewelry in the shop again if I want to avoid discussing historical hairstyles."

I was babbling because I was nervous. As I came closer to the bedroom, I could hear the distant lazy sounds of Roxy Music spinning about Avalon.

Hot damn. Saint was in a mood.

"Babe?" I asked with a chuckle. "Should I strip down before I get to the bedroom?"

I was in the hallway now and decided to err on the side of naked by beginning to unbutton my shirt. By the time I entered the candlelit bedroom, I was topless and half-hard. There was no sign of Saint in our bed.

"Don't tease me, Saint-Michel-des-Saints," I warned. "I'm the new master of edging, remember?"

I heard a muffled thump from somewhere above and realized where he was.

My hidey-hole.

I stripped down to my underwear and entered the closet. Sure enough, the trail of keys on the floor led straight to the ladder in the back of the small space. The music got louder as I climbed up.

When I poked my head through the hatch, I nearly fell off the ladder. There, in complete almost naked glory, was the love of my life lazily stroking his hard cock through the thin fabric of a sexy jock.

"Fuck me," I muttered. "I should have chartered a jet. Had I known this was what was waiting for me…"

"Get up here."

I finished making my way into the small space. The fairy lights hanging from the low ceiling set off the gold and silver of my key collection. They hung from gold thread, making the entire space glow with a warm and honeyed ambiance that only served to make Saint Wilde look more like a fitness cover model than a... well, hell. He'd actually landed on the cover of a fitness magazine recently. Granted, it was North Texas Gymscape doing a profile on Twist's new co-owner, but still.

He was hot as holy fuck.

And he was all mine.

"What're you doing up here in your skivvies?" I asked, reaching forward to snap an elastic strap on his hip. The jock he wore was one I hadn't seen before. The waistband said Pistol Pete and the straps themselves were red, white, and blue.

"Where are my black sequins?" I teased, crawling forward. "It's New Year's Eve, not Fourth of July."

"Sequins itch. And the selection wasn't all that great at the thrift shop."

Had I not known he was joking, I might have gagged.

"I feel underdressed in my utilitarian boxer briefs," I admitted.

"You're sexy as hell in anything. Or nothing. C'mere."

I finished crawling across the piles of blankets to where he lay. As I stretched out between his legs, I took the opportunity to run the tip of my tongue over the defined muscles of his hairy thigh. One of my new favorite things was stopping by Twist and watching the clients drool over him. The first time it happened, I was overcome with insecurity and jealousy.

But then Neckie had burst out laughing and pointed out the undeniable truth. Saint only had eyes for me.

Sure enough, after she told me that, I'd noticed the truth of her words. When I was in the same room as Saint, his eyes were locked on me like industrial magnets. The look on his face was sometimes affectionate, sometimes predatory, but always, always possessive and claiming.

And I loved every minute of it.

His adoration of me had very quickly helped convince me my fears of being unworthy were unfounded. Saint made a big effort to make sure I knew how much he loved me.

Case in point: the naked sailor in my favorite nest.

His grunts of pleasure filled the small space, and I looked up to catch his stormy gaze.

"How'd it go at the gym today?" I asked. "Any takers on your New Year special?"

"It was packed. My personal training spots are full through February already, and the Jumpstart Grinder class is on a waitlist. But I don't want to talk about work. I want to suck your dick."

That was enough to finish filling my cock in about half a second. "Then what are you waiting for?"

Suddenly I was on my back looking up at the lights and golden keys spinning idly around Saint's blond hair like a halo. My underwear was missing, and my knees were next to my shoulders. The sound of Saint's mouth caught up to my ears right when I felt his beard stubble on the sensitive skin of my rim.

"Jesus *fuck*," I croaked. "Yes. That. Mmm-*more*."

I held my knees back to give him access to whatever the hell he wanted to lick and suck down there as I squeezed my eyes closed and tried not to shoot off in the first ten seconds. Saint's mouth moved over my balls to my shaft and ran a hot tongue up its length.

"You smell good. Taste good." His muffled voice warmed the skin of my inner thigh, which reminded me of Christmas morning when he'd woken me up with his mouth while we were in his grandfathers' bunkhouse bedroom. Before I'd come fully awake enough to realize where I was, I'd screamed so loudly through my orgasm that half his siblings held up scorecards when we arrived at breakfast.

I ran my fingers through his hair. It was longer on top than the sides and I loved running my hands through it. Sometimes when we watched a movie together he'd lie on my lap and let me play with his hair. Most of the time it resulted in a sleeping Saint who would be quickly joined by Milo curling into a tight ball on his warm lower back.

As he licked and sucked, Saint finally made his way up my body to lay claim to my mouth. I grabbed the back of his head and held on, wrapping my legs around his back to keep him still. He devoured my tongue and rubbed his scratchy cheeks against mine.

"Missed you," I mumbled into his mouth. "Love you."

I felt his cock slide against mine and groaned.

"What time is it?" he asked. "Midnight?"

"No. Like, seven? I think?" My head was spinning enough to make me unsure, but I remembered it being six something in the car.

"Want to wish you happy New Year's," he said before nibbling my ear lobe. "Gonna be a good one."

"Mm-hmm."

"Best one ever. You and me. Milo."

My heart soared. "Mm-hm," I hummed again, arching up into him in search of release. "Gonna be better if we close out this year with an orgasm."

Saint's big, warm hand wrapped around our cocks and began to jack us off together. It felt so fucking good, I threw my head back and arched into him even more.

"Oh god."

"Want to see you come," Saint said through quickening breaths. "Please, Augie. Can't... can't..."

His thumb swiped over the head of my cock, throwing me over the cliff with a gasp. My entire lower body contracted with a bright, searing explosion of nerve endings.

"*Fuckkkk*," I cried.

"Yes," Saint hissed as I felt his warm release against my skin. "Fuck. So good, baby. God, you feel so good like this."

He leaned in to kiss me some more, slowing it down until it was the barest of brushes against my lips. Finally he collapsed beside me and rested his head on my shoulder. I handed him a box of tissues so he could wipe off his hands.

"Why do you have a box of tissues up here?"

I thought back to the night I'd first met Saint Wilde, when I'd been too afraid to sleep in my own bed but plenty brave enough to mastur-bate one or five times in my hidey-hole to the memory of the stacked navy SEAL who'd touched me all evening in the gym and then bought me a drink at the pub after.

"No reason," I said, blushing. "I read books up here. Sometimes they're tearjerkers."

"Liar," he said with a grin. "You got the word 'jerk' right, but if you need these tissues for reading, the only book I can think of is Jacking Your Beanstalk."

"Shut up," I said with a bark of laughter.

"How To Choke A Chicken In One Easy (Repeated) Step."

"Oh my god, you're terrible."

"Lone Rangering. Dotting the I. Me Before You. Grilling Salami for One."

"I hate you right now," I insisted. He was laughing just as hard as I was. Tears streamed down both our faces. "Bet you're glad we have these now, huh?"

He handed me one to wipe my eyes with. When we caught our breath, he glanced at me with so much raw affection in his eyes, I was shocked into silence.

"That night I followed you home, you know."

"You did?"

Saint reached out and pushed a piece of hair off my forehead. "I was worried about you. Wanted to make sure you got home safely."

"Even then?"

"Even then."

We spent the next few hours teasing, snuggling, planning, and pulling as much pleasure out of each other's bodies as we could. And when midnight finally came, we were too busy enjoying the moment to even notice it was a whole new beginning.

Want more stories, bonus scenes, and exclusive content for free? Sign up for Lucy's newsletter and visit www.LucyLennox.com to see what free stories are listed today!

LETTER FROM LUCY

Dear Reader,

Thank you so much for reading *His Saint*, book five in the Forever Wilde series!

If you're unfamiliar with the series, check out the first book *Facing West* which is about Nico, a tattoo artist from San Francisco, returning to his small-town Texas roots to take custody of his sister's baby. There he meets the local uptight physician, West Wilde, who thinks this urban punk is in no way prepared to take on the care of a newborn. And he's right.

There are already five novels in the series with more to come, so please stay tuned. Up next will be Doc and Grandpa's story as they travel to California to confront Grandpa's long-lost sister.

Be sure to follow me on Amazon to be notified of new releases, and look for me on Facebook for sneak peeks of upcoming stories.

Feel free to sign up for my newsletter, stop by www.LucyLennox.com or visit me on social media to stay in touch. We have a super fun reader group on Facebook that can be found here:

https://www.facebook.com/groups/lucyslair/

To see fun inspiration photos for all of my novels, visit my Pinterest boards.

Happy reading!
Lucy

ABOUT LUCY LENNOX

Lucy Lennox is the creator of the bestselling Made Marian series, the Forever Wilde series, and co-creator of the Twist of Fate Series with Sloane Kennedy and the After Oscar series with Molly Maddox. Born and raised in the southeast, she is finally putting good use to that English Lit degree.

Lucy enjoys naps, pizza, and procrastinating. She is married to someone who is better at math than romance but who makes her laugh every single day and is the best dancer in the history of ever.

She stays up way too late each night reading M/M romance because that stuff is impossible to put down.

For more information and to stay updated about future releases, please sign up for Lucy's author newsletter on her website.

~

Connect with Lucy on social media:
www.LucyLennox.com
Lucy@LucyLennox.com

ALSO BY LUCY LENNOX

Made Marian Series:

Borrowing Blue

Taming Teddy

Jumping Jude

Grounding Griffin

Moving Maverick

Delivering Dante

A Very Marian Christmas

Made Marian Shorts

Made Mine - Crossover with Sloane Kennedy's Protectors series

Hay: A Made Marian Short

Forever Wilde Series:

Facing West

Felix and the Prince

Wilde Fire

Hudson's Luck

Flirt: A Forever Wilde Short

His Saint

Twist of Fate Series (with Sloane Kennedy):

Lost and Found

Safe and Sound

Body and Soul

After Oscar Series (with Molly Maddox):

IRL: In Real Life

Free Short Stories available at www.LucyLennox.com.

Also be sure to check out audio versions here.

Made in the USA
Columbia, SC
09 May 2019